THE
MAPLE COURT

Books by Joan Elizabeth Lloyd

THE PRICE OF PLEASURE

NEVER ENOUGH

CLUB FANTASY

NIGHT AFTER NIGHT

THE SECRET LIVES OF HOUSEWIVES

NAUGHTIER BEDTIME STORIES

HOT SUMMER NIGHTS

MADE FOR SEX

THE MADAM OF MAPLE COURT

Published by Kensington Publishing Corporation

THE MADAM OF MAPLE COURT

JOAN ELIZABETH LLOYD

KENSINGTON BOOKS
http://www.kensingtonbooks.com

KENSINGTON BOOKS are published by

Kensington Publishing Corp.
850 Third Avenue
New York, NY 10022

Copyright © 2008 by Joan Elizabeth Lloyd

All rights reserved. No part of this book may be reproduced in any form or by any means without the prior written consent of the Publisher, excepting brief quotes used in reviews.

All Kensington titles, imprints and distributed lines are available at special quantity discounts for bulk purchases for sales promotion, premiums, fund-raising, educational or institutional use.

Special book excerpts or customized printings can also be created to fit specific needs. For details, write or phone the office of the Kensington Special Sales Manager: Kensington Publishing Corp., 850 Third Avenue, New York, NY 10022. Attn. Special Sales Department. Phone: 1-800-221-2647.

Kensington and the K logo Reg. U.S. Pat. & TM Off.

ISBN-13: 978-0-7582-2372-2
ISBN-10: 0-7582-2372-2

First Kensington Trade Paperback Printing: May 2008
10 9 8 7 6 5 4 3 2 1

Printed in the United States of America

This book is dedicated to all the fabulous folks who've read and enjoyed my books over the years. Your kind letters, your visits to my Web site, and your consistent support have made all my work so worthwhile.

Chapter

1

Thirty-four year old Pam DePalma strode through the ground floor of her beautifully decorated, almost palatial home on Maple Court and smiled. Good. The cleaning crew had been through and everything looked perfect. The silver gleamed, oak and cherrywood had been polished to a high shine, windows sparkled, carpets were free of any trace of tread marks, and furniture pillows had been plumped to the correct softness. Wonderful.

The following morning the caterers would arrive and take over, prepare the hors d'oeuvres she'd selected, then carefully arrange them on silver and crystal trays and plates. She'd listened to the reports on the radio and knew that the mid-July weather would cooperate, as it always did for Chase's parties. She wondered whether it would dare do otherwise, although, as always, she had a huge tent on standby just in case.

At three that Saturday afternoon the uniformed staff would begin to circulate as she greeted guests and made sure everyone had been introduced to everyone else. She'd done this dozens, maybe hundreds of times before and was sure everything would progress like clockwork, with none of the guests aware of the amount of planning it took to bring off a party for a hundred people and make it look effortless. And as always, Linc would arrive early and tend bar in case of any trouble.

She heard a car pull to a stop at the top of the long driveway and walked toward the front door. As she opened it, a strong masculine hand was reaching for the doorbell. Chase Hobart jumped slightly, then a wide grin spread over his strong features. "Pam. You always know everything, don't you." He hugged her and bussed her lightly on the forehead. "How are all the arrangements going?"

"Come on in and have a look around. Everything's great, and you'll particularly love what I've done in the back. I took your suggestion and had the garden service put several more large potted ferns and jungly flowering plants around the spa. It really does give a lot more privacy and makes it look like some secluded forest glade."

"I thought it might," he said. Chase exuded power and wealth. He was not very tall, with very short, prematurely gray hair, neatly trimmed chestnut brown beard and mustache, and surprisingly blue eyes. He was the major stockholder in the Wall Street firm started by his father and already thriving when he had taken over about ten years before. Now it was almost legend in the business, as was he, and he encouraged that image with wealthy and lavish entertaining.

Together Pam and Chase walked through the house and out the sliding glass door, onto the large flagstone patio, and into the early evening. Since it was midsummer the sun was lowering toward the horizon, slowly painting the sky in ribbons of gold and pink. Pam smiled with pride. The backyard was as well manicured as the inside of her home. The grass was freshly cut with the light smell of clippings still filling the air. Summer flowers bloomed everywhere, her rose garden was in full bloom, and large oak and maple trees provided areas of deep shade that felt private. Tables had already been set up, some in bright sun, others in the semidarkness of fully shaded areas.

Her gaze took in the entire lawn and pool area, then they

THE MADAM OF MAPLE COURT

strolled around as Chase, the perfectionist, carefully examined everything. Pam smiled to herself. He trusted her skills but never left anything to chance. "It looks fabulous," he said finally, as she'd known he would. This was the third party she'd thrown for him and his various business associates, in addition to the occasional private entertaining she did for him. "Everyone should be tremendously impressed. I assume you have arranged for a few extra 'ladies'?" Although he didn't wink, there was mutual understanding in his voice. The "of the evening" following the word "ladies" was understood.

"Marcy and I have five women selected and I know you'll approve. Actually, two of them have been at your parties in the past," she said.

"I always admire your taste, love."

"Thank you, kind sir," she said, inclining her head. "How are you doing?"

"I'm doing great, especially now that I'm here. I need some of your tender loving care."

"You know that love has nothing to do with what we do." She had known from the start that Chase was that consummate lady's man who made every woman he met, no matter how casually, feel like his one and only.

"Just a turn of phrase, darling. You know I love my wife. You're just a sex object."

"And I don't object," she said, repeating a teasing phrase they used often. She was, in fact, with him for no reason other than sex and friendship and she liked it that way. Her life was complicated enough without another entanglement. Of course there was money involved, too. "Have you talked to your wife about your sex life?" she asked.

"Stop hounding me, Pam," he snapped. "Anna has nothing to do with this. She likes her upmarket life with sex only every now and then. She's even suggested we redo her dressing room so we'd have separate bedrooms. She's content with the way things are, and so am I."

"You keep telling me she's content, but content isn't happy. And from what you've told me, I'm not so sure she's even content." She thought back on her years with Vin. She had been just like Anna, content but never happy. At least Anna had her children.

"She loves my money, and the kids, and that's that. She doesn't really care what I do as long as the bank account is sufficient for her and the children. Butt out!"

"I'm sorry, Chase," she said, lowering her voice. "It's just that I care about you and I don't—"

"I said butt out." His voice had an angry ring to it. "When I need a marriage counselor I'll hire one. For now, you're hired for other things."

Phew. She'd obviously hit a nerve, as she had a few times before when she'd brought up the same subject. She was indeed hired for other things, so why was she beating her head against a wall? It just made her head hurt and made Chase angry. After all, she wasn't in this to be a marriage counselor. If he was convinced that his wife didn't care about their life, so be it. "I'm sorry, Chase. I'll back off," Pam said, taking Chase's arm and pressing it against the side of her unfettered breast. She wore a flowing deep purple and gold caftan, with nothing beneath. At just five feet tall, Pam's lush body fit snugly against Chase's side. "Do you have to run off or can you spend a few minutes in the hot tub?"

"Mmm," Chase purred. "I thought you'd never ask."

"I don't have to do the asking, you know. I'm always available."

"I know, love, for a fee."

"A woman's got to make a living," she said with an upward quirk of the corners of her mouth.

"I totally understand." They walked to the spa and stepped into what appeared to be a rain forest glade. "This came out exactly as I thought it would. I'm glad my suggestions worked out."

THE MADAM OF MAPLE COURT

The glade had been his suggestion, and a few clever additions by her landscaper highlighted the effect. Right here, thirty miles north of New York City, stood this little slice of heaven. She flipped a switch and hidden lights came on, barely noticeable now in the late-afternoon sun, but very effective if people stayed late the following day and wanted to soak after dark. Hidden devices would also fill the area with almost odorless insect repellant spray. Everything had been considered. "I think it's gorgeous," Pam said softly. "Shall we try it?"

She stood on tiptoe and kissed him lightly on the lips. It took only a moment for him to bend over, slide his arms around her, and deepen the kiss. Since he was only five seven, she knew her diminutive size made him feel tall and physically powerful. Making a man feel like more than he really was made her size a great asset to her profession.

He'd left his suit jacket in his car, so she unfastened his tie, unbuttoned his shirt, and pulled it from his shoulders. She placed it on one of the wooden benches around the large tub, then deliberately removed both his cell phones from their belt clips. She raised a quizzical eyebrow, and after a few moments' hesitation he nodded, and she turned them both off. "Much better," she said, her voice low and throaty. She backed away from him and sensuously unzipped the caftan and let it fall to the paving stones until she stood before him, gloriously naked.

"God, you always overwhelm me," he said, unbuckling his belt.

She pushed his hands away. "Let me do all the work. I'm sure you've had a long day, but remember our rules. No climax until I allow it." She could tell he was aroused by the obvious bulge in the front of his slacks. She loved knowing she could get this reaction from a man.

He let out a long sigh. "Yes, ma'am." He rolled his shoulders and Pam walked around behind him.

She pushed him down onto a bench and began to dig her thumbs into his deltoids, deeply massaging his shoulder muscles. As she felt him relax and his muscles ease she expanded her stroking and rubbing to his upper arms, then down his back. He had wonderfully soft skin. She bent over, her breasts pressing against his neck, and reached down to slowly caress his lightly furred chest. "Feel better?"

"Mmm," he purred. "You always know just what I need."

"I certainly do." After several minutes of stroking, she finally said, "Stand up."

Obligingly he stood and she quickly removed his tasseled Gucci loafers, slacks, shorts, and socks. He needed little urging to climb into the steaming water. "God," he said, letting out a long groan as he settled onto a submerged bench, up to his shoulders in heated water, "that's just marvelous."

Pam turned the controls until the spa was bubbling and churning, then climbed in and sat across from him. "Okay, tell me about your day."

He looked startled, then his face settled into a wide smile. "You do know what I need." She understood all his needs. Some of her male friends wanted someone to talk to almost as much as they wanted sex, and Chase and his wife didn't seem to share anything anymore.

She spent the next several minutes listening, asking the occasional pertinent question and letting him unburden himself of the problems of his always-hectic week. Pam knew how few people he had with whom he could be honest, knowing nothing he said would go any farther. What he needed as much as her body was a place and a person all his own, where he could unwind before going home to a house filled with the hollow noise of three school-aged children and a distant, uncaring wife. She also knew that despite the fact that it was Friday evening, his briefcase would be filled with work and he'd be up most of the night, on the phone to the Far East, Russia, and eventually much of Europe. Weekends were merely additional workdays for men in his position.

Finally he wound down and rested his head on the rim of

the tub. She slid beside him, then kissed him lightly on the shoulder, letting him set the pace. He raised his head and smiled at her, tangling his fingers in her short, deep brown curls and massaging her scalp. "You're so right for me. How about let's run away together or get married when I get my divorce?"

She laughed, as she had the other dozen times he'd made the same offer. She realized that she didn't know whether he was actually getting a divorce, although he always talked as if he were considering it. No matter. "I like it just the way it is, darling. Marriage would spoil everything and you won't ever really get a divorce. You love your children and I often suspect you also love your wife."

"Let's not talk about my kids or Anna. Come here." He pulled her so she straddled his lap and they kissed for a long while. His hands wandered over her back, then to her breasts. She loved the way her breasts felt in the spa, buoyant in the bubbling water, her flesh alive as his hands artfully caressed and teased her.

He lifted one breast out of the bubbles and licked water off the turgid tip. She felt her nipples harden as the combination of his nibbles and the cooler air tightened them and her vaginal tissues swelled. She moved so his cock rubbed her through her carefully trimmed pubic hair. They played like that, stroking, caressing, biting and teasing, for several minutes until the timer shut the spa motor off and the jets and bubbles ceased. She stood and took his hand. "Out here," she said.

She flipped another switch and streams of heated air warmed the area at one end of the tub. She laid him on his back on one of the benches and found a condom in one of the several caches she had everywhere around the house in case she needed one.

As she leaned over him she allowed her nipples to rub over his chest, then moved away as he reached for her. Finally he growled and she remained still so he could cup one breast in each hand, kneading her heated flesh. She kissed his neck, then nibbled her way lower until she nipped at his flat nipples. Many men didn't have sensitive nipples, but she had discovered early on that Chase's were as responsive as hers, and she felt them become erect beneath her lips.

She straddled the bench and moved inexorably down his body, licking his belly and playing with his navel. By the time her mouth reached his groin, his cock was hard and throbbing. "Want me?" she said.

"Stop being demanding and suck me," he said.

She shook her head slightly and smiled indulgently. "For right now you're the boss." She took his erect penis into her mouth, pulling and licking until he was jerking and needy. "You always taste so wonderful," she said, his juices blending with the slight chlorine taste of the spa water. With a long sigh he gave himself up to the pleasure that her mouth gave him as she used her teeth to scratch along his shaft. Her fingers found his sac and squeezed lightly, then her fingernail scraped the tender area between his anus and the base of his sac. As she grasped his erection she heard his breathing quicken and she felt him tighten his muscles, trying to control his need.

When he grabbed for her hips, she said, "Remember the rules? You might be the boss the rest of the time, but when I have your cock in my hand you do it my way. You don't come until I say so."

"Of course," he said, gritting his teeth against his urgency. Finally she unrolled the condom over his rock-hard cock and again straddled the bench. She wrapped her hand around him, found her opening with the tip of his penis, and slowly lowered herself onto him until he was just an inch inside. How many times had a man entered her like this? She couldn't count, but it never failed to excite her.

When she grinned and held her body still above him, his hands grasped her hips and tried to pull her down. "Not yet," she said. She lowered herself, allowing him to slowly fill her, then, when he was totally encased within her, she squeezed

THE MADAM OF MAPLE COURT

her vaginal muscles and felt him jerk. She knew exactly how he liked it, so she slid her hand beneath her, found his anal opening, and rubbed her finger around the rim for a moment. Eventually she couldn't keep her body still enough to stay in contact with his ass, but she knew he was now beyond caring. And, of course, he also knew that she would not allow him to come until she had.

He growled low in his throat as he drove himself deeper into her over and over. She found his rhythm and rode him until she felt her climax deep inside her. She reached for it, found it deep in her womb, and let it overtake her, her vaginal muscles clenching and relaxing around the hard cock lodged in her.

"Now, Chase, now!" she yelled and, with a loud roar, he came, then collapsed back onto the bench. She lay atop him, their breathing rapid, their bodies wet with sweat and slightly salty water. Slowly she rose, climbed from him, and disposed of the condom. She scooped up several handfuls of hot spa water and sluiced them over his calming body, then took a towel from the heated closet beside the rock wall and slowly dried him, then herself.

As she slipped her caftan back on she asked, "Can I make you a quick bite to eat?" Last time they'd been together they'd shared a sandwich before he left.

He was almost completely dressed by then and slipped his feet back into his loafers. "Thanks, Pam, but I think I'll just do a drive-through. I've got a case full of work and there will be faxes waiting at home."

"Okay, if you insist."

"Business before pleasure," he said.

"Nonsense. This was all pleasure, but I understand that you don't have much time, with the party tomorrow and everything. The invitations said three, so I'll expect you mid-afternoon. Will you be driving by yourself or coming with some of the guests?" She knew better than inquire whether his wife would be coming. He'd snapped at her the last time she'd asked.

"I'm picking up several of the men on the way here." He kissed her forehead. "It's great that you do all of this for me."

"Parties and the rest, that's my business. I'm very well paid for these shindigs."

"For everything else, too." He smiled and she knew that he was not the least upset by the knowledge that an extra thousand dollars would be included in the "entertaining" charges to cover the previous hour of their special kind of amusement. Extra would be hidden in the bill as well for the ladies attending the following afternoon, and more if they made his associates "happy" afterward. He'd already told her the names of the men who might want some extra companionship, and he'd write everything off on his taxes as business entertaining.

He slid his arms around her shoulders and kissed her again. They understood each other completely. Together they walked through the elegant house to the front door. "I'll see you tomorrow," he said, then walked out to his BMW.

After he backed down the long driveway, Pam wandered to the end to pick up her mail. She pulled a stack of letters, circulars, and catalogs from the box and flipped through them. In the middle of the stack was a plain white envelope addressed in block letters with no return address and no stamp. Curious, she tore it open and pulled a sheet of plain white paper from it. The words glared at her, spelled out in letters cut from a magazine.

You will be punished again and again for what you're doing.

She stared. She'd wondered about a few recent incidents, flowers dug up, scratches in her car, feces left in her driveway. Now she was convinced that those weren't just random acts. Her breathing quickened and she put her hand against her breastbone. Someone knew everything and was making trouble, torturing her slowly before letting the bomb drop. Her mind whirled and she couldn't separate her fear from her anger. No, not now! Now, when everything was going so well. Someone knew. She wanted to scream. She wanted to curl up in a little ball and cry. She wanted to call someone to come over and help her. She looked again at the letters on the page.

You will be punished again and again for what you're doing.

Screaming or crying, she knew, would get her nowhere, and there was no one to call. Not yet. Marcy? What did this mean for her? No, she couldn't involve Marcy yet. Linc? Of course, but not yet.

Her hands began to tremble and her breathing gathered speed as adrenaline poured into her body. She felt her heart pound. It was all over. Her lovely life, her business, all over. She felt prison bars close around her and pictured the headlines. THE MADAM OF MAPLE COURT ARRESTED FOR PANDERING AND PROSTITUTION. And Marcy would be dragged into it. PROPRIETOR OF CLUB FANTASY JAILED. Pam couldn't bear it if her best friend got into trouble because of her.

At the sound of a motor she looked up and saw a shiny black SUV slowly pull into the cul de sac and circle, the woman behind the wheel seeming to stare at her from behind large dark glasses. She glanced at the license plate. HOBART3. Chase's wife? Could she be responsible for the note? It had to be her. That car being here was too much of a coincidence. It made sense if she really did care about him. Of course. It had to be. Shit! Was this all about to blow up in her face because of Chase's wife? Shit, shit, shit! What now? Should she confront the woman? Find out how much she knew? Tell her it was all just sex? Should she just move, get out of town? Shut it all down? Damn, damn, damn!

She looked back at the SUV as it lurched forward and peeled rubber out of the cul-de-sac. Pam shook her head slowly as tears gathered behind her eyelids. How many people would suffer now? Gary? Rob? Linc? All her friends and clients were involved. It would all come out. Did she regret any of it? she wondered. Not really. Until now it had all been a wonderful adventure.

Who could have guessed back eighteen months ago when she got the terrible news, that she'd be here, like this now? She sighed and tried to still her pounding heart. What now? She gathered her scattered wits, turned, and headed back up the driveway. The Madam of Maple Court. Who could have guessed?

Chapter

2

A year and a half earlier

"Pam," Mark Redmond said, "I don't quite know how to tell you this, but I've gone over all the records I could find since Vin's death and, well, there isn't a great deal of money." Mark had been Pam and Vin's accountant for more than ten years. "You won't starve, and if you live frugally you can get along okay for several years, but I had hoped for more."

"I'm sorry, Mark," Pam DePalma said, shaking her head slowly and tightening her stomach muscles as if to ward off a blow. "I'm having a hard time taking this in. We're not filthy rich, but we're pretty well off. Right?" She'd been trying to come to terms with the reality of the automobile accident that had killed her husband of twelve years on a snowy road in Westchester County, New York. It had happened two weeks before and the numbness hadn't lessened.

She'd just turned thirty-three. Attractive. Educated. Charming. So what? What was she going to do for the rest of her life without Vin? Her life had been so tied up with his, entertaining his clients, traveling to meet with wives of business associates, attending the right clubs, losing at bridge to the right people. *My God, what now?* What would she do all day? His death had left a gigantic hole in her life. Vin's business entertaining and the charity work he had insisted would improve their image had occupied so much of her time since he'd started his own firm that she had virtually no life of her own. Neither she nor Vin had any family to speak of, so now with his death she was truly alone. How was she going to keep going? She was usually so practical, so on top of things, but this had thrown her into a tailspin. She couldn't take it in, make it make sense.

Not much money? How could that be? It had been Vin's decision, one that Pam reluctantly concurred with, to leave Haskell & Roth and form his own advertising agency more than three years before, and DePalma Advertising had been an immediate, raging success. He'd taken several of his largest clients with him when he left H&R and just last month, although he admitted that things were in a momentary dip, he had assured her that he was about to land several major new accounts.

Now Mark was telling her that she didn't have a lot of money. Would she have to get a job? What did she know how to do? She could live frugally. She didn't need much, but she and Vin had enjoyed good living: expensive restaurants, lavish meals with expensive wines, frequent trips to Europe, designer clothes, an exclusive country club, all to enhance their image—his image—and she'd grown used to that lifestyle. What had gone wrong? Unless Vin had been painting a rosier picture for her than reality would have dictated, there should have been more than enough money to carry her through. To what? Without her husband could she just sit around and await Social Security?

"Pam?"

She refocused on what the accountant was saying. "Sorry, Mark, I guess I was somewhere else. What about the agency? Aren't there assets there?"

"I can't give you any specifics. You'll have to talk to Oren Stevens about that. He takes care of the corporate books. However, from what he tells me, after all the corporate debts are settled, there's not much left there, either."

Mark's look was almost pitying. "Unless there's money in the company that I don't know about, and that's always possible, of course, you have enough in the bank to last for two to three years if nothing changes and you live within your new means. The one bright spot is that much of the mortgage will be paid up, so those payments won't drown you. When Vin refinanced last year, the bank insisted on mortgage insurance, so that will pay off much of the remainder of that debt. However, in addition to what's left of the mortgage there are still taxes on the house, which are exorbitant, homeowner's insurance, and maintenance, in addition to general living expenses."

He leaned forward in his leather chair and propped his elbows on the desk. "You don't have to do anything for a while. Take some time and figure out what you're going to do with the rest of your life. You're a young, attractive woman with many, many years ahead of you. Relax and think everything over. You've got plenty of time."

She looked upon Mark as a friend, so she had to believe that his awful news was the truth and not exaggerated to make some point or earn an extra fee somehow. Still incredulous, she whispered, "What you're telling me can't be true." Vin had assured her time and again that he was making well into six figures a year and if anything ever happened to him she'd be well taken care of. He did have a habit of painting dreamy pictures for her, however. She had always been the practical one, he the eternal optimist.

"I've gone over everything several times," Mark continued. "He used to be well insured but, over my objections, he cashed in most of his life insurance policies about a year ago and plowed the money into the business. Since there are no children to provide for he probably thought you both would be fine until things were better financially. He kept saying that the business was about to turn a corner."

Pretty pictures. Pam sat back in the leather chair opposite Mark's desk and stared out the large window behind him. *It should be raining to match my mood*, she thought, but the November sun was bright and there was only a hint of winter in the air. Near tears but still clinging to hope, she said, "He told me he was making almost half a million a year."

"During the first two years that DePalma Advertising was in business he was, but not recently. I assumed you knew that he lost several big accounts about a year ago and had to cut staff. The firm's income dropped off quite a bit after that and he took almost no salary to keep it afloat, then plowed most of his personal savings into it." Mark looked straight into her eyes. "You must know that, of course. You're the secretary/treasurer of the corporation and signed all the tax returns."

"Come on, Mark, be real. You know I trusted Vin, so I didn't pay much attention to any of the documents. He showed me where to sign and I signed." She stopped and thought back. Just last month she'd signed several forms. He had folded the multipage document so she hadn't really seen anything but the last page. Had he been deliberately hiding things from her? As she thought about it, she realized that he probably had. She was sure he believed that things would turn around and hadn't wanted to worry her, so she had continued to live up to what she thought his income was. They'd gone to Egypt and Israel the previous fall and had traveled through the Burgundy region of France with business associates just six weeks ago.

Mark stared at her, then shook his head. "I'm sorry, Pam. I thought you knew at least some of this. I guess this comes as more of a shock to you than I'd anticipated. Vin should have kept you informed." He reached across his desk and squeezed her hand. "I'm really sorry about all this." He released her hand and pulled a typed piece of paper from his top drawer. He glanced at it. "Being practical, here's what I would advise. The Corvette was totaled in the accident, so the insurance will take care of that. Both the other cars are leased and I think you should turn in his Mercedes and pay the surrender charges." He slid the paper across the shiny surface of the maple partners' desk until it lay in front of her. "I hope you don't mind, but I took the liberty of making up a tentative budget for you from what I know about your lifestyle. If you want, give me power of attorney over your bank accounts, then just forward all your bills to me and, at least for the moment, I'll take care of paying them for you. If we do that for the short run I can polish the budget and make up some projections. We can get together in a month or two and figure out what to do next."

"I'm grateful to you, Mark," she said as she looked down at the page. She didn't really see any of the individual numbers, just the enormous total at the bottom marked Monthly Expenses. It looked like a fortune.

"What happened to the money from the refinance he did last year?"

"Vin invested the cash in the business, but in the end I'm afraid it didn't help. In my opinion DePalma Advertising was well on its way to closing shop even then and now, of course, will have to be liquidated."

What would Vin have done then? He'd have been devastated. He had put so much of himself into DePalma Advertising. Was the accident that killed him really just an accident? They didn't have any children and he must have known that the next best thing, DePalma Advertising, his legacy, was on the verge of bankruptcy. Could he have done such an awful thing? The thought that he might have driven into the bridge abutment deliberately flashed across her mind, then she dismissed it. No, he was too much of a "glass half full" kind of guy and would have thought things were about to turn a corner. Not thought, known. He'd have been sure he could make everything better by the sheer force of his will.

Pam recrossed her legs, smoothed the skirt of her dark gray wool suit, and took a deep breath. As she stared at the paper on the desk she realized that much of her monthly budget was being sucked up in the house. The house. God knew she loved it, but it was, indeed, a money pit. "I never realized how much it cost to keep the house going. Even without the mortgage the monthly outlay is amazing. There are a lot of memories there but maybe I should consider selling it. That would make things better, wouldn't it? I could move into a condo or something." She twirled her wedding ring.

Mark huffed out a breath. "Actually, no. Right after he refinanced, the town decided to try to designate most of Maple Court as a wetland and no one could consider buying. The town board hasn't made any decisions about the future of the Court yet and who knows when anything will be decided. They could decide to take the land over and condemn the houses or just prohibit sales and take a right of first refusal when you're ready to move. That might be for just pennies on the dollar, but nothing's finalized yet. I did a little investigating and the town planning and zoning boards are dragging their feet. It's a real political hot potato. Each party is blaming the other for allowing the construction in the first place, so it will undoubtedly be some time before anyone's willing to make a decision. Realistically, it could be years. Meanwhile, sadly, that means that no buyer would touch the house."

The house. Vin had spent amazing amounts of money on it, starting with its construction, claiming that it was an investment in his future. Maybe if she'd been able to give him children he wouldn't have poured all his energy into a piece of land. That had started it all, five years before. She shut her eyes and dropped her head into her hands. That house.

* * *

THE MADAM OF MAPLE COURT   19

"I'm home," Vin DePalma called to his wife. He dropped his briefcase on the table at the entrance to their small living room. Pam made her way to his side, her eyes still red from crying. "Babe, what's the matter?" Vin said, taking her in his arms.

"I got my period today." You'd think after all these years she'd be used to it, but it always disappointed her deeply. The doctors said there was always hope, but she thought they probably said that to every couple.

Vin's face fell, then brightened. "I'm sorry, babe, but it's okay. Maybe next month."

Maybe next month, maybe next month. How long had they been saying that? It just wasn't going to happen, doctors or no doctors, and it was her fault. Vin had tested fine.

"It will happen, so cheer up," Vin said, setting her away from him. "Anyway, I've got great news."

She took a deep, cleansing breath, then stood on tiptoe and bussed her husband's cheek. As short as she was, she always seemed to be standing on her toes. She forced her face into a smile. "That's wonderful. I need some good news. Tell me."

He took her hand and guided her to the sofa where they settled side by side. "I ran into Jake Preston at lunch. You remember him, the art director at H&R? Well, he heard that the promotion is a done deal." Vin had been up for partner at Haskell & Roth for almost six months but they'd been delaying any announcement for one reason after another. Pam had her doubts that it would ever happen. She knew the partners from business lunches and office parties. They were powerful, wealthy men, and she wondered whether they'd ever be willing to turn part of the profits over to a new partner. She suspected that men like that didn't like to share.

Everyone knew that Vin was landing and servicing more and larger accounts than the firm had ever had, and his annual bonuses had showed it. He earned enough that he insisted that Pam never work, but he wanted more. Always more. Always a bigger stack. This year his bonus hadn't been what he'd expected, but he'd assumed that the partnership deal would make up for the shortfall.

"That's fabulous," Pam said and, as they settled on the sofa, she kissed him again, this time with obvious enthusiasm. Why trouble him with her concerns when he obviously didn't want to hear them? "Did Jake have any idea when an announcement might happen?"

Vin draped his arm around his wife's shoulder in a familiar gesture. Since he was over six foot one, he towered over her and liked to cuddle her against him. Not yet thirty, he had straight, dark brown hair, deep-set eyes that were almost black, and a swarthy complexion that heightened his slightly foreign attractiveness.

He nuzzled the top of her hair. "I keep hoping it will be soon. There's a partners' meeting at the end of next week and I have a feeling that they'll approve my appointment then and announce it immediately afterward."

"What if they don't?" she said quietly.

"They will, but just in case, I've been quietly sounding out a few of my big accounts and they've hinted that they'd go with me if I went out on my own."

Out on his own? Open his own firm? She knew that several small advertising firms had gone under in the last year. The future of start-ups wasn't guaranteed by any means. Hadn't the dot-com bubble taught anyone anything? "That's a big step, Vin."

"I know, but I won't have to do that anyway. My partnership is in the bag."

"Oh, honey, I hope you don't get your hopes up," Pam said, resting her head of brown curls against her husband's biceps. She had been pretty in college, when she and Vin first met, all soft curves and deep hazel eyes, a girl that men wanted to cosset and protect. Vin, a bench warmer on the basketball team, had sat behind her in a history class and they'd begun dating. They'd married while in their senior year.

When they'd graduated he'd gone to work for H&R and she'd stayed at home, in their cozy little apartment in White Plains, hoping to get pregnant quickly and start the family they both wanted so much. In the meantime, however, she'd been bored. When she suggested that she could get a job, however, he'd been adamant. "Not a chance. Enjoy your leisure time now because after the baby comes there will be little enough of it. I make enough so you can play bridge every afternoon if you like, so take advantage."

When nothing happened after a year of trying to get pregnant, they'd both been tested. The fertility specialist had talked to Vin, then suggested several regimens, and over the ensuing few years they'd tried them all. To no avail. When she'd finally brought up adoption he'd been adamant. "If I'm going to raise a kid and give him my name I want him to be my blood, and my legacy." Finally she'd become content to be part of the country club set. She often gazed at the women around her, all busy with their children, many saying how they'd like to be her, free from the responsibilities of raising "the little brats," but saying it with such love that she'd often had to fight back tears. Vin seldom said much, but when he was frustrated or annoyed he brought up the lack of children and, although it was unstated, she was sure he blamed her.

Now he cuddled her closer. "I won't count my chickens," he said with a long sigh, "but I know how much they need me and how many accounts might follow me, so they can't risk my going elsewhere or opening my own shop. It's just that the waiting gets so frustrating."

"I know," she said, turning her face to kiss the hand that rested on her shoulder. "But you make a good salary and you're well respected within the agency and the advertising community as a whole. You won that award just last year, so partnership is really only a title."

His body stiffened. "Awards are one thing, but this is different. Partnership means my name on the letterhead and a piece of the action. I want that." His voice rose. "I've had enough of salaries and skimpy bonuses. I want an equity share in the business." He stared off into space. "I'd be the youngest partner H&R ever had."

She slid her arm behind him and hugged. It was the only thing she could do. "There's lots of time."

Another long sigh shook his body. "I know. It's just that I work my butt off and I want recognition, both the applause and the big bucks." Mostly, she thought, the big bucks. That was the way he measured his success, as, she guessed, most men did.

"I know, darling, and I'm sure you'll get it eventually." She took a breath. "Did you look at any more houses today?" She knew the change of subject might lift his spirits. They'd been searching for a house to buy for almost a year. At first, whenever the real estate lady called, Pam had accompanied her husband to open house after open house. After the twentieth perfectly acceptable one he rejected for some reason she couldn't fathom, she decided to let him to weed out the chaff, then visit only those that made the final cut.

He brightened immediately. "Actually, I think I've found a solution to the whole house problem."

She sat up and turned to face him, a wide smile on her face. "Tell me," she said.

"Well, you know that piece of land down by the stream off Maple Row?"

"The one that the builder's had so much trouble getting the town to approve because of the marshy areas along the waterway?"

"Yeah. I've been exchanging e-mails with the guy and he thinks he's found a way to create oddly shaped parcels that the town might just go along with. He says we can get in on the ground floor and he'll build to suit."

"I thought we'd decided that building a house would be too expensive."

"It's more than we'd planned to spend, but I think it'll be worth it. We're close enough to the city to lure lots of clients to great parties there. I think the partners will be impressed, too."

"We really shouldn't buy something just to impress people." She listened to herself and realized how self-righteous she sounded. But they'd gone over the numbers several times and discovered that the cost of building the kind of house Vin wanted would be astronomical. And she knew that once the house was begun, he wouldn't settle for less than the best.

"Pam, relax." His voice took on a slightly patronizing tone. "I won't put us into debt just to impress a bunch of folks I don't care about, but this would really be a great deal. Think of it. Only half an hour from the city and less than ten minutes from the train station. We can throw parties, have taxis pick people up at the station and ferry them to the new place. Everyone will be green with envy." He was talking faster now. "The builder will have to cut his price since the frontage will be severely limited by the shape of the parcels. We can probably do the whole thing for under five hundred thousand."

Five hundred thousand dollars sounded like a fortune to her, but Vin seemed to take it all in stride. "You've done quite a bit of thinking about this, haven't you," she said. It wasn't a question but a statement of fact. She didn't really mind him weeding out the unsatisfactory houses, but she was a little annoyed that he seemed to be making these big decisions without consulting her.

"I guess I have, and it's really ideal. I knew you wouldn't stand in my way. You've never said a thing against the idea." She looked at him and raised a dubious eyebrow. "Okay," he continued, "I know I should have been discussing this with you, but until the last few days this house had been only a slight possibility. Now it seems it might just happen and I want to be there with a down payment and a previously arranged mortgage when it does. It's my dream."

So many things "might" happen. Most of the time, if she shut her mouth and just went along, the things didn't happen and she was saved from having to put up a fuss. She pictured the property he was talking about. He'd taken her to see it when the possibility of buying it had first arisen, but that had been almost five months before and she hadn't heard anything about it since. The area certainly was beautiful, though, tall oaks and maples interspersed with pine and hemlock. Fields of wildflowers on either side of a meandering brook. It would be quite a spot for a modest home. The land would be pricey, but they might be able to afford it if the cost of the house could be kept within reasonable limits. But could Vin rein in his desires? "It sounds fine," she said, unwilling to dampen Vin's high spirits, "and it might work as long as we're careful and build something modest, maybe around two hundred and fifty thousand dollars. When will the builder know?"

"Actually, I should know about both the promotion and the house within the next few weeks." Vin put his feet on the coffee table and held her close, seeming to sense her unease. "Relax, baby. It will all work out. When I make partner there will be a big increase in my compensation and, with a cut of the profits, we'll be able to afford anything we want."

Chapter
3

Three months passed and, since Vin still didn't have his partnership, he was talking more and more about forming his own agency. Work had also begun on "the house." Funny, Pam thought, she always thought of it in quotes. The builder had named the cul-de-sac Maple Court and had arranged six houses on pie-shaped, four-acre parcels in such a way that the frontage on the court itself was barely wider than the driveway but the land opened out in the back all the way to the stream.

At first the house had been kept modest. They'd met with a well-known local architect and discussed a three-bedroom raised ranch. She'd been delighted with the ideas the architect put forth, but Vin seemed dissatisfied. "What about something colonial, with maybe four bedrooms upstairs?"

"Sure," the architect had said, "we can do that," and he'd begun to sketch out a design. Plan after plan was changed and finally, as she had with house hunting, Pam let Vin meet with the architect himself. Only later did Pam find out that Vin had added bedrooms, baths, and a second family room until the final plans called for a building of almost seven thousand square feet, not including the three-car garage. There were two fireplaces, one a unique arrangement that could be opened to either the dining room or the living room and one in the master suite. There was an area set aside for a large, covered outdoor patio with a built-in grill, sink, refrigerator, and spacious cabinets. The twenty-five by fifty in-the-ground pool and some distance behind it the hot tub that seated ten were surrounded by a decorative wrought-iron fence with a locking gate to protect them from children. It would all be elaborately landscaped so that the pool would be surrounded with flowers and flowering trees. People bathing in either would barely be able to see the house.

As they looked at the final drawings together Pam was speechless. "When did all these changes happen, and why on earth do we need five bedrooms?" she asked.

"I know we haven't got any children," he said, and by his expression she felt he was again digging at her inability to give him a son, "but we'll be doing lots of weekend entertaining. Folks who don't want to go back to the city can sleep over."

When he used the "no-children bomb" she lost her desire to rein him in, so she shut her mouth.

Vin started DePalma Advertising several months after ground was broken, and both the house and the business were going so well he pooh-poohed Pam's suggestions that he forgo some of the amenities. In the end "the house" took the better part of six months to complete but Pam had to admit that Vin, the builder, and the architect had created something special.

The downstairs was dominated by a cathedral-ceilinged entrance hall and enormous living room with a full guest bath, a dining room that could house a table for twelve, a media room that would eventually be filled with two big-screen TVs, a game console, VCR, CD and DVD players, and the biggest speakers Pam had ever seen.

The kitchen was a wonder. Red and gray granite countertops and what seemed like acres of cabinets, a built-in range top with four ovens—one conventional, one convection, and two microwaves—and what looked like an industrial stainless-steel refrigerator that was big enough, as Pam told people, to hold several dead bodies. As she shopped for furniture Pam kept trying to get Vin to set a budget, but he assured her that they could afford anything she wanted. "Get the best," he said. "You never know who we might want to entertain."

Pam was usually a judicious shopper, but at Vin's insistence she'd hired a decorator named Carlys who'd selected antique after antique for both the downstairs and the upstairs. Pam finally accepted that she could and should spend outrageous amounts on things she cared nothing about, but, she reasoned, Vin cared and that was enough for her. With Carlys's help, the entire house looked like something out of *House and Garden* magazine. To Pam it was more a showplace than a home, but each time something was added Vin's smile was her reward.

Outside, the landscaping cost a small fortune since the builder had been forced to remove several big trees. Once it was done, however, even Pam saw that it had been worth every penny. The house, set back a hundred feet from the base of the driveway, looked like it had magically grown out of a beautiful forest glade, surrounded by azaleas, rhododendrons, and lilacs, with bulbs of every description and dozens of hybrid rose bushes, enough that in addition to the lawn care service to mow and fertilize, they had to hire a separate landscaper just to tend the plants. Vin also insisted that she hire a full-time housekeeper. "You'll be busy with committee meetings and entertaining my clients, so you won't have time to look after such a big house." She'd sighed and allowed herself to be steamrolled. It was always easier just to go along.

The other five houses on Maple Court were built in the same vein, large yet not ostentatious. As the families moved in, Pam became nodding acquaintances with the owners and their wives, the CFO of a major clothing manufacturer, the vice president of a brokerage firm, a very high-priced divorce attorney, and the architect who'd done most of the work on the DePalma house. "You see, even he thinks it's a good investment." Eventually the builder even decided to keep one parcel for himself but hadn't built on it yet.

"What do you think this house would sell for?" Pam asked Vin one afternoon after they'd been living on the court for several weeks.

"I've been keeping up with values as the houses were finished, and I'd say these would go for close to one point five mil."

"One and a half million dollars?" Pam blurted out, aghast. She'd long before lost track of what they were spending. Of course it hadn't *cost* anywhere near that, she assured herself. Values were skyrocketing and they were just benefitting from a good investment. "Holy . . ."

He grinned from ear to ear. "I told you we didn't have to worry about money. Nothing but the best for the DePalmas."

Several weeks after they moved in Vin decided to host a housewarming party. "I'll invite some of my best clients and their wives, too, along with several other potential accounts I've been courting. Maybe fifty or sixty of the best people. They'll all be green with envy and they'll quickly realize how successful I've become. I'd love to rub Haskell's face in it, but I can't think of a way to invite him. Partnership? Who needs it?"

Pam had wanted to invite a few of her friends from the old neighborhood, but when she mentioned that he said, "We'll have a separate party for them. This one will be purely business. DePalma Advertising will pick up a good part of the tab as a business entertainment expense and I'll deduct the rest from our taxes."

While the art director at DePalma created designer invitations, Pam hired a caterer and began the job of getting the house ready for the "grand housewarming." Now she thought of everything about the Maple Court house in quotes. The day before the party, the house swarmed with cleaning people

THE MADAM OF MAPLE COURT

and decorators. Although most of the affair was to be outdoors, Vin had informed her that he would be giving folks the 'nickel tour' so the entire house had to be scrubbed, polished, dusted, and scented from top to bottom. Funny, she thought as she looked at the gaggle of people, they'd just moved in a month ago and already people were able to find things to clean.

The morning of the gathering, florists arrived. Fortunately the weather was fabulous, the day clear and warm as only a few perfect days in May can be in the New York area. All the new bushes and trees had been carefully trimmed, and gardeners had all but clipped each blade of grass with scissors the day before. In addition, bowls and vases of fresh blooms were delivered and placed strategically around both the main floor and the upstairs. Even the bathrooms were festooned with greenery.

As Pam looked around she realized that, were she to plan this gathering, there would be much less of everything. *Less is usually more*, she thought. They could do without the overly fussy floral arrangements and the bowls of hand-selected chocolates and nuts from a New York City chocolatier. To Pam it was ostentatious and screamed "new money," but early on Vin had insisted that he wanted to do it all with the best of everything so she'd demurred as usual.

Then the caterers arrived with truckloads of ingredients. As Pam walked into the spacious kitchen she could barely see the appliances. A chef was directing the assembled multitude with the finesse of an orchestra conductor, while his minions stuffed mushrooms, deveined shrimp, made mayonnaise from scratch, and did a hundred other tasks to create finger food for the hundred guests Vin had invited. Pam shook her head in awe and walked out into the backyard.

That too had been transformed. A dozen small tables with sparkling white tablecloths had been arranged around the patio. There was a small wooden floor for dancing beside a raised platform for the string quartet, which would be replaced late in the afternoon by a three-piece band for dancing. Originally Vin had wanted to have someone barbecuing steaks to order, but the caterer had flatly refused to have that "smoky mess" all over his yard. *His yard.* Pam could only smile. Thank God it was only one afternoon.

When the guests began arriving and the valet parking staff began to shuttle cars to the parking area at the elementary school several blocks away, Pam accepted that it had all been worth it. "This house is amazing." "I can't get over how lovely the grounds are." "It must have cost the earth." "I hadn't realized how well Vin was doing." "And look at that pool. I gather it's heated, too." "And it's got a spa, too, with a sauna."

She had bought a new outfit for the occasion, a gauzy silk blouse patterned with swirls of deep blue and turquoise, over full, matching deep blue silk pants. She wore large silver and turquoise earrings and a thick matching bracelet and necklace. She'd had her soft brown hair cut and blow-dried in the city in a sophisticated jaw-length style that curved beneath her chin and accented her oval face. At Vin's insistence she'd even had her makeup done that morning, and she had to admit that the soft mauve shadow and liner made her brown eyes look deeper and slightly exotic.

For hours she worked the room as Vin had suggested. She moved from one group to another, making sure that everyone was entertained. Several times she carried a tray of champagne flutes to be sure that all the guests were feeling relaxed. She fielded compliments on the house and the party with an innate charm that she hadn't realized she had.

The small combo began playing at five-thirty, and several couples made use of the dance floor. At six the guests adjourned to an elaborate buffet and took plates to the tables. By ten that evening the moon had risen and finally everyone had departed.

"That was quite a party," she said to Vin as they dropped

THE MADAM OF MAPLE COURT

onto lounge chairs beside the pool. "I think everything went really well."

"It certainly did, and a few very big people said they'd call me next week. It certainly showed how far I've come."

"Everyone seemed to have a great time." After several minutes Pam huffed out a breath and swung her legs off the chair. "Let me change into jeans," she said to Vin as she looked around at the masses of glasses and plates cluttering every horizontal surface, "and I'll get started cleaning up this joint."

He grabbed her by the wrist and pulled her onto the chair beside him. "Forget everything. I arranged with the same folks who cleaned up yesterday. They'll be here first thing tomorrow morning and they'll take care of everything." He kissed her lightly on the top of her head. "You were a wonder, darling," he said, holding her close. "Even Eugene Banner Senior commented on how charming you are and what an asset you are to me. He really meant it. You were fabulous."

She had no idea who Eugene Banner Senior was, but Vin's tone showed that he was impressed, so she was, too. "I didn't do much," Pam said, glowing under his praise. "The people you hired did most of the work."

"You held it all together. Next time you'll be able to direct and organize everything."

"Next time?"

"Several of my clients wondered whether they could use the house for their office summer and Christmas parties and I said we'd think about it. Can't you picture a Christmas party: big tree in the corner, fire in the fireplace, eggnog, the works. I didn't promise anything, and I wouldn't without checking with you, love, but it would mean a lot to me. I'm incredibly complimented that anyone would even suggest it."

"I guess," she said. It would be a lot of work, but if it would advance Vin's career . . .

"Listen, you take to this like the proverbial duck to water.

You were the most charming hostess I've ever seen and it means a lot to me, and to my future."

She laughed and punched him in the ribs. "You know flattery will get you anywhere with me."

"It might be flattery, but it's also true. Will you do it? For me?" He stroked her face and turned her toward him. "Please?" He kissed her and his hand found her breast.

Pam sighed. Vin was getting deeper and deeper into his image, and appearances were becoming more and more important. Pam often thought that even the vacations they took were planned as much for the cachet they gave him at the office as for the pleasure they would give the two of them. *What the hell?* She kissed him back and slid her fingers through his hair. *What the hell? If this is what he wants, why not?*

Over the next few months, to further enhance his reputation at the office he began to buy hand-tailored suits, monogrammed shirts, and Italian leather shoes. He became a technojunky, getting a PDA before any of his cohorts and one of the fanciest cellular phones made. He was on his way up. Way up. That had been more than two years ago, she thought. And now?

Pam pulled herself back to the present. "Where did the money go, Mark? I really thought we had lots."

"Frankly, Pam, I haven't a clue. I know he lost a few good clients, but I thought he still had some. I must admit that I was a little surprised at the state of his finances."

"It all went into the business? He took almost half a million out of the house last year. Everything's gone?" Pam slumped in her chair. "I'm in shock."

Mark reached across the desk and took Pam's hand. She sensed there was something going on beneath his calm exterior. "I can imagine." He lowered his voice and seemed almost conspiratorial. "Pam, I don't know whether I should say anything to you, and I don't mean to imply anything illegal or im-

THE MADAM OF MAPLE COURT

moral, but maybe there are accounts I don't know about. Secret ones."

"You mean that Vin might have been moving money to the Cayman Islands or something?"

He looked uncomfortable. "I don't know what I mean. I'm pretty sure Vin was an honest man." She watched him make a decision. He gazed directly into her eyes. "I've known you and Vin for many years, and it's just that there's not as much money as I thought there should be, either, and I can't imagine where it might have gone. I suspect that he's been either hoarding cash or spending it on something besides the business. I hadn't wanted to bother you, but frankly I'm stumped and you deserve to know what was going on."

"Something beside the business? Like what? Other women? Gambling?"

Mark sat up straight and looked miserable. "Let's not jump to any conclusions. Please." He clasped his hands on the desk. "Let's do this. You take some time and then go through the papers in his desk at home. See whether you can find anything—records, bank statements, credit card bills, anything like that, anything that might give a hint of where some of this money might have gone. I'll give you a complete list of everything I know about and you can compare what you find with that. Maybe there are bank accounts I don't know about. Let's hope so, anyway."

"Why don't you come out to the house and look for yourself?"

"I'd rather you did it. If there turn out to be tax implications I'd rather find out all at once." He didn't say, or not at all.

"What if we find something illegal? Should we go to the police or the IRS?"

"Let's consider that if, and it's a very big if, the time comes. Take your time and call me when you've had a chance to look over his things. Don't hurry. Take a few weeks if you want to."

Chapter

4

It was almost three months before Pam finally got up the courage to look through Vin's office for any of the information Mark had alluded to. Oren Stevens had called frequently, keeping her abreast of the developments at the agency, and several times he'd asked her to come into the city to sign papers. However, it was all just dotting the i's and crossing the t's necessary to close the business down. He'd asked her whether she wanted to go through Vin's office but she declined, so he'd packed up several large boxes and had them delivered to the house.

Mark had also called from time to time but he kept saying that she could let any investigating slide, so she kept putting it off. What if she found that he'd been doing something illegal? What if he'd been being blackmailed or something? What if any of the things she signed in ignorance would get her into some kind of trouble? She was sure that whatever she found wouldn't make her happy and so she delayed, and delayed, and delayed.

It was now almost four months since Vin's death and she was surprised at how little she'd mourned. She was sad, and confused, and lonely, but she kept waiting for the deep pit of grief that she thought she ought to be feeling. Day after day she examined her soul, but that misery just wasn't there. She wasn't happy, but she wasn't devastated, either. The membership at the country club had another six months to run and the people had been supportive and urged her to get back into the swing of things, so she'd slowly begun doing some of the things she'd done before.

She spent her days playing bridge, which bored her a little, and had quickly gotten back to her work with her favorite charities. In the beginning she'd joined because Vin insisted that mingling with the rich and dedicated would be good for his image, but from the beginning she'd enjoyed the work: keeping up with mailing lists, designing Web sites, and particularly planning fund-raising functions for anywhere from a dozen to several hundred people, a skill she honed with the frequent gatherings she organized for Vin. She became a prominent hostess, someone a group could come to. Occasionally she donated the use of her home and she quickly discovered that she was good at that kind of enterprise and earned a lot of praise from those around her. No one questioned the fact that since Vin's death, although she donated her time, she no longer wrote large checks to the various organizations.

At first the women she worked with were solicitous and careful not to mention Vin, but eventually they began to treat her easily. None of the women were friends, exactly, but they were familiar. The women she'd been close to earlier when they lived in White Plains all had children and they had less and less in common, so they eventually drifted apart. Real friends, people she could talk to about serious things like feelings and fears, didn't exist.

Now that she had a little distance from her husband she found she was able to organize her thoughts and think more clearly about her marriage. Who was this man she had been married to for all those years? Did she know him? As she thought about it she realized that, over the past few years,

THE MADAM OF MAPLE COURT

they'd led separate lives, intertwined yet distant, twin circles with only tiny overlaps.

Vin had his business and it had taken inordinate amounts of his time. He was seldom home before ten or eleven, attending business dinners, taking prospective clients to sporting events and Broadway shows, working on campaigns until all hours. Of course they often entertained together and she had learned to love Broadway, although sports still left her cold so Vin went on forays to Yankees or Knicks games without her.

Did she love him? *How did that question get into my brain?* she asked herself as she finished her shower one morning. However it got there, it was a valid question, one she could now think about with some objectivity. Love? She wasn't sure she knew what the word meant. Didn't love include trust? She'd been worried for months that he'd been doing something illegal and so she'd put off looking through his things for fear she'd find out something she didn't want to know. But wouldn't she jump to his defense if she loved him? Wouldn't she immediately and vigorously deny that he could have been doing anything illegal?

It was time to find out everything, no matter the risk. She'd been putting off digging into her own finances, too, and had let Mark handle it all. Strange. She could do a creditable job with the computer programs that took care of the finances at two of the larger charities she was involved in, but she knew next to nothing about her own. That had to stop, too.

The morning was bright and unusually warm for late winter, and as she walked through her bedroom she realized that work would have to begin on the landscaping of the house. It made no sense to let things go. She'd have a good look at the budget Mark had made up for her and see whether she could afford to continue the kind of outdoor work that had been done for the past few years.

She glanced at Vin's wide closet and realized that she'd also have to do something about donating Vin's clothes to any one of several charities. She wondered which one could make good use of his thousand-dollar suits, hundred-dollar silk ties, and the shirts that weren't monogrammed.

Trying again to put off her trip to the den, she wandered through the four guest bedrooms, now smelling just a little musty. As she opened the windows in each to let the rooms air out, she looked around. Mark had told her she needed money. That might be less of a problem than he realized. The furniture in these rooms had cost the earth and she could easily sell the expensive stuff and replace it with good, classic contemporary pieces. She'd have to see whether Carlys, the decorator who had bought most of these pieces in the first place, could be of some help.

She could fend off the most serious financial problems for a while, but selling furniture wasn't a long-term solution. It was time to give some serious thought to what she would do in the longer term. Slowly she wended her way through the upstairs, refolding a guest towel here, fluffing a pillow there. Eventually she descended the stairs and headed for the den, squaring her shoulders as she got closer to the closed room. She had a job to do and it was time for her to do it.

The den/office was masculine, Vin's territory, done mostly in beiges and browns, with moss green, cranberry, and navy accents. She'd always thought the room a little gloomy, but Vin liked it. An oversized seventeenth-century mahogany desk stood on one side of the room, a wall of bookcases opposite. She'd read many of the volumes but Vin didn't enjoy reading. He kept them mostly for show. She was surprised that, at every mental turn, she faced ways in which she and her late husband were different. *Opposites attract*, she thought. Yeah, but once attracted what did they have to talk about?

She sat down on Vin's chair. The desk was much too high for her tiny frame, so she took a pillow off the small leather

THE MADAM OF MAPLE COURT

sofa and put it beneath her. The surface of the desk was a little dusty but uncluttered, with only a desk lamp, a computer monitor, a date book, and several pictures to mar the stark relief. She stared at the photographs: Vin with the head of a major pharmaceutical firm, Vin shaking hands with an ex-mayor of New York, Vin accepting the Ad-Man of the Year award from H&R. No personal photos. Nothing of her. She slowly shook her head. It wasn't as if her dresser was covered with intimate portraits of him, either. She pictured the highly polished silver frames filled with vacation shots: them in front of the Taj Mahal, her in front of a Buddhist monastery, them in ski clothes on top of a mountain in Switzerland. She couldn't immediately remember which mountain that had been.

Stop putting this off, she told herself and grabbed the center drawer. To her surprise it wouldn't move. Locked. She tried the side drawers but they wouldn't budge either. Why would Vin lock his desk? Did he have secrets from her? Where would the keys be? She thought about his briefcase and personal effects. She'd stored his case and the rest of the items she'd gotten from the police, still in a brown envelope, in the hall closet. She hadn't had the nerve to open anything until now. Well, she had to do what had to be done, so she steeled herself on the slow walk to the closet. Her mind drifted.

"Are you Ms. DePalma? Ms. Vincent DePalma?" the police officer who had rung the doorbell had asked. He'd looked very cold, and snow covered the shoulders of his uniform. His breath came out in little streams of vapor. It had been unseasonably cold that day.

When she saw his face she'd known that her life was about to change and she hadn't wanted to hear what she knew he was going to tell her. "I'm Pam DePalma."

"I'm afraid I have some difficult news for you. There's been an accident."

Not wanting to allow her mind to go where it needed to go,

she'd thought, *I wonder who you have to have angered to get the job of telling bad news to unsuspecting wives.* She wanted to make it easier for him. "He's dead," she said, her voice flat.

"I'm so sorry for your loss. He was on the Hutch, doing in excess of the limit in the snow, and his car went out of control and hit a bridge abutment. I'm so sorry."

She looked at the cop. He was probably no more than twenty, with a baby face, flaming red hair, and cheeks full of freckles. Funny, she must be numb. All she could think of was comforting him. When she didn't react immediately, the cop said, "Is there someone I can call for you? Family, a friend, someone from your church?"

"There's no one I need right now," she said. Was there someone she wanted to be with at this moment? She couldn't think of anyone. "It's okay. I'll be all right." She'd ushered him out and sat in the living room for a long time.

The following morning a police detective had taken her to identify her husband's remains. It wasn't the real thing, just a photograph of his face, and she could barely make out his features through her tears. The detective had put his arm around her shoulders and she'd accepted the comfort he'd offered. "That's my husband."

He'd given her a cup of coffee and suggested that she might want to see her physician and have the doctor prescribe a sedative, then he'd handed her Vin's briefcase and a fat brown envelope with Vin's personal effects inside. She'd seen the doctor, filled the prescription he'd given her, and, except for the funeral arrangements, most of which Mark had taken care of for her, and the actual event, she'd slept for more than a week. She'd spent the following week in a fog, taking antidepressants like they were candy, hoping that each morning the emptiness would lessen. Emptiness. Not sadness but an overall purposelessness. What should she do? The heads of each of her charities had called, expressed their sympathy, and told her that she should take her time getting back, if she went back at all. They spouted platitudes and told her how much they sympathized, but she got the feeling that they were thinking, *Thank God it's not me.* Both Doug Haskell and Walt Roth had called to offer their condolences. She answered all the calls with brief good grace.

Had it been almost four months already? She opened the closet door and pulled the envelope down from the shelf. She returned to the desk, tore the envelope open, and spilled the contents on the desktop. His cell phone and his personal organizer. His watch. A Lucian Piccard day, date chronograph. She'd given that to him for their tenth anniversary. She looked at the back. MTYLTT. More than yesterday, less than tomorrow. Had she meant that then? Did it really matter? He was gone and that was that.

She put the watch back on the desk and picked up his wallet. Eel skin. That had been for his twenty-ninth birthday. He'd dropped hints for weeks, saying that everyone who was anyone had eel skin wallets. Six hundred dollars later he had one, too, with his initials in gold on the front. His cufflinks, gold and ruby. He had a dozen pair with different stones, nothing under a thousand dollars. She'd sell those, along with much of her jewelry, to lengthen the time before she had to make a decision about the rest of her life. There was three hundred forty dollars inside his wallet as well as his driver's license, several credit cards, and the other pieces of plastic that his complicated life demanded. She flipped through them. No real surprises there, although what had she really known of his life?

His keys. She picked up the heavy ring. She recognized the front door key, a key to his Mercedes, now returned to the dealer, and her Lexus, as well as the key to his Corvette. She'd complained when he bought it that, since it was a standard shift, she couldn't drive it. "Of course it's standard shift," Vin had said. "You don't put an automatic transmission in a car like this. It would be silly." No sense keeping that key, she thought, nor the key to the Mercedes. She pocketed the key to her car and dropped the other two into the garbage can under the desk.

There were several other keys. She knew he kept his office keys in his briefcase, so she hoped the key to his desk was one of these. She tried each in the desk drawer lock. The third one fit and unlocked the center drawer. She opened the drawer and found nothing of immediate interest. The top two side drawers contained little more. The bottom drawer on the right, however, was filled with files. She glanced over the tabs. Vin was well organized, so they were carefully labeled with machine made labels. HSBC Bank statements. She didn't remember an HSBC account. All their personal banking was with Citibank.

She hurried upstairs, found the list Mark had given her, and returned to the den. There was no HSBC account listed there, either. Maybe it was a corporate account. Sure. That was it. It had to be. But why was the folder here and not at the office? She pulled the folder out of the drawer and opened it. Bank statements, deposits of cash—more than ten thousand a month—and transfers to pay a credit card bill. Credit card? She went through his wallet again and found an HSBC platinum Visa card.

She returned to the drawer and found the folder that contained the credit card statements. Some of the charges were for hotel rooms in the city, expensive dinners in the best restaurants, many of which she and Vin had been to. She tried to remember which credit card he'd usually used, but that kind of thing never registered. with her. She looked at the dates and opened his date book to a calendar. The charges were almost exclusively on Thursdays, evenings she almost always had committee meetings. If these were clients of De-Palma Advertising he'd have used the company American Express platinum card.

The most puzzling charges were for CF+Co. The amounts were pretty consistent, two thousand dollars almost every week. CF+Co? What the hell was that about? Another woman? She didn't want to consider that there had been anyone else, but it was difficult not to entertain the possibility.

If he'd been unfaithful, if he'd had sex with another woman, did she care? She would be hurt by the idea, of course, and hate the idea of the lies he must have had to tell her, but if she were being honest, she realized that things hadn't been going well between them, in and out of the bedroom, for a very long time. *No! Stop it! Don't go there, not yet!*

She glanced back at the credit card statement, picked a date at random, and checked it against Vin's date book. Blank. There was nothing in the book about any dinner and nothing to indicate what CF+Co was. However, there was no doubt that this was where much of the missing money had gone. She thumbed through the credit card bills. More than one hundred thousand dollars had been charged to that credit card in the last year. That was more than he could have been paying for another woman. Unless he'd set her up in an apartment in the city? But what else could this be? Blackmail? Gambling? Drugs? No, probably not drugs. She'd have known if he'd been using something illegal, wouldn't she? Anyway, dealers didn't take credit cards. Neither did blackmailers. Was he going to some back room poker game or something?

She found Vin's briefcase where she'd put it months earlier, but there was nothing inside to clear up the credit card mystery. She'd have to find out what had been going on some other way.

She logged on to Vin's computer, looked for any records of CF+Co and, finding nothing, Googled CF+Co. Still nothing. What else could she search for? Where else could she look? When she kept coming up empty, she telephoned Mark and told him about the bank account and the credit card. "I've no idea what it could be," Mark said when she'd finished. "He never gave me any such records."

"I've had several thoughts. The primary one is gambling. Anything illegal would hardly take a credit card." And women.

"Would you like me to get in touch with someone who can do some discreet inquiry? It seems to me that we don't want to do anything too precipitous. It could all be nothing."

She took a deep breath. "Not likely. Maybe you should stay out of it. Can you give me the name of someone, a detective who does this kind of thing?"

"Sure. I've worked with a guy named Gary Jannson of Jannson Security Services. He usually does corporate work, but he's a straight-up guy with great contacts and a secretive disposition." He gave Pam a phone number. "I'll call him and let him know you'll be making an appointment. Bring along the bank and credit card statements so he knows where to start." She wrote down the number he gave her and put the slip of paper in her pocket.

It was strange how finding that Vin had secrets energized Pam. She went up to the bedroom and packed some of Vin's things to give to charity. More went into large gray trash bags. Somehow it felt more like a cleansing of her mind than her bedroom. She went to the local Wal-Mart and bought new sheets and when she got home, put them on the bed. She also vowed to make an appointment with Mark and take back control of her finances. She was ready to reenter the world for real.

Finding that Vin had some kind of a clandestine life made it easier for Pam to deal with her feelings, or lack thereof, too. Whatever she felt, it was okay and she'd deal with whatever the detective found out. She could handle it.

When her energy flagged she went down to the kitchen and made a cup of espresso, then went back into Vin's den and looked at the credit card statements more carefully. It seemed that the charges began just over a year ago. What had

THE MADAM OF MAPLE COURT 45

changed then? Anything beside the business going badly? Was this woman his ego boost?

As she sipped her coffee she went over the past few years of her marriage. She remembered incidents, arguments they'd had about nothing. She remembered one in particular. He wanted her to help out with MADD, Mothers Against Drunk Driving. "It's a great cause. The son of the CEO at one of my accounts was killed by a drunken driver about a year ago and they've gotten really heavily into it. You could meet them, sort of accidentally, and seem really hot to help."

Mothers. She couldn't get past that word. She'd never lost a child, never even had a child. How could she possibly relate to women who'd suffered as they had? "Vin, no. I'd have nothing in common with them, and I really don't have time. Between battered women, leukemia and save the wilderness, I've got all I can handle."

"You don't know anyone who had leukemia, nor do you have anything in common with low-class women whose husbands knock them around from time to time, probably with good reason."

Pam remembered being horrified at his reaction. Low-class women? Good reason? Who was this man she was married to? However, as always, she'd kept her mouth shut. Could she get involved with MADD? It would be good for Vin's career. She clamped her jaws tightly. How long had she been keeping her mouth shut about important things? Too long? "Not MADD. I'm really sorry and I'd love to help you out with your business, but no."

"Come on, honey. It's just another place to use your gifts of organization. You could even use the house for another fundraiser. The Shepards could come and it would do me so much good."

"I'm really sorry, Vin, but I'm firm on this. I just can't."

"Won't, you mean."

"Whatever word you want to use, it won't happen."

"Because you can't have children? Is that what this is all about?"

She'd almost changed her mind, but then shook her head slowly. "No. I just don't want to."

Vin huffed out a breath and folded his arms tightly across his chest. "You have to do what you have to do, of course." Pam could tell he was furious, but she just couldn't do what he wanted. That had been about a year before, around the time the charges started.

As she sat at Vin's desk with the credit card bill in her hand, she wondered whether she should have read things into that conversation. He'd used all his tricks. The "you can't have children." The body language. The "it's for the business." Had that been the first time she'd refused him? She tried to think of another time and couldn't. His methods had always worked before.

From then on she'd gone into the city to meet him on fewer and fewer occasions. She hadn't really focused on it until now, but they'd begun to drift apart. Drift? She was still on the same course, but he'd started to move increasingly rapidly in a different direction. Maybe the other woman met his needs better than she could. When had he stopped loving her? And she had still loved him deeply.

Stop conning yourself and think seriously. Had she still loved him deeply? Had she still loved him at all? She tried to sort it all out. She liked him. Didn't she? She didn't really know anything anymore.

Pam took a deep breath. Examining her feelings wouldn't help her now. She'd do that when she'd found out whether she was right about the other woman. She pulled the phone number out of her pocket and dialed. "Jannson Security Services," a soft, cultured woman said.

"Good afternoon. I'm Pam DePalma and I think Mark Redmond called a little while ago about me. May I talk to Mr. Jannson, please?"

"Let me see whether he's got a minute to talk to you. This has been a very busy afternoon." There was an unexpected warmth in her voice. Pam made a great many calls for her various charities and she was used to rather impersonal receptionists. Maybe this was his wife or something. Whoever she was, her comfortable attitude made things easier for Pam, and she imagined, for the people with the kinds of problems one hired a private detective for.

She heard the phone connect. "Gary Jannson."

"Mr. Jannson, I'm Pam DePalma. I think Mark Redmond talked to you earlier about some work I need done."

"Of course." His voice was warm and somehow comforting. She could picture angry wives trusting him to find out the dirt on their husbands. She was doing pretty much the same thing, except that Vin was dead. "Mark only gave me the barest outline of what you need. Can you come into the office one day soon? I'll see what you've got and we'll talk about what I can do to help."

What he can do to help. Nice way of putting it. "That would be fine." He gave her the address of his office in White Plains and they made an appointment for two days later.

Chapter

5

Pam expected the offices of Jannson Security Services to be in a slightly seedy building on the outskirts of White Plains, but when she arrived at the address she found a seven-story steel and glass building in the heart of the business district. She drove around until she found a municipal parking lot and put enough money in the meter for three hours. She had no idea how long she'd have to wait.

She was nervous and it surprised her. She hadn't anticipated the trembling in her knees as she crossed the street to his building. What was she afraid of? Maybe it was as simple as fear of knowing that she'd finally find out what had been going on. She'd been able to talk herself in and then out of several scenarios over the past forty-eight hours. It couldn't be any of the things she'd been thinking. CF+Co was sure to turn out to be something totally innocent. If it wasn't, did she really want to know? she asked herself for the thousandth time. Yes, she needed to find out.

The company office was on the fourth floor, and when she opened the door she found as lovely an office as she could envision, a look she'd tried to get for DePalma Advertising, warm, accepting, friendly without being too intimate or too flashy. The furnishings in the reception area were in muted shades of off-whites and browns, ranging from ecru to toast, with accents of deep royal blue. A gigantic sofa upholstered in a nubby oatmeal tweed was flanked by several matching chairs and two done in tan leather. The landscape over the sofa was probably not an old master, but had the feel of quality. A low white ash coffee table was covered with current issues of everything from *House Beautiful* to *USA Today*. They didn't look particularly well thumbed. She wondered whether that meant that not many people were left waiting for long or that the company's clients brought their own work.

She was five minutes early but when she introduced herself to the receptionist, a fortyish woman with little make-up, neat hair and, Pam was sure, sensible shoes, the well-turned-out woman said, "Of course, Ms. DePalma. Mr. Jannson will be with you in just a moment."

She buzzed him and almost immediately motioned to a hallway. "Through there, first door on the left."

As Pam walked toward the door the receptionist had indicated, it was opened by a man who was the antithesis of everything she'd expected. Rather than being someone like Columbo, Gary Jannson was of medium height, with a head full of blond curls that would have done beautifully on a fashion model. Or an angel. His deep blue eyes flashed and his smile was broad. He extended a well-manicured hand. "Ms. DePalma. It's nice to meet you."

He ushered her into his office, done in the same calming color family, this time in shades of eggshell and caramel. Calming? She realized that her heart was pounding and her palms were sweaty. She smoothed them down the flanks of her deep green pants and slipped the matching jacket off her shoulders, draping it on the back of a leather chair. Her blouse was silk, patterned in thin forest green stripes on an off-white background, her jewelry simple, classic chunky gold. She made herself as comfortable as she could while Gary Jannson made his way to his chair and settled easily. "If you don't mind, Ms. DePalma, I'm going to make some notes as we talk."

"Of course. And it's Pam. We'll never get anywhere being formal."

His smile widened, showing even, white teeth. "Good. I'm Gary. Only my father rates the Mr. Jannson stuff. Can I get you some coffee? A soft drink or a bottle of water, perhaps?"

"No, nothing, thank you." She was too nervous to think of putting anything in her stomach. She inhaled, then realized that she didn't quite know where to begin. She shifted in her chair.

"I'm sure this is difficult for you," Gary said, "so why don't you take your time and tell me what the problem is."

"You spoke to Mark Redmond?"

"He told me only that you might need some discreet inquiries made. He didn't elaborate."

Pam took a deep breath. "I guess that's for the best. It's not something I want everyone and his brother to know about. I need to know what CF+Co is." She said the name as Cee Eff Plus Co.

"Just that?"

"I won't know whether I want anything else until I know the answer to that question."

Gary swivelled his chair around and tapped a few keys on his computer.

"I already tried Google," Pam said.

"Okay. I have a few other resources. Let me see what I can find." His long, slender pianist's fingers flew over the keyboard. Occasionally he'd make small humphing noises. "I can't find anything right off the top. Are you sure they exist?"

She handed him one of the credit card statements. "I see," he said, looking them over. "Maybe you'd better tell me a little more about why you want to know about them."

She spent the next few minutes telling Gary only the bare minimum, that her husband had been killed in a traffic accident and she'd found these statements about which she'd known nothing before.

"I'm sorry about your husband's death, Pam."

"It's been almost four months and it's not quite as raw as it was."

"Are you afraid he was leading some kind of secret life?"

"I don't know anything more than what I've shown you. I don't know what it means at all. All I know is that, to my calculations, he's charged almost a hundred thousand dollars to this company in the last year or so."

"It doesn't take much to create an identity to make the credit card companies happy. It could be almost anything."

"I know that, but there are a few things at the top of my list."

"Like?"

"Another woman. I thought this might be some real estate venture where he'd set up someone in her own apartment, like that."

"What else?"

"Drugs, gambling, I don't know. How many illegal activities take credit cards?"

"A lot more than one might expect, actually. Why don't you let me put one of my best financial guys on this and I'll get back to you in a day or two?"

"I assume you'll want a retainer."

He grinned. "I take credit cards."

She smiled for the first time since she entered his office. She reached into her purse and withdrew her checkbook. "How much?"

He told her his hourly rate and she wrote a check for five hours of his time. "Of course my associates bill at a slightly lower figure. Don't worry about the money. It will take care of itself, and if there's anything left over when we're done I'll be glad to refund it."

THE MADAM OF MAPLE COURT   53

She dropped her chin. "One of the problems since my husband's death is that my funds are limited."

"We'll cross that bridge when we come to it, Pam. Don't be concerned. I promise I won't rack up thousands of dollars of expenses without consulting with you first. This should be pretty straightforward."

"That's fine." She didn't like the idea of coming across as some poor waif, but maybe she should get used to that image. She really didn't want to get into details with this man, but he was so easy to talk to that she almost poured out the entire story. She could see why people trusted him to find out their deepest secrets.

"Good. If we have to go into things more deeply I'll ask for specific authorization and give you estimates. No surprises. For now, let me see what I can find out about CF+Co."

She stood and extended her hand. His grip was firm and his hands were soft. It was the first time she'd noticed anything about anyone since Vin's death, and she felt good about it. "I'll call you when I have anything to report." He'd taken down her name, address, and both her home and cell phone numbers.

"Thanks, Gary. You've made this easier than I expected."

"I'm glad of that."

As the door closed behind Pam, Gary leaned his chair back and steepled his fingers. She was quite a woman, straightforward and seemingly not afraid of what she might find out. She was also very attractive, in a comfortable way. She wore her hair loose and it swung around her face when she moved. Her make-up was understated, as were her clothes. Simple, yet classic.

CF+Co. He wouldn't have to bill her much for actual investigation. He had known immediately what it was, a high-priced brothel. He'd known about Club Fantasy for several years, since a client had wanted them checked out to be sure he wouldn't be blackmailed for indulging in some of his more exotic fantasies. From everything he knew, they were totally honest without any black marks against the character of any of their employees. He knew of the owners, Jenna and Marcy Bryant, both now married. He knew that Jenna lived in upstate New York with her husband and a few children. Several years before, she had left any direct connection to the club, but her twin sister Marcy, also married with several children, still ran it from her apartment in the city, although she didn't participate in the activities inside the club's brownstone in the East Fifties.

What went on within the walls of the club was a deep secret, but he'd heard through his client that almost any erotic fantasy could be fulfilled. And because of its list of well-known members, the club was free of most law enforcement involvement.

Why hadn't he told Pam about it? He considered that question. When he'd first investigated it, he'd been horrified, but as time passed and he thought more about it and talked to his client, his opinion began to change. Now he believed in what the club did, provide safe and fulfilling entertainment for local and out-of-town business types at a hefty fee. The fact that Vin DePalma had shelled out two thousand dollars a session didn't surprise him, and that he visited regularly once a week wasn't unusual. The fact that Pam hadn't suspected anything was more of a surprise.

He thought about her. What about her sex life with her husband had been so unsatisfying that he'd had to go elsewhere? He realized that there were many men who wanted to try things that they didn't think they could discuss with their wives, and many men seemed to have more powerful sex drives than the women they'd been married to for ten or twenty years. He suspected, however, that had Vin discussed things with his wife, she might have been amenable. He had no coherent idea

THE MADAM OF MAPLE COURT

why he thought that, but there was something in her attitude. She hated having to probe into her late husband's life, afraid of what she might find out, but she knew it had to be done so she was doing it. He reasoned that had Vin come to her and told her he needed something he wasn't getting, she would have made an effort to satisfy him.

He sat back at his desk and let his mind wander, allowed himself a moment to focus on his newest client. Might she be interested in being something more than a client? *Don't be silly.* It was much too soon after her husband's death. But he couldn't get her quiet strength out of his mind. He visualized her hands, soft and well manicured, but with business-length nails. He wondered how they would feel raking down a lover's back.

What in the world led him to think about her that way? He didn't really know, but there was a spark in her that he sensed might be amazing if tapped. He knew he was being very unprofessional. She was a client and he had a strong rule about not dating clients. His firm dealt mostly with computer security, but he did do some detective work for spouses wanting information on the doings of an errant husband or wife. He met people at their most vulnerable and, although he had the opportunity to date and even make love with wives who needed someone with whom to prove their attractiveness, he'd always demurred.

Pam attracted him, but as he straightened and turned to his computer terminal, he vowed that he would keep their relationship professional. Strictly professional.

On Pam's drive home she briefly thought about the attractive man she'd just met. He was sexy, in a cherubic sort of way, but she certainly wasn't in the market for anyone right now. After all, Vin had been gone for less than six months and she was in mourning, wasn't she? She touched the ache inside and found as always that it wasn't sadness. Rather, inside the emptiness there was only a lack of direction.

She'd read a couple of articles on death and dying since the accident and she knew the stages everyone went through. She wasn't following the pattern. Why hadn't she wept? Why had she just accepted Vin's death and not denied it had happened, or railed against God, offering to trade her life for his? Didn't she care enough?

She deliberately changed the direction of her thoughts, considering the ways she'd have to cut back on expenses. Most were small in the great scheme of things, but every dollar would be important. Right after she had talked with Mark she had told her housekeeper that she'd have to cut her back to only one day a week. Pam didn't think she could or wanted to do the daily stuff herself, but she had little choice. She couldn't afford someone every day. The housekeeper told her she'd look for another job, but that her sister did day jobs.

She'd been putting things off, but she knew now that it was time to replace much of the furniture in the upstairs. She had no idea how to go about selling the furniture, and she wanted to be totally private about it. When she got home from her visit with Gary—she thought of him as Gary, not as "the detective"—she talked to Carlys, the woman who had sold her the pieces in the first place, and was delighted to discover that for a reasonable commission, the decorator would take care of disposing of the items and replacing them with drastically less expensive equivalents.

She and Carlys began upstairs and continued through the downstairs. They agreed on several more pieces that could go and that would raise significant cash. Pam was shocked to learn, for example, that a small pie crust table, one she didn't like and always bumped into, would sell for almost twenty-five thousand dollars. When she toted up what she could make, she was delighted to learn that, if Mark's budget figures were in the ballpark, the money she got from the downsizing, as she thought of it, would take care of her expenses for another year.

As she'd suspected, the landscapers weren't going to be as

THE MADAM OF MAPLE COURT

easy to downsize. She talked to the company representative and learned that most of the work they did was necessary to maintain the property. He was quite understanding and told her that even with his men doing only what was necessary, it would still cost a lot. This didn't seem to be a place where she could or should cut back. She had to keep the place in tip-top condition in case she was able to put it on the market.

Two days after their initial meeting, Gary Jannson called and asked her to meet him in his office late one Thursday afternoon. Thursday, she thought. Vin's charges to CF+Co were always on Thursdays.

She accepted Gary's offer of coffee, then they settled in the corner of his office on a small angular sofa. After the initial pleasantries, he said, "I don't know exactly how to tell you this, but I discovered that CF+Co is the billing name of a place called Club Fantasy, a very high-end fantasy fulfillment service. The money is routed through several shell corporations but eventually it can be traced it back to the business, a brownstone in the East Fifties." When she looked puzzled, he said, "It's an escort service that caters to very rich men with unfulfilled desires."

She processed, then blurted out, "You mean a whorehouse?"

She watched his shoulders rise and fall, then he nodded. "That's exactly what I mean."

"Vin spent two thousand dollars a week on a whore?" she spat.

Gary reached over and squeezed her hand. "That seems to be the situation. The place is very hush-hush and they keep a very low profile. They've had no trouble with the police in the five years they've been in business, possibly because they have customers who keep them below the radar. I don't know anything about what specific activities your husband was engaged in, but I can try to find out if you're sure you really want to know."

Pam hadn't heard anything after the words "escort service."
"It's a whorehouse?" That couldn't be. She and Vin had a
great sex life. Didn't they? Pam tried to remember her sex life
with her husband. It had started very hot. While they were
dating they couldn't keep their hands off each other. If she
were being honest, however, over the years they had been
married, Vin had become less and less interested and she'd
ceased caring. They had shared a king-sized bed until his
death, but their lovemaking was sporadic at best, and plain
vanilla when it did happen. It was probably because she
couldn't conceive. Vin must have decided that there was no
point in making love to a barren wife. "I didn't think he cared
that much about sex." The words "with me" went unspoken.

"Take a deep breath and please don't tell me anything you
will regret later."

He was very sensible. Her hands shook and she felt her
pulse pounding. A whore. He spent all their money on a
whore. She pictured a frowsy blond with too much makeup,
wearing a tight teddy and four-inch heels. "I want to meet
her." She didn't know why, but it was vitally important to see
the woman who had been fucking her husband. Fucking.
She'd seldom thought in vulgar, four-letter words before.

"I don't think that's such a good idea, Pam," Gary said
calmly. "You now know what was going on and you really
should let it go. Move on."

She felt her anger rising. "Let it go? When some prostitute
took all Vin's money?"

"She didn't take it, he gave it. That's quite different."

"You sound as though you condone what she did."

"I neither condone nor condemn it, and after all, she had no
obligation to you. Vin was the one who wandered."

"Wandered. Interesting way to put it."

"I've learned over my years in this business that there are
usually reasons for everything in life and, in this case, sleeping
dogs are better left undisturbed."

THE MADAM OF MAPLE COURT

"There's more to this than either of us know, and I want to find out what was really going on. I'm sure the check I gave you will cover a little more of your time. Make it happen." She felt heat rise in her face and the fury made thinking difficult. "I want to meet his whore." She didn't know why she needed this, focused on it so fiercely, but she did.

"Calm down, Pam. You're reacting without any thought." His voice had taken on a soothing yet slightly condescending tone. "I'd advise against this. Please let it go. You found out what you wanted to know. What can be gained by meeting the actual woman?"

Her anger flashed so hot she could barely think. "I want to see her, tell her that she ruined my marriage."

"Did she ruin something good?"

Pam tried to take a breath but her anger had taken over her entire body. She wasn't exactly sure what had made her so furious so suddenly, but now that she had a focus for it she needed to vent it. Who was she so angry at? she wondered. This prostitute? Vin? Herself for settling for a lousy sex life? Being mad at the other woman was easier than the alternatives. "I want to meet her."

"If you're sure that's what you want . . ."

"I am."

"Okay. Let me see what I can arrange, but it won't be easy. They're very private at Club Fantasy and very, very careful."

"Set it up. I don't care what it costs."

"If I do this, I have to trust that you'll keep this between you and the woman. No cops, no scenes. If I can't believe that you'll keep it all in proportion, I won't even try."

"I'll be good, I promise." Would she? Could she? She deliberately relaxed her shoulders and nodded slightly. Her voice lost its sharp edge. "I really do promise. I won't make a scene. Please, Gary, I don't know why, but I need this."

He looked at her for some minutes, then sighed. "I'll make some inquiries and see what I can do. Please, though, think it over for a few days when you're calmer and can get everything back into perspective. You husband's gone, and what went on before his death has no real relevance now."

"I know, but this is important to me. I promise I won't change my mind and I won't violate your trust. Set it up."

It was almost a week and a half before Gary called. It was a Monday and the weekend had been tough. She'd had little to do so she'd been bored out of her mind. She dusted and ran a vacuum over the carpets in the downstairs. After a quick lunch she put her few dishes in the dishwasher and cleaned the sink. She'd tried to read or watch TV or a DVD but nothing had caught her interest. She'd puttered in the garden but the landscapers had everything under control. What was she going to do with the rest of her life? There had to be something more for her. She thought about going to the country club, but now that Vin's death had begun to recede in everyone's mind, a few of the men had begun to act differently with her. Coming on to a possibly sexually frustrated widow had become a new sport, and wives had started to view her as dangerous.

"I was wondering whether you'd been unable to arrange anything," she said into the phone.

"I was hoping you'd have changed your mind."

"I haven't," she said. "It's important to me." She'd thought a lot about why she needed this and was no closer to understanding. All she knew was that the idea banged on her brain and wouldn't let go.

"Okay. I've set up a meeting with one of the women who run the club for tomorrow lunchtime," he said. "We're meeting at a little Chinese place called Oriental Wok in the West Sixties at noon." He gave Pam the address of the restaurant. "Does that work for you?"

"Yes, but what do you mean 'we'?"

"I'm going to be there to be sure the meeting stays pleasant and nonconfrontational. Any hint of unpleasantness and I'll drag you out of there, bodily if I have to."

THE MADAM OF MAPLE COURT

"What kind of a woman do you think I am?"

"I'm sorry, but I'm not taking any chances," he said, his voice brooking no protest. "I vouched for you, for your intelligence, your integrity, and your ability to keep this a personal thing, not a public one. I'm going along to be sure nothing gets out of line."

"Out of line?"

"No violence, no tape recorders, no nothing. My trust in you goes only so far, Pam. I don't really know you at all except for the fact that you're furious with the club for supposedly ruining your marriage."

"What do you mean supposedly? Those people got their hooks into Vin and bled him for every cent he had."

"Hold on, Pam," Gary snapped through the phone. "Let's get one thing straight. He went to them. From what I was able to find out, there's never been a report of coercion of any sort at the club. They had something he wanted and he visited the place of his own free will."

"How can you say things like that?" she said, trying not to cry. She thought she'd reasoned it all out, but there was sudden pain. "What could he get there that he couldn't get at home?"

"You're the only one who can answer that," he said patiently. "I don't want you to tell me anything, but think about this. Was your sex life everything it could have been? Did Vin really get what he wanted from you in the bedroom?" When she took a breath to snap out the obvious answer, he continued, "Don't answer and try to stop the knee-jerk 'it was terrific.' Be honest with yourself for a moment. Unless you're honest, you won't be able to understand the reality of what went on."

She held her tongue, then let out a long, shuddering breath. "Okay, I'll be good. I'll see you tomorrow."

Pam clicked the End button on her cell phone. Tomorrow. She'd find out what she could about this Club Fantasy and then, if there was even a hint of anything illegal—besides the obvious, of course—she'd blow the whistle. There had to be blackmail or something like it involved in Vin's payments. He couldn't be visiting a place like that every week for sex. That wasn't the Vin she knew.

She rubbed her eyes. Recently she'd found out lots of things weren't the Vin she knew.

Chapter

6

The following morning was bright and clear, azure blue skies with puffy white clouds. As she drove south on the Saw Mill River Parkway, Pam didn't see the spring flowers or the new green all around her. Rather, she concentrated on the road and tried to steady her nerves. She wanted this meeting, but now she wasn't sure exactly why. Did she want to berate the woman for entangling her husband in some sordid business, or was she curious about what activities he'd been interested in? She had to admit that she was curious, and that curiosity had surfaced sometime yesterday. What had he wanted? Needed?

Now she had deep doubts about the wisdom of this meeting. Maybe Gary was right. Why had she wanted it in the first place? What did she have to gain from a possibly angry confrontation with a frowsy whore? Why?

Questions! So many questions. *Why does my brain always seem to think in questions?*

She took the Henry Hudson Bridge and drove down the West Side of Manhattan, deliberately taking a moment from her whirling thoughts to force herself to appreciate the blooming fruit trees along the river. Spring. New beginnings. She opened the car windows and inhaled, both to enjoy the smell of the salt water and to try to calm her racing thoughts and clear her mind. Who was she? The woman driving this car to the city for a meeting with an attractive man and a hooker wasn't anyone she recognized. What had happened to her in the past few weeks?

She tried to picture the woman who'd led Vin away from their marriage. She'd probably be tall. He liked Pam's diminutive stature, but at parties the women he looked at were usually tall. Blond? Redhead? She couldn't figure out her hair or eye color but she'd be smooth, slender, and probably wear a bit too much make-up. A trophy wife without the wife part.

She'd selected her clothing that morning with care. Armor of a sort. A navy spring suit with a severe white blouse and low-heeled navy pumps. She applied her make-up lightly and pulled her jaw-length hair into a tight knot at the back of her head. She wore a simple but costly heavy gold necklace with matching earrings. She wore nothing on her hands to detract from her channel set diamond wedding ring and the matching several carats of perfect diamond and platinum solitaire. Vin had given them to her for their fifth anniversary to replace the smaller engagement ring she'd had since they got engaged in college and the band he'd slipped on her finger at their wedding. From then on he would have her wear nothing less. She'd always liked the old rings, three diamond chips set in fourteen karat gold and an unadorned gold circlet, both of which she still kept in her jewelry box. She looked at her hand on the steering wheel. She'd sell the rocks, of course, but for now they felt like she was carrying armor.

She found a parking lot on West Sixty-fifth and walked to the restaurant, a simple neighborhood Chinese place with a small awning and a menu in the window listing rather ordinary Oriental fare. As she read, she felt a hand in the small of her back. "Checking out the dishes?" Gary said lightly.

She hadn't been looking at anything in particular, just gird-

THE MADAM OF MAPLE COURT

ing her loins. She stood there feeling totally out of her element going into this ordinary-looking place with ordinary local people to meet someone who worked in a brothel. "I guess."

"It's okay. We can go in together."

She sighed. "Thanks for understanding."

"No problem. You look very severe today."

She smiled ruefully. "I wanted to buttress myself. The more I thought about this, the more I wondered why I'm here. When I had you arrange this meeting I was so sure. It was so important for me to see her. Now? I don't know."

"We can leave now. I have Marcy's cell phone number and I can call this off."

She sighed. "No. I want to at least see her so I can picture her from now on."

Gary patted her shoulder. "I'm glad you're not so angry anymore. As you know, I was reluctant to arrange this meeting, afraid you'd make a scene or get yourself seriously hurt. You look very much in control now and that makes me much more comfortable."

Again she smiled. "Looks can be deceiving." She smiled ruefully, then changed the subject. "How will we know the woman we're looking for?"

"She'll know us. I described myself and you pretty well." He glanced at his watch. "Right on time." The hand at her back guided toward the entrance. "Ready?"

"As ready as I'll ever be."

They entered the darkened restaurant. The walls were covered with the de rigeur red and gold Chinese wall coverings and the banquettes were trimmed with the same colors. The tablecloths were gleaming white with little lamps on each table. Pam looked around and saw no lone women, so she assumed that the woman from the club wasn't here yet.

Gary gave his name to the hostess, a tiny woman in a slender Oriental dress slit up to her thigh, and they were shown to a booth toward the back. "This is Miss Marcy's regular table," the hostess said, "so I'm sure she'll find you when she comes in."

Pam slid into the booth and Gary slid in beside her. "I must confess that you'll be meeting the woman who runs Club Fantasy first, rather than the woman your husband spent time with. She wanted to meet with you, sort of size you up, before it went any further. She's a very cautious, but also a very perceptive woman. If you pass muster and she's convinced that you won't make a scene, and you still want to, you can meet Vin's lady."

Suddenly Pam felt like she was on trial and she unconsciously smoothed her skirt and folded her hands in her lap. They sat for a few minutes while the white-jacketed waiter served them ice-cold water and poured tea into tiny Oriental cups. Pam looked over the red ersatz-leather-covered menu, then put it down and played with the small gold tassel.

A jeans-clad woman hustled over to their table and slid in opposite them, dumping a huge purse on the seat beside her. "I'm so sorry I'm late. My sitter got the flu and I had to scramble to find a substitute." She extended her hand. "I'm Marcy." Pam noticed that she didn't give a last name. "And you must be Gary and Pam."

Gary shook her unmanicured hand. "Gary Jannson, and this is Pam DePalma."

"Nice to meet you both," she said as Pam reflexively shook her hand as well. "I hope this place isn't too ordinary, but the food is great and it's very convenient for me."

Nanny? Sitter? She has children? Pam was totally nonplussed. This was the famous Marcy, the madam of Club Fantasy. How could this be? The woman looked like a typical young matron, with well-styled, brown wash-and-wear hair, a white short-sleeved shirt with a small stain on the sleeve, and nothing more than lipstick on her well-scrubbed face. She seemed rather tall but several pounds overweight. This ordinary-looking, motherly woman ran a brothel that supplied Vin with a two-thousand-dollar-a-night prostitute? She hoped Gary would fill the awkward silence because she was incapable of speech.

"We have a few things to discuss," he said, filling the breach, "but maybe you'd like to order first."

"I don't have to. They know what I'm having. At some places I'm adventurous, but here I stick to what I like. Wonton soup, chicken and trees, and an egg roll. I guess I always think of Chinese food as not too fattening, but my scale always says I'm wrong. You two decide what you're having, though."

Pam and Gary looked at the menus but she found it difficult to fix on anything. She couldn't think about food. Thank heaven for Gary. "Why don't we just get some soup and egg rolls for now?" he suggested. "That okay with you, Pam?"

She could only nod.

The waiter took their order and placed small dishes of Chinese mustard and duck sauce on the table, then added two bowls of fried noodles. Marcy mumbled thanks, then grabbed a noodle, dipped it in the duck sauce, and shoved it into her mouth. "I'm sorry. The twins had me up at six and I'm starving." She dipped another noodle and munched. "They know me here, hence the two bowls of their fabulous noodles, one for me and one for the two of you."

Say something, Pam told herself. "How old are your children?" she said, trying to calm her roiling nerves.

Marcy grinned with obvious pride. "The twins, boys, are almost five and my daughter is two. In spite of everything I'd like more kids, but my husband has absolutely put his foot down." She dipped yet another noodle, then gazed at Pam with a serious expression and said, "Pam, you didn't come here to talk about my children. What can I do for you?"

"You didn't tell her anything?" Pam asked.

"I just told Marcy this was business." He turned to her. "Does the name Vin DePalma mean anything to you?"

Marcy's eyes slitted with obvious wariness. "Should it?"

"We found credit card receipts for CF+Co in his effects."

Marcy's jaw dropped. "Effects? He's dead?" She looked totally taken aback. "Oh, I didn't know. I thought he'd merely moved on."

Pam spoke up. "He was killed almost five months ago in a car accident."

"Oh my God. Pam DePalma. Of course. I should have made the connection. I'm so sorry to learn of your loss." She looked genuinely saddened.

"It's gotten better," Pam said quickly. "I just wanted to know what connection there was between you and him."

Marcy took a moment to gather her thoughts, then took a deep breath, her eyes shuttered. "How much do you know?"

Gary answered. "As I told you on the phone, I do security work and I've told Pam about Club Fantasy. Pam wants to know what Vin's connection to it was."

Marcy let out a long breath. Softly she said, "He was a customer." She shook her head slowly. "I had wondered why I hadn't heard from him in so long. I guess I assumed he'd found something else, and I hoped it had been with his wife." Pam watched her process the news of Vin's death. She looked at Pam directly. "Sorry, that was thoughtless. Oh God. Liza will be really devastated. She is, was, very fond of him."

Pam's stomach muscles tightened. Liza. That was the name of the other woman. At that moment Gary reached for her hand beneath the table cloth and squeezed. She'd let them do the talking.

"Pam was hoping you'd tell her exactly what went on between them?" Gary asked.

"I keep everything that goes on at the club strictly confidential and I have to be very careful, as I'm sure you can understand. I'll speak only in generalities and hypotheticals. I guess I need to know that you are who you say you are and why you want to know all this before I go any further."

"I assumed as much." Gary passed her his credentials, then

THE MADAM OF MAPLE COURT

took a folder from his briefcase, pulled out the *New York Times* obituary the firm had taken out after Vin's death, then passed it over to Marcy. Pam had seen it and knew there was a copy of Vin and Pam's wedding portrait. Beloved husband, yada yada yada. Marcy scanned it quickly, then looked up at Pam and nodded. "I see." She considered her next sentences, then looked Pam in the eye. "I don't know how much you knew, but suffice it to say he was a regular client of my escort service."

"I know this is really awkward," Gary said, "and we'd be grateful for whatever you can tell us. And to put your mind a little more at ease, I have Pam's promise that none of this will go any further." He looked over at her and Pam nodded.

At that moment the waiter arrived and put porcelain bowls filled with steaming soup in front of each of them and a plate of egg rolls in the middle of the table.

Marcy took a small spoonful, then said, "If there's a lawsuit here, we're pretty well insulated."

Pam jumped in. "No. No lawsuit." Nothing like that at all. Seeing Marcy as a normal woman had changed everything. She didn't want cops, just answers. "I merely want to know what he got from her that he couldn't get at home." She found sudden tears gathering in her eyes.

"Oh, Ms. DePalma, I don't quite know what to say. If you really want this, I'll be as honest with you as I can and still protect the club." Marcy took another spoonful of soup, then leaned back against the banquette. "Men come to us for lots of reasons. I know nothing about your marriage or about his relationship with Liza. I don't know whether they were more than just client and professional, but I tend to doubt it. Most of the men who come to us want very specific things, not new relationships. Just escorts."

"You say men come to you for lots of reasons. We had a good marriage and we loved each other." As she said it Pam wasn't sure she believed it anymore. Somehow, though, it was important to make that point, true or not, to Marcy.

"I'm sure you thought you did," Marcy said, again leaning forward and sipping her soup thoughtfully. "Married men visit the club because they want something from the ladies that they don't or can't get at home."

"You say that so matter-of-factly, as though it's okay. Don't you realize that your business breaks up perfectly good marriages?"

Marcy put her spoon down. "I hate to have to say this, but a good marriage doesn't break as easily as you'd like to believe. Your husband came to us for a service and we provided it. It's that simple."

Pam took a breath, her emotions climbing and falling like a roller coaster. She found herself about to yell, then toned it down. "He came to you for sex."

"I'll admit that it sometimes happens between an escort and her client. And?"

"Illegal sex," she hissed. "Prostitution."

"I'm not going to admit anything about anything, so let's play the hypothetical game. Everything we say from now on is based on assumptions that might or might not be true. However, if it were true that he came to the club for sex, it was his choice. The ladies who work for me don't ever coerce anyone into doing anything. Vin and his counterpart, if there were one, did something that people do a zillion times every day. They had sex, and I assume, since he kept returning, it was good sex."

"But it was for money."

"Again, hypothetically, if money changed hands it is illegal, but in my opinion and that of many, many others, it shouldn't be. Women have a right to do with their bodies what they wish. If they sell their services as waitresses or flight attendants, is that so very different?"

"It's totally different. This was sex for money."

"I'm afraid I don't see the difference. If we were in Nevada or Amsterdam, what the club is purported to do is perfectly legal. Here in New York it isn't. What's the difference, geography? Does that make a lot of sense to you? It doesn't to me."

Pam was having a difficult time dealing with what she was hearing. Was this woman truly defending what she did? She ran a whorehouse but was calmly attempting to take the moral high ground.

Marcy looked at the woman sitting opposite her. She'd never had an experience like this and it was bizarre at best. She wanted to trust the woman, but the man sitting beside her had such an unreadable face that she worried about revealing too much information. He could be a cop with a tape recorder in his breast pocket. Although she doubted she'd get into much trouble, what with the laws about entrapment and her connections, she didn't want this kind of publicity for the club.

Her sister and a friend had started the fantasy fulfillment business years before and they'd never had any real trouble. She didn't want to start now. However, she felt sorry for the diminutive, well-dressed wife mourning her husband and trying to understand why he'd found it necessary to seek something outside his marriage.

Marcy interviewed almost all the club's clients before allowing them to use its services and, although she remembered Vin DePalma only vaguely, she knew she always thoroughly discussed a man's reasons for wanting to hire an escort. Either he'd denied being married or he'd listened to her "take it home and try it out there" speech and ignored it, as most men did. Most men had no idea what their wives might be interested in, so she always tried to send them away with a suggestion and even a bit of opening dialogue to see whether their itches could be scratched in their own bedrooms. Several times she'd received phone calls from men saying that they were delighted at how much their wives or girlfriends were eager to share and that they'd changed their minds about her services.

She knew from her billing records that Vin hadn't done that. Quite the contrary. Vin's credit card information turned up on her computer each week and she dutifully credited part of his payments to Liza's account.

She looked Pam straight in the eye and Pam's gaze didn't drop. Marcy found, to her surprise, that she sympathized and even respected the other woman. Pam didn't shrink from what she thought was important. She was direct despite her obvious anger and confusion. She was well put together and actually quite attractive. "In many other countries," Marcy continued, "and in many other centuries, prostitution was looked on favorably. The word 'hooker' comes from the name of a Civil War general who took women with him on campaigns to keep the men happy, and there wasn't any stigma about it at the time."

"You really think that what you do is okay," Pam said, her shock fading.

"I really do." Marcy listened to her stomach grumble and picked up her spoon. She really had to get in the habit of having breakfast. She scooped up a wonton and popped the entire thing in her mouth.

"Could I meet with Liza?" Pam asked.

Marcy wasn't sure that Pam or Liza was ready for such a confrontation, so she hedged. "This whole thing is pretty unusual, and I've never encountered a situation like this before. Let me think about it."

The three at the table were silent while they sipped their soup. She watched Pam take tiny bits of hot liquid onto her spoon but then put most of it back into her bowl. The poor woman was a wreck, Marcy thought, but tough. She wondered about Pam and Vin's marriage. What had it really been like? Many men did indeed have viable marriages but wanted

THE MADAM OF MAPLE COURT

something from her ladies they couldn't get at home. Rather than have an affair with their secretary, they paid for it. No strings, no hurt feelings if and when the guy changed his mind, and no recriminations. Just a straight business transaction.

Pam's face told Marcy that their marriage hadn't been as good as Pam might have wanted it to be. "Let me talk to Liza," Marcy said finally. "I'll leave it up to her. Is that okay?"

"It will have to be," Pam said, putting her spoon back into her bowl and picking up her purse. "I think I'd like to leave now."

When Gary got up and reached for his wallet Marcy said, "I'll get this. You two haven't eaten a thing."

Pam pulled a small notepad from her purse and wrote her name and cell phone number on it for Marcy. "Please call me. Meeting with Liza is more important to me than you can realize, now more than before. For lots of reasons." With a flash of what Marcy felt was true honesty, she continued, "There's a lot I need to find out, about Vin and about myself. Please."

"Of course. I'll be in touch, one way or another."

As Gary and Pam walked toward the door, Marcy wondered about the games Vin and Liza had played. It could be anything, from a staged burglary with a little light bondage to a cheerleader with a football hero. He might have been a sheik or a pirate, a milktoast or a prison guard. Club Fantasy catered to all kinds.

Chapter

7

Pam's phone rang that evening, but it wasn't Marcy. "Pam, this is Grace Banner. You remember Banner Plastics?" She was the wife of one of Vin's biggest accounts and the couple had been to parties at the DePalma house several times. Pam liked the woman very much, although her husband was a bit of a lecher and had made several passes at her, which she'd easily and gracefully turned aside. "We met several times at your wonderful house."

"Of course I remember you. Hello, Grace. This is an unexpected pleasure." She was surprised but also genuinely happy to hear from Grace. Pam had so few friends, and particularly since Vin's death she'd been quite lonely.

"I'm glad to hear your voice," the woman said, sounding on the edge of panic. "I need your help desperately."

She needs my help? "I don't understand. What's the problem?"

"It's Belinda's wedding."

Pam had gotten an invitation to the elegant affair and had politely declined. She had no desire to spend any time with Vin's old cronies. "I received the invitation and I'm sure I RSVPed. I'm sorry I'm not able to attend." Just last-minute checking on the guest list, she assumed.

"I'm hoping that was just a polite way of saying that you're not ready to make pleasant conversation with any of Vin's erstwhile acquaintances, and I can certainly understand that. With Vin's death . . . Oh, goodness. There I go putting my foot in my mouth."

"Relax, Grace. It's been a long time since the accident. What's really going on with you?"

She could hear Grace begin to cry. "Oh, Pam, the place where we were going to have the wedding burned to the ground this morning."

With genuine sadness Pam said, "I'm so sorry, Grace. That must throw everything into chaos." Pam really liked Belinda Banner and was sorry to hear about the snafu.

"My daughter's in hysterics. We've got relatives coming in from as far away as Australia and nowhere to hold the ceremony and reception. We've called everywhere but it's just too last minute. I'm at my wits' end."

"I can imagine it's difficult." What was going on?

"I hope I can impose on you to let us use your house. The weather's supposed to be wonderful for the weekend, so we could hold the ceremony and reception outside. I would pay you what I was going to pay the other place, of course." She named an exorbitant figure. "The caterers will do all the cooking and the planner can arrange everything else. All you'd have to do is provide the location. I can have cleaning people come in both before and after if you need them, and the flowers are all arranged. Please, Pam. For Belinda and Keith."

Use the house? It was a silly idea, although she could certainly use the money. Grace continued talking. "All those parties you threw when Vin was . . . Sorry. I don't know how to say things that won't hurt you. But you really were sensational, and your house must look fabulous with all the spring flowers blooming."

Ridiculous idea. "How many people have they invited?"

"Only about a hundred."

THE MADAM OF MAPLE COURT

Without consciously considering it, Pam started to plan. She'd have to get a tent just in case of rain but she could easily fit a hundred people in the backyard; she'd done it several times before. Tables and chairs would be rented from a party supply place. They could even set up a small dance floor as they had at their housewarming. The food had already been provided for. She'd have to have the landscapers in the Monday afterward to fix the damage, but the cost would be peanuts in comparison with the amount of money Grace had mentioned. She exhaled a long breath. "I guess I could do it."

"Oh my God, Pam, really? God, you'd be saving my life. You're a fabulous friend. Can we get together tomorrow morning so we can go over everything? I'll have the planner there, too. Oh God, Pam. You're amazing. I can't say thank you enough times." They talked for almost an hour and firmed up arrangements.

In the flurry of wedding plans Pam managed to forget Liza for hours at a time. The entire week was incredibly hectic but, in the end, everything went off without a hitch. The bride was beautiful and all the guests were impressed by how gorgeous the building and grounds were. Every professional who arrived to plan and then later set up oohed and aahed about the house. She thought the florist was going to have an attack of vapors as he surveyed the tulips and early blooming roses that surrounded the yard. "Can I keep this place in mind for others who want an unusually beautiful place to hold the ceremony?" both the wedding planner and the caterer asked.

She'd never thought of using her house for outsiders, but the more she considered the idea, the better it sounded. "Of course." *For a fee.* As she watched the professional wedding planner scurry around, cell phone to her ear, Pam realized that she could do most of the tasks the highly paid wedding coordinator did.

The check that Grace Banner handed her as the last guest left was much more than they'd discussed. The money would give her more time before she had to think about going to work. That was the way Pam measured money these days.

"Pam," Grace said as she slipped off her shoes and walked over the thick carpeting toward the front door, shoes dangling from her index finger, "you've created a miracle. Several of the guests asked whether you'd be interested in letting them use your house and your services for office parties and such. What should I tell them?"

She thought only a moment. "I'd certainly talk to people about it."

"Wonderful." Grace kissed her on both cheeks. "You're a genius. Again, thank you from the bottom of my heart."

That evening Marcy called. "I'm sorry to have been so long in getting back to you, but Liza's been out of town. She got back last evening and I talked to her at length. Are you still sure you want to do this?"

"Yes," Pam said, feeling less compelled and more curious.

"Okay. I trust you to keep confidences where necessary, and for the moment Liza will keep specifics to a minimum. She'll be happy to meet with you, but you have to be ready for whatever she tells you. You might not like it."

"I think I've come to terms with most of it, but I do need to talk with her to help me figure Vin out, if nothing more. Will you be there?"

"If you want me to be."

"Please."

"Okay. How about the same place on Monday? Liza is exhausted from her vacation and will be sleeping in. These ladies keep different hours than the rest of us." Marcy's laugh was contagious and Pam chuckled along with her. Different hours, right. "She'd like to make it later in the day, say for a drink around five? Would that work for you?"

"Done."

She phoned Gary and told him of the meeting. He'd called

THE MADAM OF MAPLE COURT

several times during the previous week but Pam had been too rushed to talk with him for more than a moment or two.

"Do you want me to be there?" he asked.

"Honestly, I don't think so. Your presence will make everyone a bit nervous and I'd like to find out as much as I can without filtration."

"Okay, if that's the way you feel." She heard him draw in a great breath. "How about we meet for dinner afterward and you can tell me as much as you want to. You could call me when you're done and we could pick a place."

Meet for dinner. It was strange how those three words made her brain click into a different mode. Meet for dinner. It could be all business, of course, but from the tone of Gary's voice Pam thought there might be something more going on here. It had been so long since she'd thought of a man in "Let's have dinner" terms that she didn't trust her judgment. Was she interested in anything more than a business dinner with Gary? It was such a strange thought that for the moment she put it out of her mind. He was rather attractive, she thought as she forced the thought to the back of her brain. "Why don't we just have dinner there? The menu looked rather pedestrian, but what I tasted of the soup seemed fine."

"Okay, I'll look forward to it."

So will I, Pam thought, strangely interested. What a delicious new feeling. Vin had been gone for quite a while. Why shouldn't she be interested?

When she arrived at the restaurant Marcy was already waiting for her, dressed in a soft blue blouse and a pair of black trousers. Her face was again almost free of make-up and her hair was caught back in a black butterfly clip.

"I'm sorry if I'm a little late," Pam said. "Traffic was a beast."

"Not at all. Being able to just sit without a child demanding my attention is a delight. I turned off my cell phone and didn't even bring my PDA."

Pam slid into the booth. "Isn't Liza coming?" Pam had again girded her loins, this time in a pair of lightweight toast-colored slacks and a pale rose paisley blouse.

"She called just before I left the house and said she'd be about a half an hour late. I hope you don't mind. It will give us a few minutes to visit."

Pam's shoulders dropped and she felt her stomach unclench. She'd been prepared to do battle, of sorts, but that would have to wait. What would she talk about with a madam for half an hour? After ordering glasses of white wine, both started to talk at once. They laughed and then, amazingly, they spent the next fifteen minutes with no lull in the conversation. After covering a few of the big news stories and the health of all concerned, Marcy asked, "You said you've been really busy over the past week. What was going on?"

Marcy seemed genuinely interested, so Pam told her about the wedding. "After all the panicky moments, it all came off without a hitch. I have to say I was quite pleased and so was the bride's family." She sipped her wine.

"You sound like this is easy stuff for you."

"It is, actually. I used to entertain several times a year for Vin and his business contacts. I've gotten pretty used to it."

"You're so well organized. You said they paid you quite a sum to do the party."

Pam couldn't help but smile. "That they did, and the money will come in very handy." She very quickly told Marcy of all her financial problems, then wondered what it was about this motherly woman that made it seem so natural to confide in her.

"Are you interested in doing more of this kind of thing? I have lots of contacts, businessmen who are always looking for someplace different to entertain."

Was she interested in taking referrals from a madam? She had already told Grace Banner that she'd be interested in talking to folks looking for places for weddings and summer affairs. Marcy's offer gave the word affairs a whole new meaning. "Only if it's strictly business," Pam said, then with a chuckle added, "I mean real business."

With a hearty laugh, Marcy said, "Not my kind of business, you mean. I understand, although you'd be fabulous doing what I do. You're organized, well spoken, classy looking, and charming. My instincts have always been right and I got good vibes about you from the start."

Pam actually felt herself color. "I don't think so."

"I'm going to stop the hypothetical nonsense. My two partners and I each make more than your husband did in his best year."

Pam gasped. "You're kidding."

Marcy grinned, then shook her head. "Not at all. They don't call it the world's oldest profession for nothing. It has been around forever, and the club started almost five years ago. We do very, very nicely. And I share."

From what she knew of Vin's expenditures, she didn't doubt that Club Fantasy was a gold mine. But not for her. "Not interested, but thanks for the vote of confidence. You seem to be very well paid for what you do. How many clients do you have?"

"About three hundred."

Pam's jaw dropped. "Three hundred men pay the kind of money you get for sex?"

"There would be more if I were less selective and had more time and space. My client list includes many of the best people, men, and women, too, who are looking for my kind of entertainment. Our clients include politicians, CEOs, rock stars, sports types, just about everyone you might imagine. We give them things they can't or don't get anywhere else and we're totally confidential and discreet. Men and women have needs and wants and we cater to them."

"You mean to tell me that women pay for sex, too?"

"Sure. Why not?"

Pam's mind couldn't quite grasp the concept of women paying for sex. In the last several years she and Vin had made love from time to time, and most of the time it had been enjoyable for her. But she didn't need it, or want more than she had. Women paid for it? "I don't know why not. I just thought that women didn't need or want sex the way men do."

"Many don't, but lots of women have discovered how fabulous great sex can be. Most get it at home, but more than a few come to us for, well, let's say diversion. Actually, that's what my husband Zack used to do."

Pam gasped. "Okay, you finally shocked me. Your husband used to be a male prostitute?" She had to be saying that to make a point. She couldn't be married to a man who'd done *that*.

Marcy smiled indulgently. "Listen, Pam, there's a lot more in this world than you can imagine. Yes, Zack used to entertain women. He doesn't anymore, of course, not since we got together."

"What do these women want?"

"We live in a couples-oriented society, and women often outlive or outlast their partners. We cater to recent divorcees, widows, and just plain lonely women. Some merely want companionship, someone to take them out to dinner, the theater, or a concert. Others need a man to take them to a special event. Eye candy for the female set. They can introduce a good-looking stud to their friends and watch the envy show on their faces without ever letting on that the guy is being paid. Our gentlemen are cultured and well read, not to mention good looking. And the fringe benefit is sex afterward, if the woman is in the mood, and most of the time she is. She knows she'll get the best, too."

Pam kept her jaw locked to keep it from falling open. She must be the most naive woman in the world. "I can't imagine wanting sex that much."

THE MADAM OF MAPLE COURT

"Then, my dear, you've never had great sex." Marcy's eyes lit up. "You know, I could introduce you to someone . . ."

It was Pam's turn to laugh. "Thanks, but no thanks," she said quickly.

Marcy had been watching the entrance and suddenly her face brightened. "There's Liza," Marcy said, motioning to a well-built woman who was just walking through the restaurant's front door. When she waved, the woman waved back and headed for the table, stopping briefly to talk to the waiter. Pam looked her over, wondering what this woman had that she didn't.

Liza was not a knockout. She wasn't much taller than Pam, had short auburn hair and a peaches-and-cream complexion with a scattering of freckles across the bridge of her nose. She was dressed in white jeans and a soft lilac shirt that showed off her ample bosom. Pam looked down. She wasn't badly endowed herself. Why this woman?

Liza crossed the room and slid in beside Marcy. "Pam, this is Liza."

Liza looked at Pam with genuine sadness in her mossy green eyes. "I was so sorry to hear about Vin. Your loss must be quite painful. What can I do to help?"

"I don't know how to begin," Pam said. "You're not what I expected."

"You're exactly what I expected. Vin and I didn't talk much, but on the rare occasions that we did he told me what you looked like and lots more."

"What else did he say?"

"That you were super organized, a great help to him in his business, that you were talented and charming and, I don't know, sort of comfortable."

"I think the word 'comfortable' is damning with faint praise, but I won't go there. He gave you no details about our sex life?"

"I don't kiss and tell, and neither did he. I made it plain that once he and Marcy had talked and decided that he wasn't going to go to you for what he wanted, I didn't want to talk about his sex life with you. He wanted what I gave him and that was that."

"And what did you give him?" Pam watched Liza's shoulders rise and fall.

"I won't give you any details. Let me just tell you this. It was only sex. There was no love or anything close to that. I was a live sex toy and that was all. I want to assure you of that."

"I find that difficult to believe. Vin wouldn't have made love with someone he didn't care about."

The waiter arrived with a glass of wine for Liza and she took a large swallow. "Oh, he cared about me, I think, but I can't even say I was a friend. Maybe I was sort of an acquaintance and a sexual plaything."

Pam was getting annoyed with Liza's coy attitude. Who was she to know things about Vin and not divulge anything? "Come on, Liza. Let's lay it all out here."

Liza looked at Marcy, who nodded. "Tell her what she wants to know."

"He told me that he made decisions all day and that he didn't want to make any in his sex life. He wanted me to be in control, tell him what to do and when to do it."

"That's it?"

"That's it."

Pam considered. Liza was right that Vin was in control of everything at DePalma Advertising, almost to a fault. She could understand his not wanting to make decisions about sex. Had he made them with her? She thought about that. He had always initiated sex and the routine had usually been pretty much the same, his rolling toward her in bed, stroking her until she responded, touching her breasts, sucking at her nipples, then removing her nightgown and his pajama pants and moving on top of her. She had usually been wet enough for him to thrust into her and within a few minutes he'd climax with a moan, roll over, and fall asleep.

God, when she thought about it, it sounded deadly dull. Hadn't she realized that? Seen it? What if she had? Would that have been in time to make a difference?

Chapter
8

Pam slumped against the back of the booth. "I don't know what confuses me more, the little bit you've told me about what went on between you two or his feelings about making all the decisions. Why didn't he tell me all of this? Why you?"

"Why me? I can't answer that one," Liza said. "All I know is that he desperately didn't want you to know about the making decisions part. He said you depended on him to be strong and authoritative all the time and he was glad that you leaned on him."

"Actually, I didn't." Pam shook her head slowly, taking in what Liza had said. "I deferred to him, and that's quite different. It was just easier to let him do it all than to argue about anything."

Marcy chimed in, "That's an interesting distinction, one I don't think Vin would have understood."

"I don't think he knew you at all, Pam," Liza said. " I think he thought of you as another person who couldn't survive without his guidance, and from the little I see, you're anything but. It's really sad, when you stop to think of it."

"It is," Pam said. "He didn't know much about me, and I guess I didn't really know him either."

Pam thought about how little she and Vin had really had in

common, particularly in the later years of their marriage, and strangely how much she did have in common with both of the women who shared the booth with her. They were bright, insightful, and charming, and she could see why Liza commanded such a high price for her time. "Liza, thank you so very much for being honest with me. This can't have been easy for you."

"I'm glad it turned out this way. I think his being with me and not you was Vin's loss, and I'm sad he never had the opportunity to find out more about you."

"If I were being brutally honest, I'm not sure it would have mattered. I think our marriage would have chugged along until something, or someone, pushed just a little. Then, I think, it might very well have stalled or fallen apart altogether." Pam huffed out a breath. "It doesn't matter now anyway."

"You need to understand one thing, Pam," Liza said. "Vin didn't consider what we did together cheating. True, he didn't tell you about it, but in his mind paying for it was different than having any emotional attachment to some 'other woman.' He told me several times that he had never done what he considered cheating, seeing another woman without money being involved. He liked and respected you."

"Thanks for that," Pam said, understanding things a little better. But still, wasn't cheating cheating? Did it matter that Vin didn't consider it that way?

Liza took a final drink of her wine, then reached under the table and took her purse from beneath her feet. "I've got to run. I've got a dinner date this evening. I mean a real date, with no strings attached or money changing hands."

"That's great," Marcy said, kissing Liza on both cheeks. "Do I know him?"

"Not at all. I met him at a parents' night at Kim's school. He's got a daughter in her class. He has no idea what I do for a living and for the moment I'll keep it that way." She stood and reached for Pam's hand. "I like you, Pam, and it's been an un-

THE MADAM OF MAPLE COURT 89

expected pleasure to meet you. I can tell you now that I wasn't looking forward to this encounter."

"Neither was I," Pam said, "but I'm glad we got to know each other." She took Liza's hand warmly and held it for a moment. "In our own ways we both cared about Vin. I'm glad you gave him something he needed." She would examine the small pain and large sense of inferiority later.

"Maybe I'll see you again sometime." And with that Liza hustled off.

"I'm dying of curiosity," Pam said to Marcy when they were again settled in the booth. "Liza's got a daughter?"

"She's got two lovely girls. Tiff is nine and Kim is seven."

"Husband?"

"Not anymore. He decamped with Liza's best friend when Kim was a baby. Left Liza with nothing, and the amount of child support he pays, when he pays any at all, isn't enough for a bird to live on, much less a household with two growing girls. That's when she came to work for me."

"You're blowing all my stereotypes to hell."

With a chuckle, Marcy said, "I can imagine. You thought of us as looking like the women in the old westerns, blousey, overly made up, bosomy."

"What got you into this?" Pam asked, more and more curious about this strange, genuinely friendly woman.

"It's a long story and I'll tell you at some point. Suffice it to say that my sister Jenna and her friend Chloe started Club Fantasy several years ago and I joined the business about a year later. Jenna now lives upstate with her husband and my wonderful nephew and nieces."

"Gary told me that you two are twins. Are you identical?"

"We are and we aren't. If we dressed alike," she winked, "and I lost twenty pounds, we'd be difficult to tell apart. As it is, we're quite different. And contrary to the old wives' tale about skipping a generation, we each have a set of twins." She looked at her watch. "Which reminds me that I've got to be getting home. Zack called me just before you arrived and was on his way home. He works in human resources."

Pam couldn't surpress the chuckle. "I guess both of you do."

Marcy guffawed. "Right you are. Anyway, the sitter will have left by now and he'll be overrun with rug rats." Her smile was slightly wistful. "You'll have to meet Zack. He used to work for the club and he could give you quite a different perspective on what we do."

"I'd love to meet your husband," Pam said. "Maybe we could get together some afternoon and I could meet your children, too."

"No kids of your own?" Marcy asked. "You seem like you'd be a great mom."

It was Pam's turn to become wistful. "No children. It just wasn't possible. We had all the tests and stuff."

"Did you try in vitro and all that?"

"Vin didn't want to go through all the fuss, so we dropped it."

"That's a shame." Marcy looked at Pam's face and said quickly, "I'm sorry. I didn't mean to touch on a sore spot."

"It's okay. I've gotten used to it." Not all the time. "I always wanted children, but I've resigned myself to enjoying other people's kids. Like maybe yours."

"I'd like that." She looked at her watch again. "I'd really love to continue this, but I do have to bail Zack out." Her face brightened. "You could come over right now and meet the crew. We could do take-out for dinner."

Pam pictured Gary's blond curls and found that she was eager to sort out everything she'd heard with his help. And she found she was looking forward to seeing him and exploring the new feelings she had about being with an attractive man. "I'm sorry. I can't. Maybe another time?"

THE MADAM OF MAPLE COURT   91

"Absolutely." Marcy rose and grabbed her purse. As she slid out of the booth she handed Pam a business card on which she'd scrawled her home and cell numbers, then leaned over and kissed Pam's cheek. "I like you very much. You're my kind of people, and I don't say that often. Let's not let this founder."

"My sentiments exactly." *How bizarre is the world?* Pam thought. Here she was, making plans to visit with a madam and her family.

Marcy turned back and waved from the doorway, then disappeared while Pam sat for a few minutes trying to digest everything that had transpired. A woman that she thought she could be good friends with ran a brothel. Vin had enjoyed taking orders. Liza was delightful. Pam had been invited to become a madam. Marcy had said that she could get some business types to use Pam's home and organizational talents to create unusual parties. That was the one concrete thing that had come out of this lunch, but the intangibles were just as important to her. She'd call Marcy within the next few days and reinforce the idea of an entertainment enterprise. She grinned inwardly. Her kind of entertainment, not Marcy's.

Gary. She pulled her cell phone from her pocket and dialed his number. "I was afraid you'd forgotten me," he said.

Pam looked at her watch. She'd been sitting with Marcy for almost two hours. "I'm sorry. Marcy just left."

"Great. I'll grab a cab and meet you there in about twenty minutes, depending on traffic."

"I'll be here," Pam said.

When Gary walked through the restaurant door Pam was surprised at how nervous she suddenly felt. *This is ridiculous,* she thought. *This isn't a date. It's just a business conference.* She took a calming breath. *Who are you kidding? It feels like a date.* She wondered how it felt to Gary.

Gary's face brightened as he spotted her and walked over.

He extended his hand. "It's good to see you again. You've sounded so distant each time I called recently that I was beginning to wonder whether I was getting the brush-off."

That sounded personal, Pam thought as she took Gary's hand. "Not at all." Over glasses of surprisingly good pinot grigio she told him about the wedding.

"No wonder you've been so busy, but when I talked to you, you sounded so calm and, I don't know, put together. I'd have been a nervous wreck. You must be pretty good at this party stuff."

"I'm discovering I am. The wedding planner asked whether I'd be willing to have the house used again and I said yes immediately. Belinda said a few of her friends said the same thing. I think it would be fun. Maybe I could even become a cottage industry. Weddings and other functions. Actually, Marcy suggested it to me today also." She spent the remainder of the meal filling Gary in on her conversation with Marcy and Liza, without going into any details about Liza and Vin's encounters.

"My first impression of Marcy was overwhelmingly positive," Gary said when she finished. "She's quite a woman despite what she does to earn a buck."

"Much more than a buck, she told me." Pam's laugh was a little forced. "She even invited me to become the suburban branch of the club."

"You're kidding. She must really like and trust you."

Trust. It had become something to treasure. "She must."

"What did you answer?"

Her eyebrows rose in surprise. "No, of course."

"Why not?"

"You've got to be kidding. Me?" She lowered her voice. "Run a whorehouse?"

"Not necessarily run something like Club Fantasy, but what's so wrong with what she does? I listened to Marcy quite a bit when we met last week and I've been thinking about it

THE MADAM OF MAPLE COURT

ever since. Lots of what she said made sense. I know it's illegal and all, but why shouldn't a woman be able to sell something that's hers? She can sell her services as a secretary or a singer or even a day laborer. She can sell the use of any other part of her body. Why not sell the rest? I guess rent it out would be a better term."

"Okay, that makes sense in a strange way, but it's still both immoral and illegal."

"The illegal part is true. Immoral? Probably true as well. But what's so different about paying for it that way, rather than asking your secretary to dinner with hanky-panky afterward while your wife's home with the kids?"

"It's the secretary's choice."

"It's Marcy's choice, too, and the women who work with her."

"From what I gather she doesn't actually do it. She just keeps the books and does the scheduling. Did you know they even pay taxes as an escort service and all the women have health insurance?"

"You're kidding. What a day and age we live in."

"Yeah," Pam said. "I remember reading several months ago about that Washington woman who was arrested for pandering. Doesn't she worry about that, I wonder."

"I would guess that she feels pretty insulated, but the law is probably always a danger. She's probably got a client list that won't quit, though, and maybe that's what keeps her safe. And remember that the guys have as much to lose as she does if the police get involved."

"I hadn't considered that, but you're right." She paused, then said, "Did you know that not only does she have kids and a home life, but so does Liza? Liza's got two kids in school and a new romantic relationship with someone she met at her daughter's school."

"Bravo for her," Gary said, his deep blue eyes gleaming. "Dating is so difficult these days."

Did that comment have a double meaning? Pam wondered, but she let it pass. *No need to stick your neck out.*

By this time they'd finished a long leisurely dinner and were opening their fortune cookies. As he read his fortune he chuckled. " 'You will be successful in your love life.' " He met Pam's gaze and she held her breath. "I'd like to think I'll be successful in my dating life, anyway." He hesitated, then said, "Would you have dinner with me some other night—a dinner not involving business?"

A date. Holy shit. A real date. She hadn't been fantasizing about something that would never happen. Here it was, and suddenly she couldn't form a coherent thought. When she didn't answer, Gary said, "I'm sorry. This might be too soon for you. I didn't want to upset you."

Her brain began to function. "You didn't, and I'd love to have dinner with you sometime soon." She felt her face warming and she smiled slightly. "Strictly nonbusiness."

Gary beamed. "Great."

Okay, time to find out a few things. "Tell me a little about yourself. You know lots about me. If we're going to—well, whatever we're going to do, I'd like to know a bit more about you."

"Fair enough. I'm thirty-six, married and divorced with two wonderful children." His face lit up when he mentioned his children. "My wife lives in Riverdale and I've got an apartment less than a mile away so I get to see my girls every other weekend and lots of evenings during the week."

Trying not to be jealous of his having the children she couldn't have, she said, "How old are they?"

"Melissa is seven and Amy is five. Toni and I have been divorced for four years, but I think the kids are doing pretty well, all things considered. Toni's remarried to a doctor and the girls love him to pieces. It's really worked out fine."

"How do you feel about your wife's new husband?"

"He's a great guy, a surgeon. I like him as a person and he's wonderful with the kids." His words seemed genuine and Pam was pleased. He was obviously as nice a guy as she'd thought he was.

"I envy you your children. I wish Vin and I had been able to have kids."

"I'm sorry about that." When the silence lengthened, Gary said, "Anyway, how about dinner and a movie or something? I usually have the girls over the weekend, but maybe some evening next week."

"I'd like that." And she wasn't just being polite.

"Great. I could rent a car and come up to Westchester."

"Not necessary. Driving is second nature for me and I really don't mind coming to the city. Eventually"—if there was an eventually,—"if you want to try the joys of Westchester County, I could always drive down and pick you up."

"What do you enjoy doing when you're in the city?"

"Vin and I used to go to Lincoln Center a lot." She looked down at her hands. "Actually, I'm more of a lightweight musical person, but Vin loved big concerts. He and a friend of his used to go to the opera about once a month." Or was that a sham to cover his visits with Liza?

"I can see your mind working, and I think it's probably counterproductive to wonder about things that used to be and are no more. Whatever was, was."

"That's a great philosophy. I only hope I can abide by it. What do you enjoy doing?"

"Mostly I work, but when I have time to spend I love amusement parks. My kids and I have season passes to Six Flags Great Adventure in New Jersey. They love it there. They've got cartoon characters, rides, and food, of course. I got friendly with one of the women who takes care of one of the food areas and she occasionally looks after the girls on her break so I can I ride the roller coaster."

"The roller coaster? You're kidding."

His face lit up as he talked about it, almost as much as he

loved talking about his daughters. "Nope. I'm addicted to Kingda Ka. Did you know it's the fastest roller coaster in the world? It hits almost one hundred thirty miles per hour."

"I hate to say this, but I've never been on a roller coaster."

"Lady, you've got a thrill in store for yourself. I'll see to that." There was a double entendre in his voice but Pam chose to ignore it. "I also like comedy clubs. Many of the performers are pretty lame, but from time to time you get to see someone really talented and on the way up."

"Vin and I went with his business friends every now and then, and I usually enjoyed myself. Vin always seemed to be above it all."

"You've got to have a drink or two first."

"Vin didn't drink." She thought about it for a minute. "Probably a control thing, like most of the rest of his life." *He only dropped his guard with Liza.*

"I like to get a little mellow and laugh at bad jokes. Let me see who's doing what this week and maybe we can visit one."

"I'd like that." She looked at her watch. "My lord, it's almost ten, and I think the waiter is wondering whether he'll ever get to go home."

Gary signaled for the check. "Don't even think about it," he said as Pam reached for her wallet. "This is a date and I get to pay."

"Okay. I won't get silly about it, but from here on we share. Right?"

"When we take our first trip to the Caribbean we can split it. For the moment, I know your financial condition and, even paying child support, I make enough to take you out from time to time. Got it?"

He was right about her financial condition, and she sort of liked the fact that he was old-fashioned. For the moment, she let it go. When the waiter brought the check, Gary put his credit card on the little black tray. "How about Thursday?"

THE MADAM OF MAPLE COURT   97

"That would be wonderful." She had a date. A real official date. Amazing.

"I'll call you and we'll make firm plans."

"Are you going back to the Bronx? I can drop you if you like."

"That would be great."

After they bailed Pam's car out of the parking garage they drove north and chatted about nothing of consequence as they wended their way through sleepy streets. Gary directed her to a block of small houses and she pulled to a stop in the middle of the block. "This one's mine," he said. "When Toni and I split, I found a little upstairs apartment that the folks who live here have carved out to earn a little extra money. My place even has a second bedroom so the girls can stay over. They're hot for their bunk beds and they don't even notice the stairs."

"You sound like a good father."

With a slight smile, he said, "I hope so." He unfastened his seat belt. "Awkward moment alert," he said, then leaned forward and placed a quick kiss on her cheek. "End of awkward moment."

She couldn't help but laugh. "You're right. That was perfect." He climbed out of her Lexus and before closing the door he said, "I'm glad you needed my help. Otherwise we'd have never met and that would have been a shame."

"Right you are. Good night," she said and he closed the car door.

Chapter
9

Pam and Gary met for dinner the following Thursday evening and went to a comedy club the Tuesday after that. Pam enjoyed the evenings thoroughly and was excited by the idea of dating. She loved the careful selection of what to wear, the excitement of not knowing where they'd go, and the little flutters of her heart when she thought about possibly taking this dating thing to its logical conclusion, bed. She tried not to get too deeply into sexuality, but between her evenings with Gary and her conversations with Marcy and Liza, the idea of making love was never far from her consciousness.

Sex. Hot, sweaty sex, the kind of sex she read about in erotic novels. Did it really exist? It must, since books, magazines, TV dramas, movies, and uncountable talk shows devoted so much time to helping people to achieve it. She hadn't had any good sex since the early days with Vin. Now she was thinking that it might change, and she was excited about it.

Would Gary open up this new sexual world for her? She had no idea, but slowly she realized that she was becoming more and more curious about what that world might contain. *Patience*, she cautioned herself, *just go out there and see what's what. Meet people, have dates, and let the rest take care of itself.*

Gary seemed to be a really nice man, with a deep love of his children and an easy friendship with his ex-wife. He had explained that he didn't want Pam to meet his girls because he attempted to keep a separation between the sections of his life. At first he'd introduced his daughters to his lady friends, he explained to her, but eventually, when the women faded, the girls had been disappointed because they'd grown attached. Now he never invited a woman he was dating to do anything with his children. Pam regretted that. She would have enjoyed being with children and maybe, for a short time, she could get a taste of what she'd been missing.

On their third date, she and Gary went to a different comedy club in lower Manhattan. The entertainment was mediocre but the conversation on the way home in the car was enlightening. On the way down they'd made small talk and there had been little chance for conversation during the performance. So, when the last comedian had finished, they retrieved her car from the garage and she maneuvered through the traffic across Canal Street. "Tell me a little about yourself," he said. "Only child?"

"Does it show that much?"

"In some ways, yes. You're pretty independent and a pretty strong person. Did you know that the original seven astronauts were all either onlies or oldests? They make the best organizers, and you seem to me to be like that, too. Are your parents still around?"

"I'm sorry to say no. They died several years ago. They were older when I was born and after Mom died of breast cancer my father followed quickly of a heart attack. I think he stopped living when she died and it was just a matter of his body catching up."

"Are you sorry you never had children?"

She turned toward the Henry Hudson Parkway northbound, using the need to avoid other drivers as a moment in which to gather her thoughts. "I've always wanted kids and my parents wanted grandchildren, but it wasn't meant to be, I

THE MADAM OF MAPLE COURT

guess. What about you? Parents? Brothers and sisters? You don't sound like a born and bred New Yorker."

"I'm originally from Kansas, believe it or not."

"Kansas? Corn fields? That's quite a switch from farms to high-rises."

"Not as much as you might think. We were business types, not farmers. My family came over from Sweden when I was a baby and we all spoke both Swedish and English at home. When I was a little kid I was never sure whether the words I used were English or not. When the kids in the neighborhood teased me, however, I learned quickly.

"My folks had saved for many years before they came here, and when they arrived they bought a small mom-and-pop grocery. They were forced to close it down a few years ago when Wal-Mart and Shop-Rite arrived in town."

"I'm sorry," Pam said, steering around a minivan. "That must have been tough."

"Not really. They were ready to retire. I was long gone, and neither my brother nor my sister was interested in running the store even before the competition made that impossible."

"Brother and sister still back in Kansas?"

"Yup. Karen's been married and divorced three times. She's got three boys, one by each husband. It's been tough for her, juggling who goes where for what holiday. That's part of what's made me so careful with my girls. I see how troubled her boys are, not knowing who's what in their lives. Each time they get settled as a family they're jounced out of their security again. It's made them suspicious of any man they meet and that made me crazy about not upsetting my kids the same way."

She'd always envied families but she didn't envy Gary's sister and her brood. "I can imagine."

"My parents are the only constants in the kids' lives. I don't know why I'm telling you all this. I guess it's the price you pay for being a good listener."

"How about your brother?"

"He owns a small insurance agency in the same town in which I grew up. He married his high school sweetheart and they've got four kids. He and Sue have been married almost fifteen years and I think by now they cohabit more than love each other."

It was funny that Gary should use that word. She'd begun to think she and Vin had been cohabiting for the past few years as well. *Maybe more people do that than have really good relationships. Maybe it is an inevitable result of a couple's knowing each other too well.* "Did you have a good childhood?"

"Really good. We all helped in the store and, although I complained bitterly, I enjoyed stocking shelves. I had something to show for my work when I was done, even if it was only neat rows of cans of peas and an empty box. That's not so true for me anymore."

"Why not?" Pam asked as she drove beneath the George Washington Bridge.

"What I do doesn't ever get 'done.' I do some private work, like I did for you, but most of my firm's business is corporate. I go into an international corporation and show them how to beef up their security, both personally and in their paper and computer systems. They read my recommendations and sometimes they implement some, seldom all of them. What I suggest is time consuming and deducts from their bottom line, so they hem and haw and do the items that don't cost too much. When things go wrong, and they do more often than not, they call me back, complain, then sometimes see the error of their ways and we go back and help them put through the hard parts."

"Sounds frustrating."

"It is, a little. We've got several jobs going at the moment, all over the world."

She glanced over and watched his face, alternately illuminated by overhead lights and shrouded in darkness. "Like where?"

"We have projects going in Sweden, Russia, India, and Brazil right now."

"Wow. What about languages? It sounds like you and your staff have to speak Swedish, Russian, Spanish, and whatever they speak in India."

"Actually, Brazil speaks Portuguese, and India speaks so many languages that it's difficult to work without a translator. I hire people who are fluent in the ones I think I'll need and I have a running account at Berlitz. Most computer systems can be set up to speak English until we're ready for implementation. Then we can switch to whatever the locals speak. I'm the Swedish expert and I speak a smattering of several more languages, enough to get along as long as things don't get too complicated."

She exited the highway onto the side streets in Riverdale, stopped in front of Gary's building. Without warning, he reached over and shifted the car into Park, then cupped her head in his hands and kissed her. It was a revelation. Heat! She hadn't felt it for many years, the lava-flowing, all-consuming heat of a passionate kiss. She felt her knees shake and, despite her trembling hands, she stroked his hair and kissed him back. His tongue requested entrance and she parted her lips. Her breath caught in her throat and her pulse pounded so loudly she was sure he could hear.

The kiss lasted for long moments, each drowning in the other. Finally he sat back. "Toni and Peter are taking the girls away next weekend. How about coming to my place for a drink on Saturday, then we'll find someplace for dinner?"

She didn't fool herself. She knew what going to his place meant, and it excited and aroused her. "That sounds wonderful," she said, trying to pull herself back into the here and now from the breathless place her mind had reeled to.

"Yes, it does, doesn't it." He slipped out of the car and through his front door.

On Friday afternoon Marcy called. "Pam, I've got a lead for you. Rob Sherwood of Forest Technology is looking for a place to hold an end-of-summer party for about fifty people, mostly guys from out of town." She gave Pam the tentative date. "I thought of you but didn't want to say anything to him until I checked it out. Interested?"

"I'd certainly like to learn more." She'd had some discussions with people recommended by folks from the Banner party but nothing was definite yet. This would get her operation off the ground, and if all went well he might be the source of some more corporate work.

"Shall I have him call you or would you prefer to call him? If you make the call, I won't have to give out your number until you're sure what you want to do."

"Why don't I contact him directly rather than put you in the middle?"

"That would be great," Marcy said. "He's a great guy and has lots of friends who might be interested in using your place as well. You have to understand one thing before you sign up, however. He sometimes hires a few of my ladies to mingle with his visiting guests."

"Mingle. That's a new name for it," she said with a giggle. She'd be housing hookers. Did it matter? She considered it seriously and couldn't get too upset about it. It didn't matter, not really. Any guy at the Banner wedding, or any of Vin's parties for that matter, could have brought someone like that and she'd have never known. Actually, any of the women could have as well. The more she thought about Marcy's business, the less opposed she'd become. "That's okay as long as no one in my neighborhood knows anything."

"That goes without saying. Let me give you his number and then I'll call him so he'll expect a phone call from you."

THE MADAM OF MAPLE COURT   105

Marcy hesitated. "Let me give you something to think about from the get-go. People from his group, those who are being 'entertained,' will know where you live. We've never had a problem here at Club Fantasy, but we're also very careful not to give out any home information. Most of my calls, at least the initial ones, are made on prepaid cell phones so no one can get any information from caller ID. And, of course, Rock lives here and he's a formidable presence."

"Rock?"

"He's the bouncer, greeter, and general factotum. He's also a black belt in several martial arts and looks it. No one would ever consider messing with Rock."

"I understand, but I've got to find some way to earn a living and this is something I'm good at." She sighed. "I'm well into my thirties and I've never held a job, never earned a cent myself before Grace Banner gave me that check."

"You've worked with your charities and all. All that experience must equip you for lots of things."

"I've done lots of things, but what I've been doing doesn't amount to a marketable skill, at least not anything entry level, and anyway, entry level doesn't pay much. I don't type, I don't have computer skills more than using our spreadsheets and finding what I want on the Internet so I can make calls to donors. I've pored over newspapers and surfed employment sites on the Net. I haven't yet found an ad for a faux rich woman to help run a large company at an exorbitant salary. This party business is something I can do for starters. Maybe I can make contacts with places that might hire an in-house cruise director."

Marcy's laugh was welcome. "I think you're underrating yourself, but I do see your point. Okay, let's see what happens with this guy." She paused, then with a joke in her voice, she added, "Of course, you could always come to work for me. I could get you lots of visitors at exorbitant rates."

Pam huffed out a breath. "Me? That's silly. I've never even done any sexual experimentation. What would I know about giving good head, anal sex, or being a dominatrix?"

"It's not all kinky sex by any means, and I don't entertain, just evaluate, something I think you'd be good at. Most of what I do entails charm, intelligence, the ability to make men feel comfortable. You've got all that. You're the kind of woman men want to protect, but with a sensuality beneath that men would really respond to."

"Stop the kidding, Marcy. I know you think you're serious, but be real."

"I am, but right now you don't want to hear it and that's fine. I'll drop it. But don't think I won't bring it up again from time to time."

Yeah, right.

As Marcy had suggested, she waited a few hours, then called the number she'd been given. She considered buying one of those prepaid phones Marcy had mentioned but decided that just calling a businessman to have a discussion about a party wasn't anything dangerous.

As she dialed, she found she was nervous. Hookers or not, this might be the beginning of a new business venture and she wanted to make a good impression. "Mr. Sherwood? It's Pam DePalma. Marcy Bryant told you I'd be calling."

"Of course, but can we dispense with the last names?" His voice was deep and pleasant. "I'm Rob. May I call you Pam?"

"Certainly." She tried to think of her next sentence, but Rob saved her the trouble.

"Marcy told me your house would be perfect for my get-together. She told me quite a bit about it, including the wonderful grounds. You've even got a heated pool and a hot tub, I gather."

Marcy had never seen her house, so she had obviously trusted Pam's description. "I do, and it's lovely this time of

THE MADAM OF MAPLE COURT 107

year. Lots of things are in bloom. A few of the late azaleas and lilacs are still gorgeous and the rhododendrons are fabulous. My rose garden is my pride and joy. I think you'll like the place. Would you like to come up and see it before making a decision?"

"That would be prudent, I guess. That way we can discuss things person to person. Would Sunday work for you? Say about three?"

"That would be perfect. Do you have a car or should I plan to pick you up at the train station?"

"I have a car so I'll drive, but I understand you're pretty close to the station for the folks who'll be coming up that way."

"It's only a short cab ride. For some of the parties I threw for my husband, we hired several local off-duty taxi drivers to be available just for our guests. They dressed in polo shirts we had made and it looked like a fleet of specially selected cars."

"Clever idea. I'll see you Sunday."

"Great. I'll look forward to that." She gave him directions and they decided on three o'clock. "The weather's supposed to be nice, so bring a bathing suit."

"Good idea. I'll see you then."

As Saturday approached, Pam found herself getting excited. She and Gary had gotten to know each other, but other than that bone-melting kiss, she had no idea what he'd be like in bed. Was she jumping the gun?

Late Saturday afternoon, after a self-indulgent manicure and pedicure she drove down the Saw Mill River Parkway to meet Gary at his apartment. As she looked at her hands on the steering wheel she appreciated her carefully done, mauve-painted fingers, knowing her toes were done in the same shade. She'd debated going back to Bijoux Nails after so many months of worrying about money but she'd reasoned that one session there wouldn't dent her bank account and she really had wanted to look her best. She'd been jumpy all day and had driven the manicurist crazy. "You're having trouble sitting still," Eva had said.

"Sorry, just a little on edge."

Pam had been startled when the little Korean girl responded, "Big date tonight?"

She'd smiled ruefully. "Why do you ask?"

"You haven't had the spa pedicure in several months."

"True," she said, sidestepping the "date" question.

Later she dressed, changing her mind several times, finally settling on a pair of ice blue tailored summer slacks and a black short-sleeved sweater. She selected a pair of black designer sandals, more strap than shoe, and put them in the car. They were the very devil to drive in so she'd worn flip-flops on her way south. Since it was almost eighty degrees she had a light stole on the passenger seat only in case of over-air-conditioned restaurants or apartments.

Apartments. Every time she thought about going to Gary's apartment she got the sweats. Did she really want to do this? She'd never made love to anyone but Vin, and she thought he was probably only average in the talented-lover department. It had always been good enough, but now she began to wonder. She thought about her undies, her best pale blue lacy bra and panties.

She thought about Liza's remark that Vin didn't consider what he did with her cheating and that he'd never cheated with anyone but paid companions. She'd never even considered cheating on Vin. It wasn't that she'd been tempted and rejected the idea. She'd never been tempted, and even if she had, she would never have dreamed of acting on the impulse. Now, however, Vin was gone and she was unencumbered. She was free, single again and able to do whatever she wanted. And she found that she wanted.

She glanced at the speedometer and discovered she'd been doing seventy, so she lifted her foot from the gas and took a

THE MADAM OF MAPLE COURT 109

deep breath. How did one begin something like this? She had no idea, but then again she probably didn't have to. She'd leave the move-making to him. But what if she'd been wrong about his intentions? She'd cross that bridge when she came to it. All she had done so far was admit to herself that she wanted it, and that was a giant step.

As she got closer to Gary's Riverdale home, she became more and more tense. Although she'd spent a few evenings with him, this was different.

Since she didn't want to cruise the neighborhood looking for a parking space, she drove her car into a nearby garage, prepared to pay the exorbitant fee to avoid the hassles. She left her flip-flops in the car, walked onto the stoop in her sandals, and pressed Gary's doorbell. She heard loud footsteps on the stairs and then he opened the door.

He was not really handsome but he was good to look at, dressed in a light green shirt and jeans, with a gigantic smile on his face. "I'm so glad to have you here. I hope you're not disappointed in my little place after all I know about your magnificent house."

"Don't be silly. With luck my house will become an entertainment mecca, not a home."

They climbed the stairs and she entered a comfortable living room, furnished with overstuffed furniture in matching shades of navy, red, and cream, with an early American feel. The fabric on the navy sofa was patterned with tiny off-white eagles and the side chairs were ersatz Federal period with Wal-Mart lamps and tables. The rug was an almost industrial-looking red and navy plaid. The pictures on one wall included one obviously posed professional photograph of Gary with a lovely-looking blond woman with wide blue eyes and two little girls in matching red and green plaid jumpers and coordinating turtleneck blouses. There were half a dozen pictures of each of the girls as well. "They're beautiful children," Pam said, gazing with envy.

"Yeah, they're pretty great kids. Those were taken a year ago Christmas." His eyes glowed. "They're so much bigger now."

"This room is lovely and so comfortable."

"I'm glad it feels that way. It's half my taste and half trying to make allowances for two rather rambunctious small children. I seem to spend most of my Sunday evenings picking up toys, dolls, paints, crayons, and varied art supplies. Getting magic marker out of the carpet is a task."

She could see into the kitchen, and the front of the refrigerator was covered with children's artwork. Gary pointed to one closed door. "Their room, bunk beds, toy chest and all."

He's as nervous as I am, she realized. "You know, Gary, this is a little awkward and shouldn't be. We're grown-ups and allowed to spend an evening together without going to pieces."

"You, too?"

She chuckled. "Me, too."

"Great. I was wondering whether I was the only one taking this a bit more seriously."

"Not seriously, just momentous, at least for me. Except for Vin, you're the first guy I've dated, if that's the right word, since my first high school dance, so it's all new territory."

"I hadn't thought about that," Gary said. "That makes me feel pretty good, but now I'm under some pressure to represent all mankind."

Through her laughter, she said, "Mankind? That's quite a heavy load for one guy to carry."

His laughter joined hers. "How about something to drink?" He disappeared into the kitchen and reappeared with a bottle of white wine under his arm, two glasses in one hand, and a tray of crackers and cheese in the other.

Anticipation was making her crazy. She was sweating yet her hands were ice cold. She wanted to make clever conversation but it was as if her brain was encased in cement. When

THE MADAM OF MAPLE COURT

Gary sat beside her on the sofa, she jumped. "Nervous?" he asked.

"God, yes."

"I can fix that," he said, cupping her cheeks with his palms and kissing her into insensibility.

When he lifted his head, she said, "That doesn't fix anything. It makes it worse."

"Me, too." He wrapped his arms around her shoulders and kissed her again. His tongue entered her mouth and she brushed it with hers. Soft, not demanding but rather requesting. She relaxed against his arms and granted his wishes. Wine and cheese forgotten, his fingers glided over her neck as his mouth moved to nip her earlobe.

The technique was so different from Vin's. She didn't want to compare but she couldn't help herself—until his hand found her breast. Then all thought became impossible. He smoothed his palm over her sweater, then delved beneath and found the skin over her ribs. His hand was cool on her fevered skin. "Tell me this is what you want," he whispered.

"Yes," she said. "God, yes."

He stood and guided her to her feet, then together they walked into his bedroom. Her brain fastened on the fact that his bed was queen-sized while hers and Vin's was an extra-wide king. In this bed a man couldn't disappear to the other side.

Gary deftly flipped the beige and navy striped satin quilt aside and pulled back the navy blue sheets. Then he pulled her sweater over her head and gazed at her. She liked the look in his eyes. "So lovely and soft," he said. "So beautiful."

She was glad she'd been selective about everything she wore. As she stood transfixed he unfastened her bra and allowed it to fall at her feet. Now her breasts were revealed to his gaze and she discovered how wonderful it was to have a man look at her with admiration. And lust.

Then he was on his knees, his mouth on one nipple, his fingers playing with the other. She was in ecstasy, warmth coursing through her, gathering at the joining of her thighs. Her knees shook with the wanting, a hunger she hadn't felt in what seemed like forever.

He stood, toed off his loafers, and quickly removed his shirt and slacks, his erection making a both sexy and scary bulge in his briefs. When she reached for the button on the front of her pants he stilled her hands. "Let me," he whispered.

Hands dropping to her sides, she felt his fingers on her skin as he unbuttoned and unzipped. Finally her panties joined the rest of her clothing on the floor and he pressed her back onto the cool sheets.

He climbed over her and stroked her belly, eventually combing his fingers through her pubic hair. "You're so wet," he said as he slid his fingers toward her core.

She couldn't control the movement of her hips as her body reached for him. He yanked off his briefs and unrolled a condom over his hard shaft. "I wanted to wait, make it really good for you, but it's too much," he growled hoarsely. "I need this so much."

Then he was inside her and she felt herself filled as she hadn't been in a long time. She wrapped her legs around him and pulled him in more deeply, her hips rhythmically moving beneath him. He reared back, then drove into her harder. Again and again he pounded, making small sounds with each thrust. He came quickly, a long, loud groan announcing his pleasure.

Eventually his body calmed and Pam relaxed. Then he did something she didn't remember Vin ever doing. Still inside her, he reached between them and found her clit. She was surprised at the depth of her need as he rubbed her, pushing her upward.

She went with the feelings and felt a great swell of pleasure gather inside of her, a bubble that needed release, and she cultivated it. The spasms started in her vagina, squeezing his erection as she felt the bubble burst. He was still firm and she felt him move inside her, drawing out her climax.

So this was what all the shouting was about, she thought as she regained her composure. She must have climaxed before, when she and Vin were first so hot and hungry for each other, but she didn't really remember it. Who cared? This was wonderful, whether first or thousandth, and so different from anything she could recall.

She'd been a virgin when Vin first made love to her and he'd been the next best thing, having only been with a handful of women—girls actually. So they'd grown up together sexually. Now she'd been with a new man as a mature, dating woman and it was all she could do not to giggle.

Damn, this was fabulous! She felt like a kid with a new toy. She wanted to do it again but she knew that Gary wouldn't be up to it. Maybe later.

Eventually they got up, sipped a little wine, then had dinner at a little Spanish restaurant in Gary's neighborhood. When dinner was over they went back to Gary's apartment and, although she hoped they'd do it again, he seemed content to talk, sip wine, then walk her to her car. At the garage he kissed her again and opened the door for her. "I'll call you tomorrow and we'll make plans. Maybe one evening next week."

"That sounds great." She could hardly wait. She wanted to explore these new sensations more thoroughly. With Gary, of course. With Gary.

Chapter

10

All the way home in the car, Pam relived her fabulous evening. Now she understood why a woman would pay for sex, and maybe she understood Marcy's business a little better. What if she were never able to have another orgasm? Would she pay for it? Twenty-four hours ago she'd have said no without hesitation. Now she wasn't quite so sure. Questions whirled in her mind. Always questions.

The following morning she threw on some clothes and retrieved the Sunday *Times* from the end of her driveway. She made a pot of coffee and tried to concentrate on the Arts and Leisure section but she found herself frequently rereading an article. Her mind kept drifting to Gary. One evening next week, he'd said. The anticipation was almost more than she could stand. They wouldn't be able to meet until after seven, when Gary got home from work. She thought about offering to pick him up in the city but rejected that idea. She wasn't going to look like some poor little waif pressing her nose against the candy store window hoping for a chocolate bar. Ugly analogy.

At about two Pam looked over the house to make sure it would make the best impression on Rob Sherwood. As usual, it was perfect. Outside the grass was trimmed and the landscaping in tip-top shape. Flowers abounded. She especially liked the late parrot tulips and early tiger lilies. A few flowers remained on the azaleas, and the rhododendrons were in full bloom. In a few weeks the wild roses that provided a privacy hedge between her property and the neighbors' would be in full bloom. The early cultivated ones were already showing color and the carefully cultivated ones in the rose garden would begin to open. Soon the landscapers would also begin to add summer annuals and perennials.

Since it was unseasonably warm for late May, Pam went upstairs and changed into a pair of tailored lightweight white slacks and a caramel-colored short-sleeved silk shirt with thin coral stripes. She added only a strand of coral beads and matching earrings and finished the outfit off with tan sandals. Her only make-up was pale coral lipstick. She'd started to add blush and discovered that, possibly thanks to the previous evening, she didn't need any.

At just after three the doorbell rang. She fluffed her hair with her fingers and opened it to find a nice-looking stocky man dressed in khaki slacks and a navy polo shirt. He had a tightly trimmed beard and mustache, both as inky black as his razor-trimmed straight hair. His eyes were so deep brown as to be almost black as well. Although he was built like a fire hydrant, his pianist hands moved with unconscious grace. Behind him, a sleek, British racing green Jaguar convertible stood in the driveway. "You must be Rob," she said softly. "Come in."

He walked through the front door and looked around, obviously both appraising and appreciating. "Thanks. I have to say that the drive up here was beautiful, but your home surpasses everything I saw on the way. What I've seen of it is magnificent, both inside and out."

"I'm glad. My husband and I worked very hard on it."

"Oh. I got the impression from Marcy that you weren't married."

THE MADAM OF MAPLE COURT   117

"He was killed a while ago in a traffic accident." That had become her stock answer.

"I'm terribly sorry."

"Thanks." She found what little pain was left had been further dulled by the new life she'd just begun. "It's been six months. Let me show you the rest of the house."

They wandered through the downstairs and ended up in the kitchen. "Can I get you something? Soda, beer, wine, a cocktail maybe?"

"I'd love a beer if you have one."

She opened the double-wide refrigerator. "I've got quite an assortment. Why don't you inspect the supply and pick one yourself?"

"Wow. That's some collection," he said, staring inside.

"Although my husband didn't drink, he liked to keep a good supply around for visitors and there's no way I could drink it all."

After a long look, he picked a Budweiser. "You can take the kid out of the Bronx, but you can't take away his Bud." Pam pulled a Heineken from the fridge and got herself a glass. When she raised a questioning eyebrow and motioned to the glass, he shook his head, unscrewed the cap on his Bud, and took a long pull from the bottle.

"So you're a local kid who made good," she said as she poured.

"I'm a local kid who got lucky. I was a complete geek in school but a few friends and I had some good ideas, and bingo. Forest Technology."

"Rob Sherwood. Of course. Like Sherwood Forest, I presume. Is the Rob for Robin?"

"Very good guess. Actually my name is Elmont. Elmont Sherwood. What could my parents have been thinking? Why couldn't I have been Michael or James?" He looked a bit wistful. "Anyway, the kids picked up on the Sherwood, then added forest, then moved on to Robin Hood. When I was in elementary school I got teased almost all the time, and if it wasn't about my name it was for my good grades. I was always built like a tree stump and since I wasn't athletic and wore thick glasses I was an easy target. The kids called me Rob for short and kept after me to tell them where Maid Marian was. They kept asking me whether I'd ever 'made Marian.' For the most part I ignored it all, but eventually the nickname Robin stuck. I always hated Elmont, so I kept Rob."

Pam pictured a geeky little boy being teased by his peers and wondered how she would have survived. "No glasses now?"

"Thank God for contacts and more recently laser surgery. Now I can see well most of the time, although I still need glasses for reading small print."

"It's amazing what lenses have done for self-esteem."

"You, too?"

"Sure. Doesn't everyone use them?" They laughed together. "What exactly does Forest Technology do?"

"We make semiconductors and . . . suffice it to say that we make computer stuff." She was a little miffed that he seemed to treat her like a featherbrain, but he corrected that impression quickly. "I don't mean to gloss over what my company does, but it's really boring and not worth spending this wonderful afternoon talking about. A lot of it is government work and if I told you, I'd have to kill you." They laughed together. "If you want the spiel I give visiting royalty, the company dog-and-pony show, I can give it to you, but I'd rather see the back of your house."

"Bring your beer and I'll give you the Maple Court dog-and-pony show."

"Wow," Rob said as Pam opened the sliding door to the patio. "This is as beautiful as Marcy said." In silence he looked over the outdoor kitchen area and admired the eight-burner

THE MADAM OF MAPLE COURT 119

grill. "I have a little hibachi on my tiny twenty-seventh-floor deck. God, I'd love to have a setup like this."

"Vin, my husband, liked to cook out here sometimes on the weekends in the summer. It's got a smoker and there's even a burner especially designed for a wok. It's sad that there isn't more great weather for this stuff, although he had jalousies built so this part of the patio can be closed off and used in all but the worst weather."

She guided him out into the yard. He quickly kicked off his loafers and walked through the grass barefoot. "I remember summers when I was a kid, when I spent long hours in the Botanical Gardens. I memorized the scientific names of dozens of trees and flowers from the signs."

"I thought all you geeky types spent your time inventing computer programs."

His grin was immediate. "That, too."

They wandered to the pool. "This is wonderful. Does it require a lot of upkeep?"

"Not really. It's lightly salted so it sort of makes its own chlorine. The guy comes once a month to fix the chemicals and that's about it. It's heated, too, although I don't keep the heat on except when I expect to be using it."

She showed him the eight-person hot tub surrounded with rocky ledges. The water gurgled from it over a long series of landscaped terraces, then into the main pool. "I can turn on the heater in the spa if you'd like to take a dip."

He dipped his hand into the water, then said, "If you don't mind, I'd like that. I live in an apartment in the city and miss this kind of thing."

"Sure, that would be great. Did you bring a suit? If not, there are a few in one of the cabanas that might fit you."

"Not necessary. I just need to get my stuff out of my car."

"Great. I'll just be a minute."

Fifteen minutes later, Pam had changed into a flattering

deep cranberry one-piece bathing suit and Rob was dressed in a pair of tight black trunks. Pam found herself gazing at his well-developed body, thinking thoughts that had nothing to do with business. *Is that what one good session of great sex does to a person? Does everything become erotically charged?*

They walked to the edge of the hot tub and Pam lifted the thermometer out of the water. It was now at about a hundred degrees. "Should be perfect," she said, stepping in. Rob followed and stepped in and settled onto the ledge, shoulder-deep in water. "This is wonderful," he said with an almost animal moan.

"Want the bubbles?" she asked.

"Not really. I like the quiet."

"Me, too," she admitted as she settled opposite him, then at his urging, moved around until they were about a foot apart. They talked about several topics and quickly found that neither of them were sports fans, both liked very light classical music and western movies.

They'd been talking for almost an hour, moving between the hot tub and the pool, before Rob said, "You're an interesting woman, Pam, and I find that I like you very much."

"You're quite a guy yourself," Pam said, her nerves tingling. *Cut that out*, she thought. *You're thinking about him like a sex partner. He's a business associate and nothing more.*

Rob looked into her eyes and immediately disabused her of that idea. "Okay, let's let the eight-hundred-pound gorilla out of the cage. I gather that you're not one of Marcy's girls."

Like so many things lately, she realized that she wasn't as shocked as she would have been just a month before. "No. I'm not."

"Pity. I like women like you who are smart and not afraid to show it."

She decided to be frank. "That surprises me."

"That I like smart women?"

"No, the juxtaposition of wondering whether I was a prosti-

THE MADAM OF MAPLE COURT 121

tute and liking smart women." At Rob's puzzled look she continued, "I would have thought that looks were what men wanted. You know, big breasts, skinny hips, and long legs."

"Shows how much you know. Sure, lots of men go for Barbie dolls like the ones in the porn flicks, but for me, there's so much more. I couldn't have sex with an airhead, no matter how gorgeous her body was."

"I guess I don't know much about what appeals to men."

"What about your husband? What appealed to him?"

She thought about Liza and realized that she couldn't answer that question. "I've no idea, really."

His nod was quick, then he asked, "How do you know Marcy?"

Pam wondered how much to tell a potential client of her party business. She quickly decided that the more she lied about things, the harder it would become to remember what she'd told to whom. "He was a customer of hers," she said simply, then briefly told him about finding out about Vin's relationship with Club Fantasy and eventually meeting Marcy. "So my friendship with Marcy is pretty recent," Pam finished. "I found that I liked her a lot from the first time I met her. There was an instant rapport and it surprised the hell out of me."

"That's what makes her so good at what she does. She's quite a woman. Her sister, too." He chuckled. "You'd never believe they're twins. Despite her children, Jenna's still slim and stylish. Marcy is so soft and cuddly, sort of like you." He reached over and played with a strand of Pam's hair. She ought to gently let him know she wasn't that kind of woman, but was that completely true? Since last evening she had no idea about the erotic side of her nature. Now . . . Could someone change so drastically in just one evening?

Again she decided to be frank. "Rob, I don't know about this."

"No strings. I find you very attractive and sexy and I didn't want to let something pass without giving it a try. If you want to say no, that's fine, and it has nothing to do with whether I use your house for entertaining this summer or not. That's a done deal. The other is up to you."

She didn't know which made her happier, the money for using her house or Rob finding her attractive. Who was she kidding? The attractive part won hands down. "Until six months ago I was a suburban housewife with a plain vanilla sex life and I was content. Then Vin was killed and I languished in misery for a while."

He continued to twirl the strand of her short hair around his knuckle, occasionally brushing her cheek. "That's understandable."

"More recently I've started to date and the whole thing is new to me. I don't know how to act. Not socially, that's never been a problem. It's this new sexual freedom folks have. Vin and I dated through college, and of course made love, but there was never anyone else. I wasn't promiscuous then and now I'm not sure about the rules. If you make love to one man, is that a commitment of some kind? My new situation confuses me totally."

"And gets you a little excited, too," he said, a slight smile curving the corners of his mouth.

She smiled ruefully. "That, too. I don't know what that says about the real me."

"What would you like it to say?"

"That I'm a real person, not a sex object. That I like people, getting to know them and interacting with them outside, and now inside the bedroom."

"You've made love recently and now you wonder what you've been missing."

Her eyebrows shot to her hairline. "Why do you say that?"

"It's true, isn't it? I read people pretty well. You're sending all kinds of confusing vibes. Yes, and no, and yes again. I don't

THE MADAM OF MAPLE COURT 123

want to insult you, just make my wishes known. I find you very desirable."

"I'm very complimented and very confused. About myself mostly."

"Good. That's a first step. I've got an idea. How about we kiss? Just that. Then we go out for some dinner and see what develops. No strings, no nothing. Just dinner. And what's for dessert? You get to decide, but I can't promise that I won't try to convince you that I'd make a great sweet treat afterward."

"Do you specialize in making women like me feel uncomfortable?"

"Uncomfortably bad?"

"No."

"I've never met anyone exactly like you, but if I make you feel pleasantly uncomfortable, that's terrific. Slide over here."

She only needed to move a few inches and she wondered why he didn't slide toward her, then she realized that he wanted her to make the move. She made the decision and moved until she was thigh to thigh against him. He put his index finger under her chin and raised her gaze to his. Then he placed an almost chaste kiss on her lips. "More?" he asked.

Why the hell not? When she nodded, he placed his lips against hers and kissed her, his arms still not holding her. The kiss lingered, making her hungry for more. She placed her hands on his firm shoulders and deepened the kiss a little. Then she pulled away. "Nice," she purred.

"Very nice."

She took in a large breath and let it out slowly. "Okay, here's the most basic question." When he looked quizzical, she said, "Domestic or imported food for dinner?"

Chapter
11

As she stood in the shower a little while later, soaping herself to remove any trace of the lightly salted spa water, she thought about Rob Sherwood and his obvious interest in her. It had only been last evening that she'd been to bed with Gary. Now she was attracted to another man and aroused at the thought. What kind of woman did that make her?

Did she care? She was, after all, a mature, single woman, with needs and desires. She was free of any encumbrances and certainly old enough to make her own decisions. Gary didn't have any hold on her. They'd made no commitments. Why was she agonizing over having a little fun? She stepped out of the shower, dried off, and gazed at the clothes she'd worn earlier. As she picked up the bra, she considered, then opened her underwear drawer and found a lacier cream-colored one and a pair of matching bikini panties. Then she slipped on the slacks and shirt she'd taken off earlier.

She heard the shower in one of the guest bedrooms stop and pictured Rob getting out, naked, sexy, and aroused. She smiled. *I'm a fairly attractive woman and a man, no, two men, desire me.* She giggled. *Fabulous.* Now all she had to do was decide whether she was going to act on her desires.

When Rob had mentioned his love of Indian food, she'd

suggested a tiny nearby restaurant. "I've never been there, but it always gets rave reviews in the local papers and had a great write-up several months ago in the *Times*. It's small and very informal but the food's supposed to be the best in the area." Pam had always wanted to try it but Vin preferred his restaurants larger and glitzier, so they'd never eaten there.

They drove to the far edge of town in Rob's Jag. He had asked her whether she minded the top down and she'd said she loved convertibles, so she'd grabbed a scarf and fastened it over her hair for the ten-minute ride. They parked in the minuscule lot beside the restaurant, and as they walked to the door he wrapped his arm lightly around her waist.

The place was already filled, but the beautiful, dark-skinned hostess in traditional dress—who was also the wait-ress and the wife of the owner, she told them with pride—got a folding table from the kitchen and seated them in a corner. Vin would have been put off by the informality, but Rob took to it and even told the hostess how wonderful the aromas were. She beamed at him and Pam realized how easily he charmed women, and probably men, too. This was a man to be very careful of. She was sure women drowned in his easy, wide smile.

They ordered from a plastic-covered menu accompanied by a Xeroxed list of specials. Pam was amazed at the variety and complexity of many of the dishes offered. After reading the descriptions of the first few items she asked, "Do you know what's in these dishes? Except for the meat, most of the ingredients baffle me."

"Despite the many upscale Indian restaurants I've been to, many of these dishes baffle me as well, but I'm an experimenter and I've seldom had anything I didn't like. Should we just pick a few things? What do you like?"

"I like just about everything, too." When he caught her gaze and just stared, she realized what she'd said. "I mean

THE MADAM OF MAPLE COURT 127

everything edible." Totally embarrassed, she laughed. "I'm just making it worse."

His smile again showed his white teeth. "I think you're making it decidedly better, but let's talk first about dinner. Anything?"

She grinned, playing along with the teasing. "Anything."

"Okay, I'll take you at your word. What about heat?"

Heat! She was sizzling. "Light to medium," she said, answering Rob's question about the food. That answer was right for her sex life as well. So far.

He ordered two appetizers and then asked the waitress/hostess for her suggestions for the main course. As the waitress mentioned a few dishes, Pam was amazed. Vin would never have asked for advice. He always knew what he wanted and indecisiveness made him crazy. Rob also ordered a bottle of cabernet. "This should be a big enough wine for any dish they can throw at us."

The conversation was filled with erotic innuendos and double entendres, and the sexual tension was so thick she thought everyone in the restaurant could easily discern what was going on. The food was as wonderful as she'd read, and, although she thought the sexuality of the evening should dampen her appetite, they both ate with gusto and obvious enjoyment.

After a dessert called orange kulfi and the last of the wine, Rob took her hand. "It's only a matter of time before I make love to you, you know."

She did know.

"I'd like to take you back to your house and show you how good things can be with us."

The moment of truth. "I think I'd like that."

His smile and obvious delight warmed her. Rob quickly paid the check and they drove back to Maple Court. As she punched the security code into the alarm system, she realized that this would be the first time she'd made love to anyone but Vin in this house. She paused a moment. Did that bother her? God, questions again. To hell with it all, she thought, she'd just roll with it all.

As they walked up the stairs, Rob said, "I think you'd probably prefer to use a guest room rather than your bedroom."

Her shoulders relaxed and she dipped her head. "You're very perceptive."

He turned her on the stairs and held her in his arms. His lips were soft and warm, asking rather than insisting. His hands stroked her silk-covered back, then slid into her hair. He was not too much taller than she was, and it was a unique feeling to be the same height as her partner. She let out a long breath and surrendered to his lips, sliding her hands up the front of his polo shirt and over his shoulders.

"You smell good," he said, nuzzling her neck.

"I don't usually wear perfume. It must be shampoo." She was making inane conversation, nervous, aroused, and barely able to think.

"Don't change it. It's sexy."

"I didn't know shampoo could be sexy." She was babbling but she was unable to stop.

"It's really not the shampoo, it's you. You're sexy, and desirable, and I want to tear your clothes off right here on the stairs."

She felt desired and suddenly daring. "So what's stopping you?"

He grinned, then picked her up and carried her to the bedroom he'd used earlier. She felt cosseted and cherished, yet, as her hip brushed the front of his slacks and felt the swelling there, wanted and needed. Her hunger grew, as did her boldness. In the short space of two days she'd gone from being an adjunct, a helpmate, to a sex object, and she relished it.

Rob set her down beside the bed, letting her body slowly slide down against his until her feet touched the floor. "Part of

THE MADAM OF MAPLE COURT

me is in a hurry, and part wants to savor every moment," he purred.

"Let's split the difference." She reached over and began to pull his shirt from the waistband of his slacks. He quickly unbuttoned her blouse and parted the sides. "Mmm," he purred. "Lovely. Soft and warm."

With one swift motion he pulled his shirt off over his head, then stood facing her. He slid his fingertips down through her cleavage, then out her collarbone, pushing her blouse from her shoulders. Everywhere he touched, it caressed her like a warm brand and she let her head fall backward. He stroked her ribs, then her neck as he nibbled her throat and ears.

She was awash with sensations, heat and electricity flowed into her from everywhere he touched. She locked her knees to keep them from buckling. Then he unfastened her bra and let it fall to the floor. "You have beautiful breasts," he said softly, "and your nipples show me how much you want me."

His lips found their erect tips and he mouthed her flesh. Then his teeth took tiny bites of her skin, moving ever closer to her swollen buds, then finally sucking until her vaginal muscles throbbed with need.

She dragged off his belt, unfastened his slacks, and pulled them down, along with his briefs. There was no doubt as to his desire for her. His erection was thick and pulsing and she felt it against her as he guided her to the bed. While she flipped off the spread he found a condom in his pants pocket and unrolled it over his shaft.

"I want you," he said as he stretched out beside her.

"I want you, too," she said, and he rolled on top of her and pressed his cock against her. Reflexively she wrapped her legs around his waist and welcomed him inside her.

He filled her, starting down the path toward the satisfaction she needed so much. His mouth found her mouth and his hands slipped beneath her, cradling her ass and pressing her more firmly against him. They were fused from genitals to lips, and for a second they didn't move.

Then he pulled out and slid back inside over and over, long slow strokes interspersed with quick jabs of his cock. Her body wanted to find a rhythm, but his lack of one kept her off balance. She wanted, needed. "Please," she moaned, but he took his time. "Please," she begged, "I need you so much."

"Oh, Pam," he cried, "you're so hot."

"You make me hot," she managed to say.

Finally, with a sound that was almost a growl, he thrust deeply several times and came. Then, before she could recover from his orgasm, he pulled out and slid down between her thighs.

His mouth found her clit and he sucked, licked, nibbled until she thought she'd explode. He rubbed his mustache against her, then hummed lightly, the buzzing further inflaming her until climax crashed over her, pleasure echoing through every nerve and muscle. Then he was beside her, crushing her in his arms. "God, that was amazing," he said.

"I was just about to say the same thing."

They lay together, somewhere between waking and sleeping for several minutes, then he slowly rose. "I wish I could stay, but it's almost midnight and I have to work tomorrow."

"I wish you could, too," she said. She wanted to ask when they'd be together again, but it didn't feel right to do so. He was a free spirit, as was she, and there were no strings.

"I'll call you," he said, "both to talk about specific arrangements for my party and to make plans for us to get together again." He chuckled and his eyes roamed her naked, sated body. "Actually I'd like to get together with you again right now, but then I'd never get home."

She realized that she didn't know whether he was married, and for the moment she didn't care. That was his business. A thought slashed, unbidden, through her. It hadn't been Liza's business, either. She was just like her, she thought, becoming

THE MADAM OF MAPLE COURT

a hussy, a wanton, and she didn't mind at all. Rather she understood a little more. "I'll look forward to hearing from you on both fronts."

Later she lay in bed in the dark, unable to sleep, wondering whether she'd crossed some barrier and become something she didn't care for, but she couldn't condemn herself and she didn't regret anything she'd done in the past few days. An hour later her phone rang. It was Rob. "Pam? I hope I didn't wake you."

"No. I was just thinking about this evening."

"Me, too. I'm here in bed, naked, remembering this evening, too, and telling myself not to think too much. You shouldn't either. Let's just go with the newness and heat of it all, and enjoy it to the fullest."

"Sounds like a plan."

"Live it all for now and let next month take care of itself."

She hoped she could do just that.

Chapter

12

For several weeks Pam continued to see, and make love with, both Gary and Rob. From time to time she felt uneasy with the fact that she was dating and having sex with two men, but when she examined the situation she couldn't find anything wrong with it. She hadn't lied to either man and, although it had never been explicitly stated, she was pretty sure that each knew that he wasn't her one and only.

As spring blended into summer she was delighted that her house was being used more and more often for gatherings. She hosted a lavish engagement party for the daughter of a woman who'd been at Belinda Banner's wedding, an early-summer party for a medium-sized White Plains firm, and she had a few more possibilities for later in the summer. She had also lent her house to the local chapter of a breast cancer charity and the ASPCA for weekday luncheons. She had made financial arrangements with a few caterers, party supply firms, and quite a number of wedding consultants who came to visit and heaped compliments and promises on her and her facility. She'd even hosted a divorce luncheon and pool party for a friend of a friend of Grace Banner's cousin. Word was getting around and hosting was turning into a small, but growing business and was bringing in a small amount of money, enough to put off worrying about the future for another few months at a time.

She'd met with Mark a few times and together they'd worked out a budget of sorts that showed Pam that, with some frugality, she would have a decent length of time to plan the next phase of her financial life. Now the little she was earning with her party business would allow her still more time.

Despite her charity work, she still had a lot of time on her hands. Since her membership in the local country club was paid through December, she continued to make use of the facilities, playing tennis and bridge and keeping up her contacts with the upper echelons of Westchester County, New York, and nearby Greenwich and Fairfield, Connecticut. These were the social planners and, although they looked down slightly at her desire to "rent out" her house for affairs, she was still one of them so it wasn't too much of a smudge on her reputation.

Many of them gave her advice on the remainder of her life. "Find a good man with lots of money and get married again," several of them recommended. "Good sex. That's what it's all about. Good, sweaty, kinky sex." "Find a family man. You've always wanted kids and you could start again. You're not too old yet." "Find a man with kids. That way you don't have to go through the pregnancy and giving birth shit."

They found nice gentlemen for her, and at first she agreed to meet them at small dinner parties. Most of the men were deadly dull, and when compared with either Gary or Rob they all fell far short. She even had sex on her third date with one man, but he was as dull in bed as he was in person. She gently put a stop to the machinations of the let's-get-Pam-married association.

Rob's party was planned for the middle of July, and about a week before she and Rob were having dinner in the city at a well-known pan-Asian restaurant. "I'm amazed at how well you've got this party organized," Rob said.

"I'm getting pretty facile at it," Pam said. "Your get-together

THE MADAM OF MAPLE COURT

is for only about fifty. The last bridal shower I did was for three times that."

"You're a very talented woman," he said. "I've got one thing I need to get clear with you."

Pam put down her chopsticks and rested her forearms on the pink tablecloth. "Shoot."

"As I told you when we first met, some of the guys will bring wives or girlfriends, but others will want female companionship." He lowered his voice. "As you probably know, we always provide paid ladies to keep our visiting royalty company. Since I got your name originally from Marcy at Club Fantasy, I know you understand what I'm talking about. One of the advantages to your place is that it's large enough that if a few couples decide to disappear for a time," he winked, "everyone will think they're somewhere else in the house or on the grounds. I assume that's okay with you."

She'd dealt with the idea when Marcy had originally given her Rob's name. She thought it would be okay, but with all her other commitments, did she really need money that much? She'd be knowingly bringing hookers into her home. She took a deep breath and decided. "It's fine with me," she said, "as long as I'm not on the menu."

"Of course not. You need to arrange things with Marcy. Find out what the identifier will be this time and don't wear it."

"Identifier?"

"Each of her ladies wears some identifying item, like a charm bracelet or a pendant, to let the guys know who's who. As long as you don't have one, you're not on the menu, as you put it."

"I never thought about how a guy would know who's available." Marcy was a sophisticate and could probably help her deal with the conflicts in her own life as well as helping her arrange Rob's party. "I haven't talked with Marcy in quite a while, so I'll certainly give her a call."

The following day as she sat in her living room, she thought about Marcy. Over the months since Vin's death, Pam had realized that she had no family or real friends with whom she could discuss anything personal. She had lots of acquaintances, several of whom were becoming her customers, but when she went through her mental PDA she found no one in whom she could confide.

If she told any of them that she was having sex with two different men they would have either condemned her or grinned and winked, impressed and a little envious. If she had wanted to discuss sex and expanding her sexual horizons, which she had slowly realized she did want to do, most would have laughed and recommended books or urged her to watch Dr. Phil. Others might wonder about her life with Vin, and she didn't want that kind of speculation. Stuffy? Most of them were, and a few were truly judgmental. When they met and chatted weeks before, Marcy had seemed like someone she could talk to.

Without further thought, she found the other woman's phone number, called, and set up a meeting for lunch later that week.

As she had been before, Marcy was late and looked frazzled. "I've got to hire a full-time nanny," she said without preamble as she arrived at the table. She'd selected a small Italian restaurant with, as she'd put it on the phone, little real ambience but the best meat sauce in the city.

She was certainly right about the first part of her statement. The place was so cliché as to be almost tacky: red and white checked tablecloths, booths upholstered in maroon ersatz leather, candles in Chianti bottles on the tables, and walls covered with murals of supposed farm life in Italy, with Vesuvius smoking in the background. The wait staff spoke with thick, phony accents and as she was seated she expected someone to break into an aria from *La Bohème*. The waiter brought her a basket containing sesame-covered bread and long, thin bread sticks, along with a dish of olive oil and herbs.

THE MADAM OF MAPLE COURT

"I hope this isn't an inconvenient time for you, Marcy," Pam said as the other woman settled into the far side of the booth. Marcy was dressed in an oversized white shirt and well-washed jeans. Her hair was pulled back into a scrunchy-banded ponytail and strands of escaped hair frizzed around her face and at the nape of her neck. Pam had dressed carefully but casually, in grey twill pants and a yellow and white striped knit top.

"Not at all. You look great, glowing and happy. Me, I'm a slob when I can be, and it's necessary with my brood. You'd be surprised how professional I am with my clients, but with friends like you I'm so happy just to be me."

Friends. What a great word. "I'm glad of that," Pam said, and quickly realized that she meant every word of it. She toed off her sandals and tucked one leg beneath the opposite thigh.

Marcy's smile was genuine. "Me, too. How about a beer? They have Heineken on draft."

"Sure." They made small talk while the waiter fetched two glasses of foaming amber liquid. They ordered salads, preferring to wait and order the pasta course later.

"Rob called me and told me about his plans for the party and his need for my escorts. Let me give you the finances as I see them. I charge Rob about two thousand dollars per lady, and he's asked for five women. The fee holds whether they make a connection or not. I keep ten percent and you'd get twenty."

"Me? I get a cut? In addition to what Rob is paying me?"

"Of course." Pam was having a difficult time dealing with the numbers. Four hundred times five ladies. She'd be making an additional two thousand dollars. She never thought that hookers earned that much money and hadn't considered that she'd make part of it. "They make that much?"

Marcy lowered her voice and leaned forward. "Let me fill you in on my world. I don't rent out cheap hookers. I supply well-educated, well-bred women who are good looking—not necessarily gorgeous but certainly presentable—can make good conversation on almost any topic, stroke egos where desired, and are flexible in their sexual appetites. You met Liza. Would you have taken her for a prostitute?"

Pam clearly remembered the poised, well-dressed, well-spoken woman who'd been Vin's favorite liaison and who had two daughters in school. "Not at all," Pam said honestly, "but they do have sex for money, right?"

"Yes, but there's lots more. They're devoted to mutual pleasure. They do things with men that they enjoy, too." When Pam raised a questioning eyebrow, Marcy added, "Okay, most of the time. I don't necessarily know the proclivities of all the men who use our services, especially when I do something like Rob's party, which is a small part of Club Fantasy's business, but most of the time I match what men want with what my ladies enjoy."

"Okay," Pam said, trying to take it all in, curiosity pounding in her brain. "Like what?"

Marcy tore off a piece of crusty bread and sopped up some of the fragrant, light green oil from the plate in the middle of the table, took a bite, and chewed. Pam realized that Marcy was stalling, gathering her thoughts and deciding what to say. "You're not worried about me and my ability to keep your business between us, are you?"

Marcy looked surprised. "Of course not," she said quickly. "I have to make quick decisions about people, and I've become quite good at it over these last few years. I liked and trusted you after the first time we met. Otherwise I wouldn't have told you as much as I already have."

"I'm glad. I've realized over the past few months that I don't have many intimate friends. I have lots of acquaintances, but very few people I would call friends." She looked down ruefully. "Actually, none. Somehow I felt something comfortable when we first met."

THE MADAM OF MAPLE COURT

"That's what I try to give to my clients, a feeling of closeness and understanding that's nonjudgmental."

"You project that quite well. Let me help you with the rest of this," Pam said. "When I found out about what Vin and Liza had been doing I was shocked at first. Since then I've adjusted for reasons I'll tell you about later. I'd really like it if you were frank with me about all of it."

Marcy obviously made up her mind. "Club Fantasy is housed in a brownstone in the East Fifties. It's got rooms that we can dress up to be almost anything a man or woman has ever dreamed about: a sheik's tent, a pirate ship, a doctor's office, a football field with cheerleaders, or a bedroom with convenient places to hide or break into. The basement is a dungeon with suitable accoutrements. It's got just about everything. We fulfill fantasies using everything from costumes and odors to sound effects."

"Before I met you and Liza, I wouldn't have dreamed that Vin even had fantasies."

"Most wives have no idea that their husbands might want more unusual things; more's the pity, but many do. If couples could only communicate, I'd have much less business and I'd be much happier for them. But the men I talk to don't seem to be willing to take the risk of revealing their innermost thoughts. They don't even consider that their partner might be interested in giving new things a try. I guess my greatest regret would be the thought of a couple who's been married for, say, thirty years, each having the same desire and neither ever having the nerve to talk about it."

"You're right about that. Obviously Vin didn't, and I never knew that I wanted anything more than what we had. Actually, I never knew what I was missing."

"And now you do?"

Pam merely grinned.

"That's terrific," Marcy said, raising her glass in salute.

"Good for you!" She sipped. "At Club Fantasy we also cater to out-of-towners, men in the city on business who want the kind of good time we can provide.

"About a year ago we began to do the kind of thing Rob needs. There used to be a great escort service in Manhattan called Courtesans, Inc. They've gone out of business now and much of their party business has moved to us."

Horrified pictures flashing through her brain, Pam said, "Out of business? Were they arrested?"

Marcy laughed. "Not at all. The founder is married and long gone from the city, as is my sister. Gone out of business means just that, gone out of business."

Pam was thoughtful, trying to deal with the stereotypes Marcy continued to destroy. "Rob said you were sending five women to his party."

"I am, as long as you're willing to have such stuff go on in your house, your home. The only one who actually lives at the club is Rock, our bouncer. He looks like a professional wrestler and he's always there when we're entertaining. He gets free rent and the use of the facilities when we're not open. That's Mondays and Tuesdays. We've seldom had to use his services, but I think his mere presence ends most trouble before it starts. You'll have to decide whether you are up for having your residence made public."

Pam hesitated. The partygoers who ended up with the paid escorts would know the location of her house and might think she was fair game. "I never thought about that."

"I don't think it's a big problem. I can't see any of the men who know about my business coming around when you're not entertaining. They have a lot to lose if the police have to be called, and they know it. It is, however, something to consider. You certainly need someone around while you're hosting a party just in case anyone gets out of line. You never know what guys with lots of liquor and women might think they can do.

"I can, of course, ask Rock whether he'd be willing to front

THE MADAM OF MAPLE COURT 141

for you from time to time on the nights we're closed, but on other nights, like next Saturday for Rob's party, we should give some thought to how to protect you."

"In essence I'd be running a whorehouse." She cringed at the words.

"If you knowingly host parties in which this sort of thing is going on, I guess so. Does that sit all right with you?"

"Phew, that's a lot to take in. Six months ago I was the very proper wife of a very proper corporate executive. Now I know he wasn't so proper, and I guess I'm not, either."

Grinning, Marcy said, "Proper people don't necessarily have much fun."

Pam couldn't help but smile along with her. "I've discovered that."

"From that gleam in your eye, I assume you're making love with someone special?"

"Special? Maybe, maybe not." She realized that Marcy was someone who could help her deal with the distress about having sex with both Gary and Rob. "I've been with two guys since I saw you last." She didn't even mention the slightly boring guy her friends had set her up with weeks before.

Marcy reached out and squeezed Pam's hands. "Bravo. Sex is the most fun, isn't it?"

Grinning, Pam said, "Yeah. It is. Now that I know what I've been missing, it's sort of like a new toy."

"Are the two in question good lovers?"

"I don't think I know what that means."

"It means several different things. Are you satisfied?"

"Oh yes."

"Are they creative?"

"If you mean kinky stuff, no." She couldn't control her blush. "It's just good, hot, orgasmic sex."

"Hmm. No kinky sex. Too bad."

"Is everyone interested in kinky stuff?"

"Not everyone, but now that you've let the genie out of the

bottle it might be time for you to get a bit more adventurous before you miss the opportunity and settle down again."

"I'm not settling down so fast," Pam said, meaning every word.

"You never know. Are there things you wonder about? Things you'd like to try but neither guy is interested in?"

She decided to be completely honest. She had been reading magazine articles and erotic how-to manuals and there were things that it seemed nice people did that she'd never experienced. She had to admit that she was curious. "There are things I might like to experiment with," Pam admitted. "'There are more things on heaven and earth, Horatio, than are dreamt of in your philosophy.'"

"Hamlet, I think. And you're so right."

"Does that make me some kind of slut?"

Marcy frowned. "Oh my, such harsh words. 'Slut' is so pejorative. It makes you a woman who's not afraid to admit the desire to experiment. Bravo for you."

"I'm not so sure. It's really been bothering me. When Vin and I dated, we dated only each other. Now I'm not only dating but having sex with two men and thinking of still more exotic activities. It doesn't feel right to me."

"So stop. Pick one and end it with the other."

Pam chuckled. "That doesn't feel right, either."

Marcy dipped some more bread into the oil, chewed slowly, then licked her fingers in an unconsciously sensual gesture. Finally she said, "Only you can decide what's right for you. Just let me say this. It's not selfish to want things for yourself, and as long as you're not hurting anyone else, what's the harm? Have either of the guys asked you to be exclusive?"

Pam considered. "Gary's not ready for any kind of exclusive relationship. At least not yet. He spends a great deal of time with his children, as he should, and they are the center of his life. If he were to ask someone to give up everyone else for him, then he'd have to take the part of himself that he's

THE MADAM OF MAPLE COURT 143

spending on his daughters and share that, too. I don't think he's ready to do that."

"I think you're very wise. What about the other one? Can I guess that it's Rob Sherwood?"

She felt her face flush. "Yeah, and he's a wonderful, easy, light, no-strings kind of guy. He's not asking anything of me."

"You're right about him. He's been married twice, no kids and oodles of money. He's got bevies of women who wouldn't mind being Mrs. Sherwood number three, without a prenup, of course. It must be refreshing for him to find someone like you who isn't on the hunt for a next hubby."

"Me? Marry again? Not yet." She thought about that. "I've got some wild oats to sow, ones I never sowed before Vin."

"So sow away. I think you've answered your own question. Have a blast. Leave no stone unfucked."

Pam burst out laughing. Marcy had a way of making everything look simple and easy. "Right you are."

"Okay, now that we've got your personal future planned out, you need to be sure you're okay with Rob's party. Are you up for it?"

"Why the hell not?"

"Just do whatever you can to protect your own safety. I'll see whether Rock knows someone who could be there during the festivities, just as a not-so-subtle warning to everyone not to let anything get out of hand."

"That would be great."

"After lunch, how about coming over to the club and I'll show you around, introduce you to Rock, and we can see what we can arrange."

"I'd love it."

Chapter
13

The two women took a taxi to West Fifty-Fourth Street and climbed out in front of an unassuming four-story brownstone not unlike many others on the block. The only thing that might have distinguished it was an elaborate keypad for what Pam assumed was a state-of-the-art alarm system. She quickly realized that for a brothel, something like that would be imperative. Fortunately Vin had been a bit paranoid and had had a serious system installed in the house at the time it was built. Not only was the house alarmed, but the property was monitored with video cameras and thoroughly protected in other ways as well. Pam had never paid any attention to it, just punched the various controls to set and unset it as a matter of habit.

Pam followed Marcy into a large, comfortable front hallway that branched in several directions. To the right, a living room was low key and tasteful, with comfortable upholstered furniture and a quite unremarkable collection of tables, lamps, and greenery. A big-screen TV dominated one end of the room beside a fully functioning wet bar.

"Were you expecting black leather or a tinkling player piano?" Marcy said with a smile, watching Pam's expression.

"I guess I didn't know what to expect."

"That's the best answer to all of this, I guess. We've redone it several times to make it feel comfortable, welcoming and sort of homey, a place where if something breaks, no one cares. People are nervous enough, especially their first time here, that we didn't want to increase the stress level any more than absolutely necessary."

"Hello," a male voice called from the back of the building.

"Hi, Rock," Marcy said. "I've got a visitor. Come on out and meet her if you've got time."

"Sure. Be right there." The voice was deep, yet not so booming as to be threatening.

When Rock appeared he was wiping his hands on a kitchen towel. He kissed Marcy's cheek, then looked at Pam. "This is my friend Pam," Marcy said. "You've heard me talk about her. Pam, this is Rock."

Rock was immense, an obvious bodybuilder, with heavily muscled arms, shoulders and chest, beneath a tight black T-shirt. His upper arms were adorned with tattoos of chains around his biceps and his wrists. His black jeans covered long legs and a narrow waist and his head was completely shaved, with a large diamond stud winking in each ear. He wasn't really handsome, but he exuded masculinity and sex through every pore. He also made it plain, without any effort, that he brooked no interference from anyone about anything. In most ways Rock was exactly what Pam expected a bouncer to look like. However, he was wearing a "kiss the cook" apron and was wiping his hands on a frilly kitchen towel.

Rock extended his hand. "It's nice to finally meet you, Pam." His voice was surprisingly smooth and cultured. "Marcy's talked quite a bit about you." When their hands were almost touching, he shook his head and snatched his arm back. "Sorry. No hand-shaking right now. I'm still wet and a little smelly."

Smelly? From some sexual ritual? Semen, perhaps, or vaginal secretions?

"Don't look so shocked, Pam," he said with a wide grin that

revealed his even, white teeth. "I've been making osso buco. It's one of my specialities, and my hands are all covered with lamb fat."

"Rock's been taking gourmet cooking classes and we've all been benefitting from tasting his creations," Marcy said. It was all too complicated for Pam. Friendly madams, gourmet cooking motorcycle types?

"How about you all come to dinner tonight?" Rock suggested. "I've got enough to feed an army, including strawberry-rhubarb pie and homemade ice cream for dessert. Actually, if you bring Zack and the kids, that sort of is an army."

Marcy inhaled and closed her eyes at the delicious aroma. "Smells like an offer that's too good to pass up. I don't think Zack has anything planned. I'll call him in a few minutes and make sure. First, though, I want to discuss something with you." She outlined Pam's plan to host a party for Rob and his friends. "I don't think Pam should do this alone, at least not without someone like you to front for her."

"You're right there. I'd love to help, but since it's on a Saturday you know that I can't."

"Of course not. I was hoping you might know someone," Marcy said.

"I can't quite advertise for a bouncer for a sex party, can I?" Pam added, trying to joke her way through her momentary disorientation.

"Let me give it some thought. Can you stay for dinner, too, Pam? I'll ponder while I cook. I'm sure I can come up with someone."

The odors coming from the kitchen were wonderful and Pam was relaxing beneath Rock's charm. "If you're sure it's not an imposition."

"Not at all. You're more than welcome."

"Okay," Marcy said to Rock. "With that set, you go back to work and let me show Pam around." She turned to her friend. "Just give me a minute to call Zack."

148   *Joan Elizabeth Lloyd*

"Why don't you keep me company in the kitchen while Marcy does her wifely thing? I've heard a lot about you, Pam. You must be quite something for Marcy to trust you so implicitly. She's very protective of us here and I haven't known her to do this sort of thing with anyone before now."

"I'm complimented."

"You should be. And if she trusts you, I do, too." He started to walk away. "Follow me into the kitchen and I'll tell you all our secrets."

Together they walked to the back of the building. The kitchen was modern, with just about every small appliance imaginable on shelves and counters around the room. At the far end was a door to a small backyard. "When Jenna and Chloe first started this business it was to keep from having to sell this building, and the yard was one of the primary reasons." He ushered her outside into a diminutive walled courtyard with a fountain dribbling water over rocks down to a small fish pond. One small area had been turned over to a small vegetable garden, with vines of ripening tomatoes, zucchini, and cucumber plants. What looked like the green pepper plants she'd seen in the farm stores were the only things that weren't thriving. When he caught the direction of her gaze he said, "I never had any luck with peppers but I try every year."

"This is sensational," she said, genuinely admiring what he'd done. "I wouldn't have imagined this sort of thing existed in the middle of Manhattan. You live here, right?"

"Yup. I've got the whole thing to myself Mondays and Tuesdays and most of the daytimes the rest of the week. When the club is entertaining, I show myself, then keep to my room."

"Marcy told me that the club is closed early in the week. How come? I'd think they could make appointments for those days, too."

"Indeed they could, and sometimes I have to talk Chloe or

Marcy out of doing just that, but it would be just too much. Chloe and Jenna made that a rule early on. Otherwise they'd never have had any time to themselves."

Wilting from the July heat and humidity, Pam followed Rock back into the air-conditioned kitchen where he began to efficiently chop a green pepper with a huge chef's knife. "Store bought, and much better than mine will ever be."

"Can you tell me about Chloe and Jenna?" Pam asked.

"Sure. No secrets. They started the club almost six years ago and Chloe still works here. She loves it and makes great money, enough to spend the entire summer in Europe every year. Jenna is Marcy's sister. They're twins, you know."

"Marcy mentioned her. She lives upstate now with her husband, I gather."

"That's her. They each have a single child and a pair of twins, although Marcy had her twins first. Jenna's twins are just two years old now and my godson is five." He beamed when he spoke of the children. "I assume you'll meet Marcy's group tonight, and Zack, too, if he can make it."

Curious, Pam continued, "What's he like? Zack, I mean."

"He's wonderful and has turned into a real company guy: suits, ties, overtime and all. With his background I didn't expect that. He's in human resources." He chortled.

"So Marcy told me."

"Well," Rock said, attacking several carrots with the knife, "him being in human resources is a bit of a family joke. I don't think I'm telling you something you shouldn't know. Zack originally worked in the business."

Her jaw almost dropped. "I thought Marcy was kidding when she told me that. You mean to say that he owned something like this?"

"He worked here."

Holy shit. Marcy's husband really had been a male prostitute. This entire group of people was getting stranger and stranger. But Marcy and Rock seemed so normal. She wondered whether Rock was also an "entertainer." He probably was. There must be hundreds of women who wanted him, and not for his cooking. He was one sexy man.

"Linc Frawley."

"Pardon?"

"Linc Frawley. It's really Washington Lincoln Truman Frawley. His mother was a history teacher and she got a bit carried away with names when he was born, I guess. Needless to say he hates the long version, so he goes by Linc. He'd be perfect for your party. He's an imposing presence but he dresses up well, too. He could be your bartender and bouncer. I think he even rents a room somewhere in Westchester. You're near the Clintons, right?"

"I don't think they'd like the connection, but yes, they live within several miles of me." Linc. She pictured a hulking black man, maybe with dreadlocks. Phew. *Stop the stereotyping, Pam, she warned herself. Most of the ones you used to have have already been exploded.*

Rock's chopping was rhythmic and efficient and he continued to work as he talked. "Linc's trying to become an actor. I think half of New York is, too, but he might just have a chance despite his maturity. He's in his early thirties and right now he's working for a temp agency to keep himself in groceries. He also does some work with us from time to time. That doesn't bother you, does it?"

Another male prostitute. Until recently she'd never even thought that they existed. "Of course not." Well, not too much.

Marcy walked into the kitchen and Rock said, "Linc Frawley. He'd be perfect."

"Definitely. I should have thought of him immediately," Marcy said, brightening. "You're right. He'd be great. Let's just hope he's available. Give him a call and see whether he can join us for dinner. He can meet Pam and we can see what his schedule is."

THE MADAM OF MAPLE COURT 151

Rock dried his hands on a towel and grabbed his cell phone from its clip on his belt. "You ladies go tour the joint. Is Zack coming tonight?"

"Sure is. He'd have to be a real jerk to turn down your osso buco. He'll stop and pick up the kids from the sitter." She took Pam's arm. "Rock has obviously shown you the backyard. Isn't it the best?" She beamed with pride when Pam raved about the courtyard. "Okay, come on and let me show you around the rest of the place."

As they climbed to the second-floor hallway, Pam said, "Rock seems nice."

"Okay, I know you must be curious about him. Let me give you the rundown. I've no idea exactly how old he is because he hasn't changed in the five years I've known him. He lives in a two-room suite on the first floor. Over his objections we broke through a wall a few years ago to make his living quarters bigger and more luxurious. My sister Jenna met him when she and her friend Chloe started Club Fantasy. Their mentor, a woman named Erika, introduced them, insisting that we couldn't leave this building and the business inside unprotected. Rock's got family on the West Coast, but he's a very closed-mouthed person so I don't know much more."

"Interesting guy."

"Just FYI, he's bisexual, leaning mostly to relationships with other guys, but to the best of my knowledge he's never lived with anyone nor had a serious, long-term relationship. I emphasize the 'to the best of my knowledge part' because as much of a friend as he is, he's super private."

"Tell me about the guy you're recommending for my party."

"Linc is just the opposite of Rock. He's outgoing, fun, totally open, and strictly heterosexual. He's attractive and very sensual and he attracts women like a dog does fleas. Take care you don't get burned."

"I've got as much as I can handle with the two men in my life right now."

"Three isn't many more than two, but take care with Linc. I would hate to see you hurt."

"Advice taken," Pam said.

For the next hour Marcy showed Pam around the interior of the brownstone. There were four rooms on the second floor devoted to fulfilling differing fantasies. A Western room catered to would-be sheriffs and damsels in distress and a doctor's office contained an exam table, cabinets, and one mirrored wall. Another room was arranged like a desert oasis, cleverly done with fake trees, sand on the floor, and one wall covered with burlap to simulate a tent wall. A brown awning was held up with thick wooden poles. "The better to tie you up, my dear," Marcy said with an exaggerated leer and a twirl of an imaginary mustache. "Seriously, the sand used to be a bitch to clean up, even with plastic sheeting beneath, so we decided to just leave this room this way. It's amazing how popular it is. Sometimes folks have a vague idea that they want a power fantasy and when I suggest this 'oasis' they jump at it."

They walked to the "all-purpose" room and settled on the bed. "This room can be rearranged for a number of common fantasies. The hooker entertaining a guest in a hotel room, a wedding night, a burglar breaking in and ravishing the occupant. It's seldom empty."

"I gather the place is closed Mondays and Tuesdays."

"At first Chloe and Jenna entertained every night, but it got to be too much. It was difficult at first to turn clients down, but once the place began to pay its way they decided on sleep rather than cash."

"I'd take the cash right now," Pam blurted out.

"Are things that difficult?" Marcy said, looking concerned.

"No, not really," Pam said. "I'm okay for the moment, but I have no idea about the future. I'll have to get a job eventually, for both money and something to do with my days. Right now I feel like a slug. I play bridge, attend committee meetings,

THE MADAM OF MAPLE COURT   153

and basically slide through life. I can't seem to focus on doing anything."

"Eventually it will be made known to you."

She sighed. "I know. I'm hoping my party business takes off."

"I'm sure Rob can help with that. I know the money is a great lure, but you don't have to have parties with my girls in attendance just to make a buck. If it makes you the slightest bit uncomfortable then it's not worth selling your soul. I need for both of us to be entirely sure this is okay."

Pam considered, then said, "It doesn't bother me nearly as much as I thought it would. Intellectually I still have a few doubts, but in my heart, I think it's kinky in the good sense. If some of the ladies are paid to be there, why should it matter to me?"

"What if they take over a bedroom?"

"What they do in private is no skin off my nose. Should it be?"

"Not at all. You'd be doing what I do—provide a location for fun and games."

"You make it sound so easy. Maybe I'm beginning to understand the morality issue, but it's illegal and I still worry about that."

"Jenna, Chloe, and I have ways to keep the officials at bay."

"Secrets?"

"Just the names of our clients is enough incentive to keep the powers that be at arm's length. Remember that government official who had to resign when his name turned up in that Washington madam's little black book? No one wants that kind of trouble."

"I guess not."

"I think most people, if they thought about it, would agree that what we do, although technically illegal, isn't all that bad. It's private, totally safe health-wise, and not one of my employees has ever done anything out of line. No drugs, no blackmail, no nothing." Marcy had obviously made this speech before, including to her, but the reassurance was necessary and Pam slowly relaxed. She really wanted to do this despite her reservations.

"That's quite a record."

"I work very hard to keep it that way."

Pam had been wondering something, so she finally asked the question she'd been wanting to ask. "You never worked here?"

Marcy's laugh was genuine. "Not ever. Not my thing. Jenna did for over a year before she married Glen, but not since. I've always been the organizer, so once I got comfortable with the situation here I took over the bookkeeping, scheduling, and doing the interviews, both with prospective clients and women wanting to work here. I'm very good at sizing up people very quickly and I haven't been burned yet." She stood and adjusted her jeans. "Enough of that. Let me show you the rest."

By the time Zack arrived at just after six with three children in tow and the family had been introduced to Pam, the house smelled even more fabulous and the aromas wafting from the kitchen made Pam's mouth water. The baby, Eliza, moved like lightning, so Zack quickly perched her lightly on his hip where she contentedly chewed on the end of his tie, at least for a moment, until she yelled a firm, "Down, Daddy." The twins were identical, and at first Pam was grateful that they were wearing totally different shirts with their bib-front denim shorts. Quite quickly, however, their differing personalities made it easy to tell them apart. William, older by more than a minute, was outgoing, talking a blue streak, asking questions about living in the country. "We visit my cousins upstate a lot," he said, "and I like it up there. Do you have a cow?"

THE MADAM OF MAPLE COURT   155

"No," Pam said when she could get a word in edgewise. "Does your Aunt Jenna have one?"

"No, silly," William answered. "They don't live on a farm. But there's a big one nearby and we visit every time we go there. I like cows."

Patrick was quiet, seemingly content to build with a collection of multicolored cars and trucks Marcy retrieved from a closet.

Zack was very attractive but obviously very much in love, and he kissed his wife soundly and grabbed her bottom from time to time when he thought no one was looking.

At six-thirty the doorbell rang and Zack let Linc in. Black with dreadlocks indeed, Pam thought when she first saw him. No, Linc Frawley was anything but. Pam knew immediately that he was as dangerous as Marcy had said. There was obviously a lot of black Irish in his background. His jet black hair was long enough to curl slightly over his shirt collar and his piercing blue eyes seemed to be able to see into one's very soul. His profile was all angles but his sensual, Elvis Presley mouth softened any hardness, lips slightly thicker than necessary and his habit of licking them with his tongue made her pussy throb. *This is silly,* she told herself. *It's like some bad romance novel.* But she couldn't deny the jolts of pure lust that speared through her when he caught her eye. *He must be very good as a male prostitute,* she thought, *if my body's reaction is any indication.*

Rock appeared from the back of the building and shook Linc's hand heartily. "It's good to see you, man. It's been a while."

"Good to see you, too," Linc said, his voice deep and resonant. "How've you been doing? Good to see you, too, Zack."

"Zack, Rock, and Linc," Marcy whispered. "Sounds like a nursery rhyme or a vaudeville team."

Pam couldn't help but giggle.

The three men talked for a while and Pam became totally involved in replying to William's constant questions. "You know you don't have to answer," Marcy said after the fifth "Why?" in a row. "He'll go away if you stop responding, but he knows he's got a sucker right now so he'll keep it up until you're ready to explode."

As the three men talked, Zack kept both eyes on Eliza, who was taking blocks from the gigantic box Rock had dragged out of a closet so she could build a castle next to her brother Patrick. When her activities got too close, Patrick merely moved his traffic arrangement a little farther away.

While the children played and the men caught up on their recent pasts, Pam's gaze kept straying to Linc. The three men were of similar height, all just over six feet tall, but somehow Linc stood out in the group. Lust at first sight, she realized. *Stop it! Just stop it!* Was this what she'd become now that she was having sex with two men?

The conversation broke up and Rock grabbed one twin under each arm and spun them around. While William squealed, Patrick merely grinned. "Do more, Uncle Rock. Do more," William kept yelling.

Linc picked up Eliza and nibbled at her neck. "I miss my sister's kids," he said to Zack with a slightly dreamy look in those exquisitely blue eyes. "I really have to get out there soon and get my fix."

"Where does your sister live?" Pam asked, eager to get to know him a little better. She didn't stop to examine her motives.

"You must be Pam. Hi, Rock told me a little about what you need. I guess you've figured out who I am, and we can talk business later. My sisters and their broods are in the Chicago area and I miss them like crazy. If you want to get into modeling or acting, though, you've got to be here in New York."

"Is that what you want to do ultimately?"

"I try not to think about ultimately. I'd just like to know I can get into showbiz, then I'll figure out where to go from there. I'm willing to think about next week, but further than that can take care of itself."

"Good plan, as long as you have no ties, no responsibilities."

"That's me. No ties. No nothing."

"I see you two have met," Marcy said. Rock motioned everyone toward the back of the house. "We can talk business after dinner."

Rock had set up a table in the kitchen with a high chair and two booster seats for Marcy and Zack's children and a wrought-iron table and chairs in the backyard for the grown-ups. "The kids are pretty good and while we eat we can see them easily," Zack said. "I'm just as happy to have a little quiet."

"I need to be in the kitchen for a bit, so I'll keep an eye on them. You all eat like adults for a change."

"Rock, you're a prince among men," Zack said.

"I know that," he said, lifting Eliza into her high chair. "I'm terrific." He nibbled on her neck until she was helpless with giggles.

"And modest, too," Linc said. "But I'm sure Marcy and Zack are grateful."

Chapter
14

Rock turned out to be a fabulous cook, and dinner was superb. Pam got to know and like both Rock and Zack, but she tried to avoid dealing with Linc. She needed to get some perspective on him before she thought about him too deeply. She remembered Rock's comment that Linc dressed up well. She looked at his simple short-sleeved denim shirt and jeans with a well-developed but not flamboyant body beneath. He dressed down well, too. She couldn't stop the vision of him naked that flashed through her mind. *Stop it. You're behaving like a silly teenager looking at some rock star.*

"Will it?" Linc asked.

"Sorry," Pam said, refocusing on the conversation, "I'm afraid I was woolgathering. What did you ask?"

"Marcy's told me about the party, and I wondered whether this would be the only time I'd be needed or will this kind of entertaining become a habit at your house?"

"Interesting question," she said. "I don't know what Rob, or anyone else for that matter, will want in the future."

Marcy chimed in. "I have a few ideas for your place if you're not too turned off by Rob's party. After all, we can't do any outdoor or country type stuff here." Pam watched the wheels turning in Marcy's head. "For an additional fee to my customers, I could hire a limo and transport clients up to your place and they could meet a lady there. Making love in a garden, or in the pool. Or," she said, planning as she spoke, "I could book your place for multiple encounters, like several guys who want to party together."

"I remember several weeks ago you had something you had to turn down," Zack said, lifting Eliza onto his lap. "Did you have a good dinner, sweetums?" he asked her as an aside to the main conversation. She patted his face and then, with a grin, took a cookie from his plate. "God, she's got me just where she wants me," he said, shaking his head slowly.

"Right. Those three guys from lower Manhattan who wanted a party with lots of space. Your place would have been perfect, Pam."

"Don't get ahead of yourself, Marcy," Pam said. "I'm still not sure about all this."

"You take all the time you need to be comfortable with whatever decision you make, but just remember the kind of money we're talking about."

At that moment a pair of little dynamos ran outside and attacked their mother. Patrick climbed onto her lap with William grinning but remaining in the background. "Uncle Rock says we can have ice cream but only if you say it's all right," Patrick said. "Can we, Mommy?"

Marcy looked at the people at the table. "William always puts Patrick up to asking stuff like this, the little conniver."

"He takes after you," her husband said.

Marcy nodded in agreement, then said to her son, "You may have a small ice cream as long as you ate your dinner."

"Rock says we did okay," William said, "and what's a conniver?"

Everyone laughed and Zack said to his son, "That's what you are, my love. Just like Mommy."

Pam knew that Marcy was manipulative, but she wasn't being talked into anything she didn't really want.

THE MADAM OF MAPLE COURT

161

"Much as I'm enjoying myself, I've got to get home," Linc said, pulling a business card from his wallet and offering it to Pam. "Here are my numbers, both home and cell. I'm certainly interested in coming to your gathering, and I agree with everyone that you need someone to be there just in case, if only for the guy who's had too much to drink."

She'd told him the plans for Rob's party. "Does the date work for you?"

"No problem."

She rose. "I've got to get going, too," she said, "but first let me help with the cleanup." She gathered several plates and carried them into the kitchen.

Rock took them from her and put them into the dishwasher. "No need, Pam. This will only take a few moments."

"Take him up on his offer and beat it, Pam," Zack said.

"Right," Marcy chimed in. "This is the first and last time you'll be company here."

After a moment's hesitation, she agreed. "I'm driving back to Westchester," she said to Linc, "and I gather you live up that way. Can I give you a lift somewhere?"

"I've got my own car," he said. "Miracle of miracles, I actually found a spot on the street."

Pam walked out through the front door and turned right toward her garage, while Linc turned left. With a wave he said, "It was nice meeting you, Pam, and I hope there's a future in this entertaining of yours. It should be fun for both of us."

Was there a double meaning there or was she just hoping there was? Hussy! "I think there might just be."

"Great. Call me and we'll firm up arrangements."

Firm up. He would firm up well, she thought, then pushed the thought away. Would everything always be a double entendre for her now? More questions. "Will do," she said, and as she walked down the street she found she was glad she'd be alone on her trip home. She had quite a bit of thinking to do.

As she drove north, she thought about the morality of dating, and of course having sex with, two men at the same time, and now lusting after a third. Rob and Gary were wonderful fun, no ties, nothing serious. She knew Gary pretty well, at least as well as she could know someone after a dozen dates, and she had fun with Rob, both out of bed and in it. But she didn't love either of them, nor did she see a long-term future with either. Did she care? Not right now.

Then there was Linc, an actor and part-time male prostitute. There was some kind of chemistry between them, at least on her part. Had he reacted the same way? She had no idea. As attractive as he was, this kind of chemistry must happen all the time, and she certainly didn't want to become some kind of Linc groupie.

Then there was Rob's party. She was actually going to become some sort of a madam, inviting men and women into her house to have sex. Okay, okay, it was just a business party and she was not taking an active role in it, but still it would be in her house, with her knowledge. And Linc would be there.

The Madam of Maple Court. Quite a title.

She went over her discussion of prostitution with Marcy in her mind again. Why didn't she see anything wrong with it? Of course men should be home with their wives. Hadn't she been deeply hurt by Vin's defection? Why didn't men discuss these things with their wives rather than take out their frustrations with hookers?

How would she have reacted if Vin had asked for new, creative things in the bedroom? She hoped that she would have been supportive and adventurous. She was afraid, however, that she would have been a little taken aback and negative. Would Vin have decided to change the subject? That might just have happened.

So what now?

When she got home she called Rob. "I talked to Marcy and we've agreed on the details for the party. She'll provide ladies and I'll have a bartender who'll double as a bouncer."

THE MADAM OF MAPLE COURT 163

They talked for an hour, finalizing the budget and agreeing on food and drinks and agreeing on a time schedule. "Did you and Marcy agree on a signal for her ladies?"

"Marcy's worked that out quite cleverly. All her employees will be wearing a thin gold ankle bracelet with a tiny heart charm with a ruby center. So all the guys have to do is gaze at their legs, something guys do all the time anyway."

"That should work fine. By the way, I won't be able to stay with you afterward," Rob said. "I'll have to go back to the city with some of the guests."

"No problem."

"I miss you. I'm pretty tied up until the party, but how about the following week?"

She could hear the leer in his voice and she laughed. "I look forward to it."

She saw Gary for a quick lunch near his apartment on Tuesday of that week. "I'm so sorry this has to be so brief," he said after he kissed her hello. "I've got to pack. I'm taking a late flight to Stockholm for an important client." She loved the way he said Stockholm; it sounded so exotic. "I'll be gone for at least a month."

"Oh. That's too bad," she said, meaning it. She would miss him. She liked him a lot and he'd been hinting that she might spend a day with him and his children. She was dying to meet them. Children. Delightful little girls she could get to know. "I'll miss you."

"Me, too, Pam."

He was distracted during lunch and after gulping only half his coffee he stood, leaned down, and kissed her soundly. "I'll call you." Watching his back as he rushed out the restaurant door, she sighed. She really would miss him.

Linc did dress up real nice. He showed up at her house about an hour before the party was scheduled to begin, dressed in black slacks, a deep burgundy shirt and matching silk tie, hair slicked back and a small gold stud in one ear. "I look like a hood out of general casting," he said, "but I thought it would be appropriate."

"You look great," Pam said as she ushered him inside. Although it was almost seven, the sun was still well above the horizon. The weather had been poor all week but had cleared up that morning, so the evening was comfortably cool and tendrils of vapor danced in the lights above the heated pool water. The yard was lit with colorful lanterns and candles and she'd had the property sprayed with insect repellant to keep out the mosquitoes.

"This place is a fantasy come true," he said. "I could enjoy living here. What a place for an orgy."

"This isn't going to be an orgy," Pam snapped. "There will be lots of married folks here with their wives, husbands, or partners."

"Hey, chill out."

Chagrined, she said, "I'm sorry. I'm a little nervous about this whole thing."

"I'm sorry I joked about it." He put an arm around her shoulders and hugged her. "I shouldn't be flip. I know it's your first time hosting a party like this and it must seem really strange."

"It does."

"You'll be just fine, and you look fabulous."

She knew she did. She'd selected a halter-top jersey dress of white, with a black Greek key design around the waist and skirt bottom, and slipped on tiny white sandals. She'd put on a necklace of large white and gold beads with matching drop earrings and added a white and gold enamel cuff around the upper arm. Vin had always hated that cuff, and when she'd noticed it in her jewelry box she'd added it because she could. She had also removed her wedding band, stowing it in her jewelry box, and moved her diamond engagement ring to her right hand. She had intended to wear nothing on her left, but when she noticed the dent where the ring had been she added a cocktail ring with a flat onyx stone. "Let me show you where everything is," she said, then walked around pointing out the three open bar areas with adjacent tables of hors d'oeuvres and finger foods.

There were tables set up for folks who wanted to sit and talk, and the usual small dance floor. The DJ she'd hired was setting up his equipment and waved at her as they passed. She surveyed everything and it all seemed to be in order.

Linc let out a low whistle. "Quite a setup. This is really fabulous. I can see why parties are your specialty."

Rob arrived about ten minutes early with several friends, both male and female. Some of the women wore simple summer slacks and blouses, others were dressed to the nines. "I brought a bathing suit," one woman said. "Rob said you have a heated pool."

"I do, and it's a delightful temperature," Pam replied. "I hope you'll enjoy a dip while you're here. The spa is behind it," she said, pointing. "Just follow the little stream."

"Oh, I certainly will."

Pam showed her where the cabanas were and indicated a large pile of fluffy towels. "There are also several spare bathing suits for both men and women, so spread the word and please urge anyone who wants to make use of anything here."

Rob drew her into the den and closed the door behind him. He kissed her deeply on the mouth. "I can't tell you how great this place is, and you're wonderful." He glanced at her hand. "You've removed your wedding ring. Bravo!" He pulled a small jewelry box from his pocket. "A little token of my gratitude for all this."

She didn't take the box. "I'm being well paid," she said. "You don't have to add anything more."

"This is personal," he said. "Please."

She took the box and, hoping it wasn't anything too serious, untied the ribbon and pulled off the paper. Inside was a small, almost lacy, pendant, a spray of tiny flowers each in a different semiprecious stone. "This is lovely," she said, impressed by his good taste, "but I can't accept it."

"Of course you can. It's just to say thank you for everything." He grinned, showing even, white teeth. "And I do mean everything." When she hesitated, he added, "Please. It would make me happy to see you wearing it. Tuck it away and put it on the next time we're going to be together."

With a sigh and a smile at the lovely piece, she slipped it into the top drawer of the desk. Ironically, it lay beside some of Vin's secret credit card statements, the ones that had started everything.

A half hour later the house and yard were filled with people. Marcy's ladies arrived separately and deftly slipped into the throng, looking as though they belonged, tiny gold bracelets gleaming around slim, shapely ankles. They looked not unlike any of the women there, attractive but not gaudy. A tall black woman with a generous figure immediately gravitated to a still taller steel-gray-haired man who, after a glance at her ankle, welcomed her into the group of men he had been talking to with an arm around her waist.

A blond in a gauzy pink dress was quickly approached by a heavyset man in a pair of beige slacks and a burgundy golf shirt, and a brunette with amazingly blue eyes that Pam suspected were enhanced with tinted lenses was ushered into a group in which several men and women were talking animatedly. Every so often voices were raised in a heated exchange, from which all Pam could hear was, "The president is an asshole." Another group laughed heartily at a joke one of the women had told. Everything was going along beautifully.

Pam kept her eye on the revelers, making sure that everyone had a drink and something to eat and that no one was standing or sitting alone who didn't want to be. She saw Linc deftly mixing drinks, pouring wine and soft drinks, and neatly and easily fending off several women, smiling yet keeping his distance.

THE MADAM OF MAPLE COURT 167

"Hello," a masculine voice said from behind her. "My name's Samuel Andala, and you don't seem to have a drink."

"Thanks. I'm not drinking right now."

As the man moved around her, she caught him looking at her ankle and she grinned and preened a little. Amazed, she looked at him again. He was of average height, pleasant looking with gray wings at the temples of his chestnut hair and steel-rimmed glasses. *Holy shit*, she said to herself as he again looked at her ankle. *He's interested, hoping I'm available.* It was the most amazing compliment she'd ever received, and her ego swelled with it. "Who are you here with?" he asked.

"This is my house, and I'm a friend of Rob Sherwood's."

"Ah," he said as if she'd made some kind of confession. "That's too bad." Did he know about their relationship? Who cared? They made small talk for several minutes, then he wandered off, probably in search of one of Marcy's girls.

Rob found her just after one a.m. and again pulled her into the den. He kissed her soundly, then thanked her effusively. "You were fabulous. So many folks told me how great the party was and what a beautiful setting. A few asked when we would be here again. I can't thank you enough, darling."

Darling? "No thanks necessary, Rob. I was glad to do it, and well paid."

He kissed her again. "I've got to get some of these guys and their ladies back to the city. I'll call you in the morning."

"Wonderful."

It was after two a.m. when the final guest left and the last band member and caterer had departed. She and Linc collapsed onto the sofa, looking around at the mess. "Can I give you some help cleaning up?" he asked.

"Not necessary. Housework has never been my thing, so I always have a maid service come in after a party and clean everything, including the carpet, where necessary."

With a long sigh, Linc kicked off his black loafers and put his bare feet on the coffee table. She noticed that he had long, sexy toes. When had she begun thinking toes were sexy? "I'm glad. My feet hurt."

Pam unbuckled her sandals. "Mine, too." She wiggled her toes. "Much better." Her feet joined his, propped on a pile of napkins. Just to avoid any trouble with anyone returning after the party for who knew what, Marcy had arranged to have Linc stay over. "You can stay in any guest room you like. Would you make sure everyone's gone from up there before you crash?"

"I already did. Several of the beds will need clean sheets, but everyone's gone."

"Great."

"Listen, I'm sort of juiced. Are you too tired to talk for a while?"

"I'm high as well. I think the entire thing went well."

"I've tended bar at lots of professionally run affairs, and this was as good or better than any. I don't think there was anyone who didn't have a great time. Having Marcy's girls here didn't bother you?"

"I was afraid it would, but it didn't. I never even thought about it."

"Good girl. I'm with Marcy on all this." He sighed. "What a great party."

"Thanks. It's hard work, but I've done it lots of times and I've gotten pretty good at it."

Linc ran his long, slender fingers through his hair. "I gather from Marcy that you used to do this for your husband."

They talked about her past for a few minutes, then she asked, "You're from Chicago originally?"

"Yup. My family is in retail. Dad is a vice president of a department store chain and Mom is an office manager. I have two sisters, both married with two kids each, and a brother, still single."

She learned that he'd graduated from the state university with a degree in business and, after a few years of working in

THE MADAM OF MAPLE COURT

the Midwest, had come to New York four years before to try his hand at acting and modeling. "My parents think I'm some kind of nutcase, but I've always wanted to perform and I decided that if I didn't try it before I was thirty I would never do it."

"Any success?"

"Some. Very limited. I did a few bit parts, one walk-on in an off-Broadway show that lasted for only two weeks, a few commercials, and several menswear catalogs."

"That sounds like quite a bit."

"Not when you try to pay the rent. So I moved into an apartment over the garage at a friend's house, rent free, and I do temp work. I'm a whiz with a spreadsheet, and," he seemed to hesitate, then continued, "I work with Marcy from time to time."

"That blows my mind," Pam said, feeling she could be honest with him. "It never occurred to me that women might want a . . ."

He tilted his head to one side. "Let's call it an escort and leave it at that."

She found this conversation more than a little arousing. She was talking about sex with an attractive, single man, in her living room, and she felt her pussy twitch. What would he be like in bed? He should be very good. After all, he got paid for it. She fantasized for a moment, then shut off that part of her brain. She wasn't about to find out. She floundered for conversation in the sudden silence. "Do you like that kind of work?"

"Being an escort? There's nothing better. I get to go to fabulous parties, like this one, with interesting women, or I get to fulfill their fantasies and be something I never dreamed of being. Acting and sex. What could be better?"

"What kind of fantasies do women have?"

"You're a woman. What kind of fantasies do you have?"

This conversation was getting very uncomfortable. "I don't have any."

"Bullshit. Of course you do. Everyone does." His hand found hers on the sofa and he idly stroked the backs of her fingers. "Wouldn't you like some knight in shining armor to make long, leisurely love to you, make you come over and over?"

She felt heat rise in her face and tiny tingles all over her body.

He laughed. "I'm sorry, I'm making you uncomfortable. I guess I was hoping I could interest you in a little nightcap."

"Me?" she squeaked.

He turned and cupped her cheek. "Of course you. You're lovely, unattached, and after an evening like this I often like a little drink and whatever. And who better to share it with?" He dragged his feet from the coffee table and wandered to the elaborate bar that had been set up in the corner. "What can I get you? How about something outrageous? Maybe a tequila sunrise?"

What the hell. "I've never had one."

"Great. Something new to start off this part of the evening." He efficiently poured orange juice and tequila onto ice in a shaker, then poured the cold mixture into two glasses and trickled grenadine down the side. "I make a beautiful sunrise, if I do say so myself."

The drink shaded from deep rose at the bottom to bright orange at the top. It was indeed beautiful. "It's wonderful," she said as she took the icy glass in her hand. "Thanks."

"It tastes even better than it looks," he said, sipping his drink.

It tasted delicious and, since she was nervous and thirsty, she swallowed it quickly until half was gone. She felt the warmth down to her toes. "Are you trying to get me drunk?"

"Would you mind if I were?"

She thought over that question. He was interested in making love to her. That was all too obvious. Was it just because he was there and he was horny, aroused by all the beautiful,

THE MADAM OF MAPLE COURT 171

desirable women who'd been coming on to him all evening? Or because it was a warm summer evening and maybe he'd been sampling the alcohol? "Why?"

"Why what?"

"Why are you trying to get to me?"

"Why not?"

"Okay, enough of answering questions with questions. Why do you want me?"

He didn't deny it. "Because I think we could have some fun together."

"You hardly know me."

"Does that matter?" Then he laughed. "Okay, now I'm answering a question with a question again. You asked me why." He considered. "Because I enjoy making love. It's one of my greatest pleasures, and I love giving pleasure to the ladies I'm with. It's really just that simple for me. No entanglements, no declarations of undying affection. Just fun and games in bed."

"Without love it's like hiring a hooker."

"Without caring, you're right. Love has nothing to do with it, but caring does. I care about women, love them as a species, and I enjoy good sex. Isn't that enough?"

She sipped her drink. God, she was tempted. "I don't know."

"Let me try to convince you."

Chapter
15

He lifted her hand to his lips and kissed the palm. Then he swirled his tongue against her skin, making a tingling, wet circle. Between the alcohol and his ministrations, she was sorely tempted. Making love without any assumptions or declarations of anything. No dating in the future. Just a quick roll in the hay. No, that wasn't right. With Linc there wouldn't be anything quick about it.

His hand rested on her thigh, giving her time to move away, then he slid her skirt upward until his fingers found her skin. The jolt of heat was both exciting and terrifying. What was she becoming? Why not? As his fingers slipped up the inside of her thigh, the "Why not" was winning. And winning big. She allowed her eyes to drift shut and reveled in the sensations his fingertips were creating.

He slid his other index finger down the center of the halter top, delving deliciously into her cleavage, sliding beneath her bra and flicking over her erect nipple. Saying nothing, he stopped what he was doing. When she opened her eyes she found him gazing into them, asking, allowing her time to say no. When she didn't, his lazy smile creased his face and he leaned forward and gently placed his lips against hers.

Sex just for fun. What a concept? It didn't seem outlandish

to her anymore. Why the heck not? She relaxed into his kiss, feeling the tingle his fingers were creating throughout her body. She snaked her arms around his neck and tunneled her fingers into his hair. It was softer than she had imagined, almost baby fine.

The kiss deepened, both participating in equal measure, and their bodies moved closer, his groin and hard erection beneath his slacks pressing urgently against her belly. She wanted this, a culmination of a wonderful evening. Her eyes drifted shut but she didn't imagine Linc was anyone else. Actually she didn't picture anyone, just reveled in the sensations that this man's body was creating.

"Wonderful," he whispered. "Just enjoy." He untied the knot that held the halter top closed and let the sides fall and easily unfastened the clasp on her halter bra. Then his mouth found her breast and he pulled hard at one nipple while his fingers played with the other. Her vaginal muscles spasmed, almost as though she were climaxing. Amazing.

He spent several minutes playing with her breasts until she wanted to scream with both joy and frustration. She wanted his cock inside her, fucking her, bringing her what she knew she needed. When she pulled at his shoulders, however, he resisted. "I'm enjoying this too much," he said, his voice hoarse. "You'll just have to be patient."

Patient? She had no patience. She wanted, needed, craved.

He parted her knees and knelt on the floor between them, pulling her hips forward and pushing her skirt up to her waist. He quickly pulled her panties off and then his mouth found her pussy. She'd had oral sex performed on her before, but it had always felt like someone wanting to get her ready for the next phase. Linc seemed to enjoy licking and sucking her for its own sake. When she moaned he licked again, causing her back to arch. His fingertips joined his mouth, manipulating her vaginal lips and caressing her clit.

Her body went crazy, out of her control. He was the puppet

master, expertly pulling her strings until she felt orgasm surge through her bloodstream. "Yes," he whispered, his hot breath arousing her to still greater heights. "Come for me."

She clasped the pleasure to her, holding it back until she could resist no more. Then she came, his mouth sucking her clit, his fingers filling her. "I can feel you come," he said. "That is so hot."

He quickly removed her clothes, then his own. His body was beautiful, lean and strong, his erection straight and thick from its nest of curly hair. As he turned his back to her to put on a condom, she saw that he had a small tattoo high on his left buttock. It looked like a heart with an arrow through it, but when she looked more closely it was not a heart, but a star.

When he turned again and urged her onto the carpet she forgot the tattoo, forgot everything but the pleasure this man could give her. And the pleasure she could give him. Then he was on top of her, slowly sliding his hard cock into her. Then he held still for a moment, giving her a chance to adjust to his girth. He guided her legs until they were over his shoulders, her pussy wide open, enabling him to deepen his penetration. Propped above her on his hands, he threw his head back and laughed, then drove hard into her, thrusting and withdrawing, finding the rhythm that gave them both maximum pleasure, his hands beneath her buttocks, cradling, guiding.

She felt another climax within her and reached for it as he pounded into her. "Again, woman. Again," he cried and she came for a second time. Then, almost simultaneously, he erupted within her.

Later they lay together on the living-room carpet, the sound of hoarse panting filling her ears. She was exhausted. She'd climaxed twice under his expertise and her entire body, though incapable of movement, glowed. She couldn't help the giggle that escaped her.

"Enjoyed that, did you?" he asked.

"I think you of all people should know."

"Yeah." She could hear the grin in his voice. "I think your screams were the first clue. I might have permanent hearing loss."

She bounced up onto her elbow, concern filling her. She knew she'd cried out loudly several times. "I'm so sorry," she said.

He rolled her on top of him. "I'm kidding, silly woman. You were fabulous and I wouldn't change any of it."

She felt the length of his naked body beneath her, still slightly slippery from the sweat of good sex, then leaned over and bit his earlobe. "Kidding? I'll show you kidding." She wriggled against him like a cat in heat and felt his cock harden yet again. "Not here," she said. "My butt is rug burned and sore."

She led him upstairs and, without thinking, into her bedroom. When she realized where they were, a stab of regret flashed through her. In her bed. In the bed she'd shared with Vin. Linc flipped back the spread and stretched out on the cool sheets, unconscious of his beautifully naked body. All the bedding was new and so was this man. With a newly liberated attitude, she looked down at Linc's gorgeous body and rampant erection. She started to lie down beside him, but he said, "I'm too tired to do all the work. It's time for you to ride me, woman!" He handed her the condom he'd grabbed from his pants pocket as they left the living room and she took it from him.

She'd never been so daring in her desire to fuck a man. Here she was going to do all the work, make the moves. With a small smile she tore open the foil and withdrew the latex. She leaned over and very slowly unrolled the flesh-colored cover over his cock, stroking him as she did. She wrapped her fingers around the base of him, squeezing as she lowered the condom all the way onto him. Then she nestled his cock in the valley between her breasts, holding him against her body and undulating.

"Enough!" he cried, grabbing her arm and leg and yanking

THE MADAM OF MAPLE COURT

her over him so she knelt over his waist. "Do it, woman," he cried as she slowly lowered herself onto his shaft. "God, woman, do it."

She laughed from the sheer joy of it. She was in charge of their lovemaking. She lowered her body until she felt the tip of him against her heated flesh. Slowly, watching the joy and need on his face, she filled herself with him. She rose and fell on his cock, using it to caress her channel from every angle she could manage. She scratched his chest with her nails, then leaned over and bit his lower lip. He was so hard and growled over and over, "Do it, do it more!"

Then she reached between them and rubbed herself where she needed friction. She came yet again with another yell and squeezed her muscles, bringing him to his second climax.

Finally she dropped against him and together they rolled over and fell into deep, dreamless sleep.

The next morning Pam awoke before Linc. As she watched him sleep she found herself wanting to make love to him again. Would it all be awkward in the daylight? She'd made love to a man who didn't love her, wasn't even a friend. He just loved sex and, unless he was the greatest actor of all time, had enjoyed making love to her. And she'd enjoyed it, too. In a short time she'd become a woman who enjoyed sex for its own sake, and she found she was fine with that. She touched Linc's hair. She was more than fine with it. She felt fabulous.

"Good morning," he said with a laugh.

"Good morning to you, too, and what are you laughing at?"

"I'm happy, and you're looking at me like I'm a hot fudge sundae. Wanna eat me?"

She found she did. It took only her nod to make his cock stand at attention. The aroma of sex was everywhere, and it aroused her.

He suddenly looked concerned. "I should really shower first," he said. "I must smell like . . . well, like what we were doing last evening."

"Let me help," she said, climbing off the bed and walking into the bathroom.

"The view from here is wonderful," he said, and as she glanced back at him she saw that he was watching her. "You're one sexy broad."

With a warm feeling inside her, she soaked a face cloth in warm water, then returned to wash him—thoroughly—wiping the warm cloth over his cock and testicles, watching him twitch in response. Finally she tossed the now-cool cloth onto the floor and took him into her mouth. He still tasted of arousal and lovemaking. She wasn't quite sure what she was supposed to do, but from the corner of her eye she watched his face and felt his body respond. She did more of what seemed to give him pleasure and finally, with a groan, he pushed her away. "I'll come in your lovely and talented mouth if you do any more of that."

She didn't think she was ready for that, so she wrapped her fingers around him and did what he showed her he liked. As she watched he erupted and semen spurted onto his belly and dribbled over her fingers. She'd never seen a man come before and it was a magical sight. She'd done this. She'd made him come. Holy shit. She'd done it.

When he calmed, he said, "You're one talented lady. You've got great hands and a spectacular mouth. You sure you're not a professional?"

He said it as a compliment, and after a moment's shock she laughed and took it that way. "Nope. Just someone who's learning to enjoy sex, just because."

"Just because." He tossed her onto the bed and stroked and fondled until she came again.

"I think I'm beginning to like this," she quipped.

"That's the right attitude." He took a deep breath. "Think there's anything left to eat downstairs? I'm starved."

The cleaning crew! She looked at the clock. It was almost

THE MADAM OF MAPLE COURT   179

nine and they would be here soon. What would they think about Linc emerging from her bedroom? To hell with it. Let them think what they would. Oh God, clothes were scattered all over the living room. She couldn't let it go. She just couldn't. "The shower's in there. I need to get our stuff before the cleaners arrive."

She threw on a coverup and dashed downstairs, grabbing clothing from where they'd thrown it the previous evening. Wow. The previous evening. It had never been like that before. Fun. Hot. Hungry and immediate. She found his shoes last, then grabbed a tray still full of crackers with various toppings and a bottle of seltzer and dashed back upstairs.

Linc was just coming out of the bathroom, a towel draped around his loins. God, he looked so sexy she wanted him again.

"Food first," he said.

"Food only," she responded. "I've got work to do today."

"Awww, please?" he said, like a kid denied a toy he wanted.

"Not a chance," she answered. "I'm sure you've got things to do, places to go, people to see."

"I do, but it's going to be difficult to leave here. I will see you again, right?" he said, stuffing several crackers into his mouth.

"You bet." And she meant it.

"Between work and a few auditions I'm afraid my appointment book's pretty full, but I promise I'll call you." He left shortly after.

Rob called about noon. "You were just great," he said, "and I can't thank you enough for doing that. I hope the presence of Marcy's women didn't make you too uncomfortable."

"Not at all. I chatted with two of the ladies and they were charming and delightful. Did everything go well with that?"

"Most certainly. I had a limo full of happy guys going back to the city."

She wondered whether Rob had frolicked with the group but didn't ask. It was not any business of hers. "That's terrific."

"That bartender of yours was quite something. I thought he looked vaguely familiar. Is he one of Marcy's employees, too?"

"He was there to make sure everything went smoothly, if that's what you mean."

"Good idea. He looked formidable enough to put a stop to anything that got out of line."

Formidable. Good word for Linc. Rock was more of a beefy presence but Linc emitted vibes that told anyone that he brooked no nonsense. And beneath his clothes . . .

Rob continued, "Are you busy Wednesday evening? How about dinner, darling?"

There was that word "darling" again. He was a wonderful man, but she didn't feel like she should be his darling. *Oh well, maybe he uses that word with other women, too.* "Sure. Sounds good."

Marcy called that evening. "I got calls today from several of the ladies who were at your house last evening and they gushed with praise. About the house—and you. You're everything I thought you were, charming, poised and a whiz with people. Everyone said that you didn't let anyone feel separate unless they wanted to. Keeping a party like that going and seeing that everyone is entertained is a gift."

Such elaborate praise had Pam's head swimming. "It was really the kind of thing I do from time to time, and I guess I've gotten pretty good at it."

"That's an understatement. You'd make a wonderful entertainer. My kind, that is." When Pam hesitated, Marcy said, "Tell me you might think about that. Would you?"

"I don't know. The ladies seemed to have such a good time and I've become, sort of . . ."

"Curious?"

It was more than curiosity. She'd become enamored with

sex. She'd made love to four men since Vin and she'd enjoyed it all, especially with Linc. He treated sex like a fun game—no ties, just enjoyment. He'd said he loved women and making love to them, and she believed every word. She thought about him in bed with someone else and there was no pain, just a wish that he have a good time. This was an entirely new mind-set for her. "Maybe."

"Can I try to convince you? We could make some beautiful money together."

"I guess there's no harm in your trying."

"That's great. How about lunch, maybe Tuesday?"

"That would work well for me." They made plans to meet at an upscale sandwich shop near Club Fantasy. Interesting. Very interesting. Could she be convinced? She didn't know, but there was part of her that was very, very intrigued.

Chapter
16

Marcy was waiting in front of the restaurant when Pam arrived. In a singsong voice she intoned, "I hired a nanny. I'm a free woman. At least for the moment."

"That's great," Pam said. She knew that Marcy loved her children, but Marcy also freely admitted that she wasn't the full-time mommy type.

"Conchita is Hispanic, well recommended, the motherly kind of woman I'll never be. She's got school-aged children of her own who will be visiting relatives all summer. She's lonely already and eager to earn extra money. The kids seem to love her, and they're already saying *gracias* and *por favor*. I've become *mami* and Zack is *papi*." Marcy couldn't suppress her grin. "She's been with me for only a few days and I already feel like a new woman."

"Does she know what you do?"

"Hell no. She thinks I run a small business, but she isn't the inquisitive type. Everything's pretty well hidden anyway and all my computer records are here with me. Always." She pulled her keys from her purse. A small computer flash drive hung from them by a clip. "Since I handle all the credit cards and calendars for the club, this little baby has saved me a lot of passwording and worry." She dropped the handful of keys back into her pocketbook. "Let's find a table."

Later, after ordering and downing a glass of seltzer, Marcy said, "Everyone raved about last Saturday night. They said you were the perfect hostess with the perfect house."

"Thanks to them all. Your ladies were wonderful as well. Had I not known"—she hesitated—"what I knew, I never would have suspected. I wonder whether Vin ever had women like yours at any of our parties."

"Would he have told you?"

"Not a chance. He wouldn't have thought I'd understand back then."

"Would you have?"

Pam considered. "No. Probably not."

"But now?"

"I get it now."

"And you're finding the idea intriguing."

Pam felt herself blush. "Yeah, I guess so."

"Don't let it embarrass you. Back when I found out what my sister Jenna was doing, I was horrified. It took me months to come to terms with it." She leaned forward conspiratorially. "Interested in hosting the occasional party for one of my customers?"

"I think I might be."

"How about doing your own entertaining, being part of the action, as it were?"

"I don't really know." She smiled ruefully. "Three months ago I never would have dreamed of saying what I'm saying now, but I'm discovering that sex is really fun and if it would be that way and I'd get paid, what could be better?"

"I can't guarantee that it will always be fun, but you can opt out anytime if things get uncomfortable, and I'd give the client his money back. I screen my clients very, very carefully and I learn what they want, then match those desires to my ladies. I've seldom had to give a refund for any reason. Both the clients and entertainers are usually happy with the arrangements."

"I never really understood what fun sex could be, just for its own sake."

"Someone clue you in?"

Pam blushed again. "Yeah," she said, dropping her chin.

"Linc?"

She jerked her head up. "Why do you think it was him?"

"I know Linc and his attitudes. He loves women in all forms and makes a good living that way. And from what I gather from all the women he's been with, he's good at it. They ask for him again and again. Just don't get involved. He's not going to settle down anytime soon."

Pam had never even considered it. Settle down just when things were getting good? Not a chance. "I have no doubts about that. He's not a one-woman, or even a dozen-woman, man. But he is fun."

The two women giggled together. "I can imagine. Remember that Zack used to entertain. They say that once that kind of guy finishes sowing his wild oats and finds the right woman, he makes the best husband." Their giggling got loud enough that several people at nearby tables looked over. Marcy covered her mouth with her hand. "I should know."

"I have no delusions about Linc."

Again Marcy leaned across the table and whispered, "Is he as good as they say?"

Pam considered this amazing conversation. She was talking intimate girl-talk about sex with a madam. "Yes."

"Bravo! And Rob? How is he?"

Pam deliberately misunderstood. "He's wonderful. He thought the party went well, too."

"I know that, and you know that wasn't what I meant. How is he in bed?"

"Enough," Pam said, mildly annoyed. "I don't want to get into a discussion about the men in my life. Sorry, no gossip from me."

"Good girl," Marcy said. "Just checking."

"Finding out whether I kiss and tell?"

"I guess I was. Remember back when Larry Flynt, that *Hustler* guy, offered a million dollars for proof from any woman who'd had sex with a politician? I've got to be really careful."

"Isn't that the guy's job, too? If some famous person wants to have sex with a prostitute, he takes his chances."

"True, but the success of my business is entirely based on my reputation, and if one of my ladies sold her story, no one would ever trust me again."

"A million dollars is a lot of money."

"Sure is, and a great temptation. All I can do is trust my decisions about both my clients and my employees. After that I take my chances. Jenna, Chloe, and I understand that and just deal with it."

"You're a brave woman."

"And," she said, "I've got a little protection."

Not wanting to go further, Pam said, "I'll bet you have."

"So, are you interested in playing with my clients?"

"It's not that easy for me."

"Of course not. If it were easy you wouldn't be the kind of woman I'd employ. I'd love it if we could work together, but you need to be entirely sure of what you want to do."

"I'm not. The money's tempting . . ."

"This is too important to your *self* to do it for the money," Marcy said. "Oh, the money's important. I know you need a source of income, but that isn't enough for you. You're interested because you're curious about sex."

Pam nodded slowly. She realized that Marcy was letting her talk it all out and she knew she needed to do that. "Vin and I had good sex at the beginning. When we dated we couldn't keep our

THE MADAM OF MAPLE COURT   187

hands off each other and that was great. Hot, sweaty, in cars and on lawns, whenever we could find time and a horizontal surface. After we got married things sort of smoothed out. Few of the highs we'd had before. And once we found out I couldn't have children, it was as though Vin lost a little of the edge."

"I'm really sorry about the children part. I complain about my kids, but you know I love them dearly."

"I know, and I'm used to my condition. It did affect our sex lives, however. Now, since Vin's death, and knowing what I know about his thing with Liza, I've begun to question things. What's out there that I know little about? I feel like I've just learned to read and now I know where the library is."

Marcy burst out laughing. "That's a unique way of expressing it, but I know exactly what you mean. Been there, done that. With Zack. I have a proposition for you." She rolled her eyes. "Interesting choice of words for someone in my business. Anyway, I have a client who enjoys getting to know new women, ones he knows will be willing to play. He likes to be seen in the best places with a different attractive woman every evening, women who are bright, interesting and willing to play afterward. This doesn't quite fit into the Club Fantasy idea, but he loves the newness, the first-time experience, and he can afford to indulge his wishes. He loves sex and occasionally ventures into slightly off-center stuff, but understands how far to go with a woman and will take no for an answer. He'll stop at any time if you want him to. Sadly, though, he only wants to be with a woman once. His desires cramp my style, actually. Several of my ladies would have loved to join him again, but he doesn't want that, and frankly, I'm running out of partners for him."

"Why you? Why doesn't he just pick up a lady or let someone fix him up with one? Wouldn't that give him the newness he's looking for?"

"I'm not really sure. The only thing I can guess is that he

wants a sure thing with no strings, no illusions. With one of my employees he knows there won't be any repercussions. No woman will have her heart broken when he doesn't call. No one will wonder what went wrong. That's the best way he could describe his needs to me when I first interviewed him."

"You've never been with him, have you?"

"I've never been with any of my customers. It wouldn't work for me. I found Zack and that was that."

"Why Club Fantasy? His isn't a fantasy, after all."

"True enough, but he wants the best, and we're it." There was no false modesty in Marcy. Club Fantasy *was* the best and she knew it. "Interested?"

Pam thought about it. This was a momentous step, but one she was intrigued enough to take. She replayed Marcy's words. "You said he likes things slightly off center. Like what?"

"Oral sex, anal sex, the occasional slap on the ass, his or yours. He'll let you know but it will be like any other first date. He'll experiment to find things you enjoy together, but he'll stop if you say so. Who knows, you might enjoy new ventures. Does this sound like something you might want to do?"

"It might just be."

"It pays twelve hundred dollars net to you for the experience."

"Damn, that's a powerful incentive."

"Not the only one, I hope. You should want to do it because it's fun, too. If you do it only for the money, in my opinion that's what makes you a whore."

"Yeah, I guess it does." Pam had to admit she was interested in new areas of sexual play. She'd never tried anything fancy with anyone but Linc, and with him it had only been a little oral and a few new positions. She thought about a few of their positions and it was everything she could do not to blush. "No, money's only one incentive. I'm also curious to know

THE MADAM OF MAPLE COURT 189

what I've been missing all these years. Would this happen at your place?"

"No. Sometimes he likes to have company to Lincoln Center for the opera or a concert. He might want to be seen at one of the restaurants where he's built up a reputation for his good taste in dinner companions. He lives in the city so you two can go back to his apartment afterward. I'll call him and see what he's got going. Shall I set it up?"

Pam let out a long breath. "Sure. I'm single, free, and able to do what I want, and I think I want to do this."

"Just think?"

Pam paused. She knew what she wanted, so why hesitate? "I want to do this."

"What about the men in your life?"

"Linc would be all for it, Rob obviously knows what's going on, although not specifically with me, and Gary? Well, he's out of town for several weeks and I'll cross his bridge when I come to it."

"That's wonderful." Marcy took several minutes to fill Pam in on the guidelines, including wearing skirts at all times, "for accessibility," she explained. "No garlic or onions before a date," Marcy continued, "and condoms at all times, without exception, and two if he wants to play with anal penetration. No drugs of any kind, ever, under any circumstances. It's a good rule to follow in any event."

"No problem there," Pam said. Everything Marcy had said made sense.

"With anyone but Matt, who's a long-time customer, I would suggest that you not play outside the club until you're a little more sure of yourself. Having Rock in residence means a lot, to everyone."

"Have his services ever been needed?"

"To the best of my recollection on only two or three occasions have we had to, let's say *ask* a visitor to leave. In each case Rock has made him understand that his presence was no longer welcome. Both times the guy arrived drunk and had smuggled more alcohol in with him. Each guy was abjectly apologetic the following day."

"Did you let those guys come back?" Pam asked, curious about the strength of the rules.

"One was a regular, and after he served a suspension like in sports, we let him back. He's been a model of decorum ever since."

"And the other?"

"Both were newbies, two of my few misjudgments, and they're gone. That was several years ago and I thought for a while that one might make trouble, but he didn't. That might have been the closest I came to screwing things up. I'm even more careful now, and I've become an even better judge of character since."

"All your guidelines seem to be sensible."

"Just a few more. No cameras or the like are allowed into the building and no pictures anywhere, even from camera phones. We have a photo setup if the client wants a film of things, but it's carefully arranged so that the client's face is clearly visible and the woman's isn't. And there's nothing on any tape that states that it isn't all just consensual sex. No mention of money."

"You seem to have thought of everything."

"I certainly hope so."

While Marcy ate her sandwich and talked, Pam nibbled at hers. What had she gotten herself into? When Marcy finished her prosciutto and avocado sandwich on a whole wheat roll she glanced at Pam's plate and her half-eaten sandwich. "Nervous?"

"Very. I think my butterflies have butterflies."

"Not surprising. Why don't we go over to the club and let me get Matt's number and tickle my fingers on a private phone line? I have only one request. Once I set this up, there's no backing out. I can understand sudden illness, but please, this is Club Fantasy's reputation, and I don't like to disappoint my customers unless absolutely necessary."

The Rubicon. "I'm for this. No backing out."

"Good. From what I know of you, I think this is a good move. And, selfishly, it's a good move for me as well."

Chapter
17

The evening with Matt was set up for the following Friday. From what Pam could overhear as Marcy held the phone away from her ear the guy, named Matt Waterhouse, was overjoyed. "Wonderful. Can she meet me at seven o'clock at Sparks Steak House? As you know, I'm pretty much a meat-and-potatoes person."

When Pam nodded, Marcy agreed, told him Pam's first name, said her good-byes, and hung up. "Done. Wear something comfortable but classy. And keep the shoes simple." When Pam looked puzzled, Marcy continued, "Slip-ons of any kind work well. Men hate to have to work—unbuckle," she winked, "except, of course, those who are into feet."

"What can you tell me about this guy?"

"He's in his late forties, only five foot five, which should be right up your alley, balding, rather plain looking and sort of nerdy. Oh, and very, very wealthy. I think he's in corporate takeovers or something like that."

"So he's got the money to indulge his appetite for the ladies."

"Right."

Friday. Wow. Her social calendar was getting really crowded. Rob on Wednesday evening, Linc sometime soon, she hoped, and when Gary got back from overseas she'd be seeing him, too. She had an outrageous thought and giggled.

"What's amusing you?" Marcy asked.

"I was just thinking of me, sitting at some stuffy charity committee meeting later this week with several stuffy Westchester matrons, knowing what's going to happen on Friday."

The two women laughed loudly.

"So is there some kind of story here?" Pam asked. "Am I supposed to be someone in particular?"

"Not really. You're a date like any other date. It's just that no one introduced you, and he's paying."

The following evening Pam met Rob for dinner at an exclusive mansion that had been turned into an upscale restaurant on a hill overlooking the Hudson. He'd noticed immediately that she wore the pendant he'd given her, and she had to agree that the beautiful jeweled flower basket enhanced the simple black dress she wore. She'd strung it on a slender gold chain so it nestled just above her cleavage, and when she'd first arrived he'd lifted it to look at it, brushing his fingers over the swell of her breasts. They talked about everything and nothing, but Pam didn't mention her plans with Marcy. During lulls in the conversation she wondered why she didn't tell Rob. After all, he knew all about what Marcy did for a living, and Pam had hosted his party.

The answer was simple. She didn't *want* to discuss her plans with him. She wanted to do it and she was afraid he'd try to talk her out of it. Was she afraid he'd succeed? Sure, she told herself, there was some of that, but in addition the whole thing was private, and none of anyone's business but hers. Reluctantly Rob confessed that he had to leave early so there could be no after-dinner plans. She drove home slightly disappointed.

Both Gary and Linc called on Thursday. Gary called in the late morning, reaching her in her car on the way to a luncheon

THE MADAM OF MAPLE COURT
195

for one of her charities. He was still in Europe, enjoying his work but missing his daughters. And her, he added hastily. He said he'd be flying back to town just for one day over the weekend but he'd be spending time with his girls. He hoped she'd understand and, resignedly, she did. She was also glad he didn't ask for a date in the middle of the madness that was her weekend.

She and Linc talked on the phone for over an hour that evening, getting to know each other. She'd had one of the most intimate experiences she'd ever shared with anyone and he agreed that it had been fabulous and uniquely satisfying, but they realized that they hardly knew each other. When he suggested dinner on Saturday, she decided that she did want to see more of him and agreed. She wondered how she'd feel after Friday, when she'd become a prostitute for real. She reasoned that it would be good to have some normalcy afterward, if having a date with a male prostitute was normal. Good Lord, her life right now was quite an adventure.

What did it say about her relationships that she'd been relieved when Gary didn't ask her out but readily agreed to see Linc on Saturday? She didn't examine her motives too carefully. This was her time in life and she could do with it what she wanted, be a little selfish for a change. So there!

Matt Waterhouse looked pretty much as Marcy had described him, so, as Pam walked into the restaurant at seven o'clock that Friday evening, she recognized him immediately. Although according to Marcy he was only in his mid forties, he was already almost totally bald, skinny, with ears that stuck out from the sides of his head. He was sitting at a table in the center of the serving floor wearing jeans and a red polo shirt when every other man in the place was dressed in a suit or at least a sport jacket and slacks. He was reading a newspaper, looking neither left nor right. As she clasped her hands together to still their shaking, she wondered that he was so calm when she was such a wreck.

She'd spent over an hour deciding what to wear. She'd finally settled on a navy blue blouse with a small white design and a navy skirt slit to the knee on one side. As Marcy had suggested, she wore simple opera pumps that slipped on and off, with taupe thigh-high stockings. Her hair was smoothly combed and curved against her jaw. Her makeup was understated, her jewelry limited to a silver choker and silver drop earrings. She had taken off all her rings.

"Mr. Waterhouse," she said to the maitre d', who nodded and almost genuflected at the mention of her liaison's name. "Of course. Mr. Waterhouse said he'd be expecting a dinner companion." She felt conspicuous and wondered whether he was looking down his nose at her. Did he know she was a "paid companion"? No, he probably looked at everyone that way, as if examining a specimen or some lower form of life who would be dining with one of his most important guests. "This way, madam." Madam. She almost laughed at his unknowing double entendre. He led her to the table she'd anticipated.

As she approached, Matt put down his paper and stood. "Good evening, love," he said, then leaned forward and bussed her cheek as if he'd known her forever. "I'm so glad you could join me."

"I'm glad I could as well," she said, not sure what else to say. The maitre d' held her chair and she settled across from this man, her first customer. She unclenched her fingers from the strap of her small purse and put it on the corner of the table. Not knowing what image Matt wanted to project, she didn't want to indicate that this was a first meeting in front of the maitre d' so she said, "It's nice to see you." She had no idea what a prostitute said when first meeting a john.

"It's lovely to see you, too." His voice was deep and, although he was making an obvious effort to keep it low, there was a force, a drive to the mellow tones. "Marcy has such wonderful taste. You look smashing."

THE MADAM OF MAPLE COURT   197

She smiled despite her jangled nerves. "Thank you, Matt."

"Is your name really Pam? I know many of Marcy's ladies use false ones. You don't have to tell me, I'm just curious."

"When I first decided to do this I vowed to lie as little as possible."

"That's a good plan," he said. "So, honest lady, tell me a little about yourself."

"There's not too much to tell." She explained that she was a widow with no children, that she lived in Westchester, and that, currently, she was involved in several charity committees. She quickly discovered that one of those organizations was a pet charity of Matt's and they talked about its great work, which was chronically underfunded.

"Do you come here often?" Pam asked.

"I'm here at least once a week. I like to be seen here and frequently run into business associates. There's something about showing up in jeans with one beautiful woman after another that tickles my piano keys."

Was he the rebel he wanted everyone to see or was he merely making the point that no one could deny him entrance anywhere? She and Vin had been to Sparks a few times, and once one of the business associates they'd arranged to meet had arrived without a jacket. The maitre d' had insisted he wear one of the navy blue ones the house kept for just such occasions. She could picture Matt telling the powers that be here that either he dressed the way he wanted or he'd dine elsewhere. Interesting man. Vin had always been so conscious of his appearance and she marveled at how unlike her late husband this man was. She decided to let that subject drop. "Since you eat here so often, you can probably suggest the best thing on the menu," she said.

"What do you like?"

There was something in his tone and direct gaze that gave the question a deeper meaning. "I like most everything," she said with one suggestively raised eyebrow.

"My kind of woman." They agreed on her entrée and he suggested a particular, very pricey but very ordinary merlot. When he'd finally had enough money to indulge, Vin had insisted that they both study wines, mostly in order to make a good impression on others. Pam quickly realized that although Vin had little flair for the subject, she enjoyed going to tastings, visiting vineyards on wine tours, getting to know vintages and how to pair food and wine. Over the months they'd studied, she'd developed a discerning palate and an amazing ability to cherry-pick wonderful but not exorbitant wines from a list. "I've been here a few times," she said, softly, as the sommelier approached, back rigid, expression set, "so I hope you don't mind but I remember some of the items on the wine list." Wine book was a better term, since Sparks specialized in their cellar. She'd discussed wines with the then-sommelier on previous visits. It tickled Vin to watch her show her stuff. "There's a really nice Chateau Troplong Mondot that was a particular favorite of my late husband's. It's a St. Emilion and it's priced quite a bit less than the one you mentioned." She knew the money meant little but her creativity might impress him.

Rather than being surprised by her perceptiveness, he seemed relieved and said, "Wonderful. I know very little about wine, so I always order one of the few I know."

"The same wine as usual?" the sommelier said as he leaned over the table.

Matt motioned his head toward her and she ordered the wine.

"A fine selection," he said, looking a bit nonplussed. "You seem very well informed."

"I like to think so. I see that the one you have listed is the 2002. Is that the only vintage you have?"

The sommelier's expression softened and his voice became more friendly. "We used to have the 1998, for a different price, of course, but we're sold out. The 2002 is almost as good."

"Fine. We'll settle for that."

At the word "settle" the sommelier started, then actually smiled. As he left the table, Matt leaned forward. "I'm impressed. You really sound like you know what you're doing."

She put her hand in front of her face to cover her grin. "My late husband was a bit of a wine snob, and I have to admit that the stuffy sommelier brought out the worst in me."

The remainder of dinner was very enjoyable and, for a while, she forgot why she was with this charming man. He said all the right words about Vin's death and she found that the pain was now nonexistent. "I think I'm happier now," she confessed, both to Matt and to herself, "than I've been in a long time."

They discussed their backgrounds and told amusing anecdotes from their pasts. He really liked the wine and quickly committed the name and vintage to memory. When the check arrived, Matt dropped his platinum credit card on the silver tray and it was whisked away by the waiter. "Could I interest you in a nightcap at my place?" he said, his voice rising over the background noise.

She was momentarily puzzled. Didn't he know she was bought and paid for? When she raised an eyebrow he winked at her. "I'd like to show you my apartment," he continued loudly.

Ah, she thought. Those at nearby tables could make out what he was saying. He obviously loved giving the impression that he had propositioned a date. "I think I'd like that, Matt."

Sotto voce, he said, "You're quick on the uptake."

"No problem."

Matt's penthouse was atop a corner building on Central Park West. Pam tried to control her jitters as they took the interminably slow ride up in the elevator. She was conscious of her desire to wring her hands but locked her fingers around the handle of her purse and stared straight ahead.

The view from the wide living-room windows was spectacular. Silently he opened the sliding door to the terrace and she walked outside, leaned on the parapet, and looked up at the stars, then down at Central Park. When he put a hand in the small of her back she jumped. "If I'm insulting you I'm sorry, but you haven't done this very often, have you?"

Should she tell him the truth? She'd thought about how to handle slightly sticky situations like this and had decided to tell the truth wherever possible. "No, I haven't. You're my first—"she stumbled over the word,—"client."

Matt slid his hand up her back and rested it on the nape of her neck. She felt his breath on her ear as he leaned close. "That's delightful. Thank you."

She turned slowly and saw his face very close. "For what?"

"For letting me be your first. It's quite a privilege."

A light breeze rippled her hair. "It's totally scary."

His laugh was rich. "I guess it is. Would you like to call the whole thing off?"

She considered, then smiled at him and said, "No. I look at it this way. If we had met under other circumstances and ended up here, I wouldn't have balked at making love to you. So how is this different?"

Matt shook his head slowly. "It isn't." Then his lips found hers. His kiss was soft, suggesting things she realized she wanted. This was a big step but one she now wanted to take. She snaked her arms around his shoulders and held him close. They kissed for a long time, heat slowly flowing through her. She tangled her fingers in his hair and pressed him more firmly to her. Then he leaned back against the parapet.

"I would like to see you," he said. "May I take your blouse off?"

She had deliberately worn items that were easy for her to remove, so she slowly unbuttoned her blouse and, as his eyes wandered hotly over her body, she tossed it onto a lawn chair. Then she unfastened the front closure of the lacy pink bra she wore. When her breasts were free, she felt a light breeze cool

THE MADAM OF MAPLE COURT 201

her skin and pucker her nipples. She'd never been partially naked like this, outside beneath the stars and moon. It was intimate and sensual.

"I like your decisiveness, and you're so lovely," he purred, pulling his polo shirt over his head. Then he pressed his chest against hers, moving slightly so her nipples rubbed against his whorls of chest hair. She let her head fall back so he could kiss and nibble at her throat.

"You feel so good," she whispered. "I like what your lips are doing."

He kissed a steamy path down her throat, then across her collarbone and back to her ear. Then his mouth found her breast and he nipped at her flesh, making her jump. He didn't ask whether what he was doing pleased her so she moved against him, moaned, and generally made it obvious that she was reveling in the sensations he was creating.

His fingers found the fastening of her skirt and it quickly followed her blouse and bra. She stood, wearing only panties, thigh-high stockings, and her pumps.

"You're beautiful."

"I'm glad you think so."

While she spoke, he pulled off the remainder of his clothing and she saw his already rigid erection. Her knees trembled, not with reluctance or fear, but from anticipation, and she realized she was soaking wet with need. She wanted him, not because it was her job for the evening but because he was a sexy man whom she liked very much and who obviously wanted her. His desire for her was a strong aphrodisiac.

When she started to remove her panties he stopped her. "I want to do that." He took her hand and led her to a thickly cushioned lounge chair and sat down, leaving her standing beside him. He hooked his thumbs over the sides of her lacy pink panties and slowly pulled them down, then pressed his face against her belly.

She looked around, aware with a small part of her mind that

they were above most of the city, with a warm breeze caressing her heated skin and a desirable man making love to her. She glanced at the nearby skyscrapers, wondering whether anyone on a balcony could see them. She found it a very arousing thought.

His thumbs gently parted her outer lips and his mouth found her swollen clit. When the tip of his tongue flicked against her, the jolt of pleasure almost buckled her knees and knocked her off her feet.

"Come," he said, guiding her to the chair beside him. Then he slid to the foot of the lounge and crouched over her until he could again find her clit with his mouth, his fingers playing with her nipples. He was an expert at inflaming her and driving her toward climax. Why did he care about her pleasure? she wondered. She was being paid to pleasure him. She didn't question any of it, just enjoyed.

As she felt her orgasm build he pulled away. He quickly found a condom and, as he put it on, he said, "I want to be inside you when you come. I want to feel it on my cock."

He slowly opened her with his erection, then manipulated her clit with his fingers until, with a long, deep moan, she came, feeling her vaginal muscles squeeze him. When she came down, his cock was quiet inside her. "Now for my pleasure."

"What can I do?"

"Just be hot, and wet, and eager." He turned her onto her stomach and stroked her buttocks. Was he going to try anal penetration? She had never done that before and wasn't sure she was ready to try. Didn't she have some obligation to do whatever he wanted? Could she? He must have sensed her reluctance. "Don't worry," he purred. "I won't do anything you won't like."

Rather than playing with her anus, he pulled her into a sort of crouch and entered her vagina from the rear. It felt strange, and his hard cock touched her in what felt like different

THE MADAM OF MAPLE COURT 203

places. Quickly she found that she was arching her back and matching his thrusts with her own. She reached between her legs, and when she cupped his testicles he began to grunt with each stroke. Finally, he roared with his pleasure and collapsed on top of her.

They moved so they were side by side and it was several minutes until they could get control of their breathing. Finally he said, "That was wonderful. You're a very sexy woman."

"I thank you, kind sir," she said, not knowing what else to say.

"I assume you know that I never entertain a woman twice. I don't know why I've made that a rule, but I have. Right now I rather regret it."

"It's your rule. Can't you certainly break it if and when you want to?"

He stopped and thought. "I guess I could, and several women have asked me to. I don't know why I originally made it, but when I made it clear to women I went out with, it made it all easier. No one is disappointed when I don't call the next day."

"I just regret your rule and I'll hope you get in touch with me again. I'll be sad if you don't."

He scowled. "Want to see me again for a fee? Having sex with me is simple enough. Easy money."

Pam allowed her own scowl to show. "Think what you will, but the money has little to do with this. Okay, it did at first, but now that we've talked and I know you a little, I'd like to see you again. Is that so difficult to believe?"

He still looked skeptical. "Would you see me for free?"

How to answer? "Marcy and I discussed that and at first I didn't understand her rule against it. However, she said that her business depends on not letting her employees entertain her clients off the books, and I agreed to her terms. So I guess the answer is no. I value Marcy's friendship and my commitments too much to consider it."

He looked triumphant.

"However, if I were free to do so, I would."

"That's easy for you to say when you can't do it."

"True, but that's the way it is. You have only my word on it and, of course, I could say anything and not mean a word of it. You have no way of knowing, except what you know about me and my aversion to deception."

He remained silent and thoughtful until he put her into a cab so she could return to her garage. "What you said is bouncing around in my head. I'll think about my rules, and about you," he said, surprising her by leaning in and kissing her soundly as she sat in the taxi.

"Please do, and I'll hope to hear from you or Marcy."

As she drove toward the Henry Hudson Parkway her cell phone rang. She pulled over on West End Avenue, checked the caller ID, opened the phone, pushed the speaker button, and balanced it on her thigh. "Hi, Linc. What's got you up so late?"

"I just wanted to be sure everything went okay."

"You knew about my meeting with my client?" She was taken aback and embarrassed that Linc knew she was now a full-fledged prostitute.

"Marcy let it slip. I worry when anything goes on outside of the building and I wanted to be sure that you were okay with everything. You're pretty new at this, and maybe a little naive."

Her embarrassment was quickly replaced with annoyance and she let it show in her voice as she pulled back into traffic. "So you don't trust my or Marcy's judgement. She okayed this guy seven ways from Sunday."

Linc spoke quickly. "Of course I trust her, but I just worry that you'll get into something you're not ready for."

"Don't sweat the small things," she snapped. She was angry at his interference and his lack of faith in her. She was also humiliated knowing he'd been thinking about her with Matt. "It's really none of your business."

"Marcy made it my business when she put me in charge of taking care of you."

"Well, stop. I can take care of myself. You can be my bouncer when you're at my place for a party, but when I'm by myself, butt out." She knew she was getting really out of line. He was only guilty of caring about her. She stopped herself and warmed as she considered his concern, and her voice softened. "I'm sorry, Linc," she said, her voice softer. "I'm really okay with all of this."

"That's all I wanted to hear. Good night."

"Good night, Linc. Thanks for caring."

"You're welcome."

She basked in his obvious affection and she delighted that she had no hangover from her first evening as a real working girl.

Chapter
18

Men. Pam's life was beginning to be crowded with them. Who would have imagined it when Vin was killed? Now she was seeing Rob, who took her to Broadway theater, concerts at Lincoln Center, and dinners at the finest restaurants. From time to time she wondered at his slightly proprietary attitude, but he hadn't asked whether she'd begun working for Marcy. He had, however, introduced her to several business friends who planned to use her house for gatherings. Occasionally he bought her small gifts, but nothing as expensive as the pendant. Now his tokens were books he'd found that he thought she'd enjoy and CDs and DVDs of performances she'd mentioned she liked. It was getting difficult to mention liking something because he inevitably found a way to buy it for her.

She had seen Linc quite a few times. They ate pizza or take-out Chinese food at her kitchen table and made wonderful, hot, hungry love afterward. He too brought her the occasional present, but his gifts were sexy magazines and books with stories of couples making love in new and interesting ways. They even tried a few new things and she slowly became more and more adventurous.

Then there was Gary. He still spent the majority of his time in Europe, but they talked once or twice a week on the phone, e-mailed almost every day, and he'd hinted that when he returned and his life got "back to normal" he wanted to spend a day with her and his children. Children. She eagerly anticipated the day she'd meet his daughters.

In addition there was her party-planning business. She'd planned and hosted or was planning several weddings and engagement bashes for wealthy friends, friends of friends, and people who'd heard of her ability to make things entertainment happen. She was busier than she'd ever been, and happier.

Nothing had happened with her personal entertaining business since her evening with Matt. Marcy had told her that since so many men were on vacation with their families and companies cut back in July and August, the summer was usually slow in her business. Pam hadn't talked to Marcy in almost a month, so she was surprised and delighted when the phone rang one afternoon in late August.

"Up for something a bit more adventurous than Matt?" Marcy asked her after several minutes of light chatter.

"Like?"

"I've got a client with a hot tub fantasy. I'm sure you and your late husband liked to do it in your spa"—Pam and Vin had never done it in the backyard, but the vision of being there with Rob flashed through her mind as Marcy continued,—"and although he does other things here at the club, Chase has always wanted to do it outdoors. We can't oblige him here, of course, except in simulation. He also likes slightly more creative things than Matt. He's married but says his wife isn't interested in playing out any of his fantasies. He's a long-standing client and we've tried to oblige his wishes several times, but I think if we can use your backyard, he'll be in heaven and, of course, pay extra for finding the locale. We'll hire a limo to drive him to Westchester and try not to reveal too much about the location of your house."

"Did you tell him yes?"

"Of course not," Marcy said, surprised. "I said I'd always ask you first."

"Sorry. What kind of off-center things does he want?"

"He likes all forms of lovemaking, oral, and particularly being penetrated anally and the power it gives his partner, things he says his wife has declared off-limits. Your wonderful yard should be exactly what he wants. And one of these days you have to invite Zack and me up there so I can see this fabulous house and grounds of yours."

"Anytime. You just have to tell me when."

"We will. In the meantime, are you up to doing kinky things at your place?"

Pam thought of Matt's terrace and understood this new guy's desires. Doing it with the breeze in your face and the stars above was amazingly erotic. Her backyard would be the perfect place, lots of privacy and open space. Was there any danger in inviting a guy here for paid hanky-panky? What the hell. "Sure. Sounds fine."

"Oh, by the way, not to swell your head or anything, but Matt called and asked whether you might be available again. He's a bit odd, isn't he? With his no-second-date policy it nearly blew me away when he asked. He did, of course, make sure I knew that this wasn't necessarily going to change his rules with anyone else. He just wanted me to ask you."

"Tell him I meant what I said. He'll know what it means. And have him call me. I've gotten a prepaid cell phone." Pam gave Marcy the number, then continued, "About the hot tub thing, anything else I should know?"

"He wants you to do all the work and he sometimes brings a little goody bag with a few toys for you to use on him. Is that all okay with you?"

What an amazing conversation. "Do I need someone like Linc in residence?" She hated the thought of having him in her house while she was making love to another man, and she didn't know how he'd feel about it either.

"I don't think so. Chase is a longtime client and I would be totally shocked if anything got out of hand, so to speak. Oh, and he's also a probable candidate for using your house for parties. He's in Wall Street and probably entertains a lot."

"It all sounds good to me." Her second "customer." She wondered at her lack of remorse. Shouldn't she be worried about her morality? No. This was her time, and as long as no one, including this guy's wife, got hurt by what she did, it wasn't her concern. And she was having a hell of a good time!

The following Tuesday evening Pam watched the Cadillac town car with darkened windows Marcy had hired for Chase Hobart's drive to Westchester pull onto Maple Court, then come up her driveway. The chauffeur had phoned as they turned off the highway just to be sure she was ready. She was.

Chase's entire demeanor screamed power and money. He climbed out of the car more gracefully than she'd ever seen a man move and walked up to the front door.

"Chase," she said, her voice warm and welcoming. She was surprised at how easy she felt, with only a frisson of the nervousness she'd had when she first met Matt. She was getting used to all this. "It's nice to meet you." She extended her hand.

"Nice to meet you, too, Pam." His handshake was firm, his hand warm, the skin soft.

"I understand you want to see my backyard, the pool and hot tub."

"I certainly do." He took a small attache case from the back seat and carried it with him.

Pam nodded to the driver, who pulled out of the driveway to find someplace to wait until he was called. "This way." She guided him through the house to the patio. "Would you like a drink first?"

"Thank you," he said, seeming relaxed yet assertive. "What can you offer?"

"See for yourself." She indicated the fully stocked bar, then showed him the large freestanding wine cellar. "I've got a good selection. There are several good vintages of both white and red. I'm a white bordeaux fan myself." Marcy had told her Chase was a bit of an oenophile and she counted on her knowledge to break down any barriers.

He set the case on a patio chair and said, "I'll have whatever you're having." A challenge?

She showed him the label on the bottle she'd selected, then, after he nodded in appreciation, with a few efficient movements opened a bottle of 1997 Pavillon Blanc de Château Margaux. "I've always been a white burgundy fan but I read an article recently on white bordeaux in *Wine News* and decided to give them another chance. I retasted one, then several. This one really knocked my socks off." She poured a small amount into a crystal glass and handed it to him. "Wonderful for a summer afternoon," she said as he closed his eyes in appreciation of the crisp, cool liquid.

"This is truly delightful." He picked up the bottle, studied the label, then set it back on the small glass side table. "You're obviously a woman of many talents."

"You've no idea," she said with a wink. Was a paid escort supposed to flirt? She had no idea how she was "supposed" to behave, so she did what she felt and she felt like flirting.

"Tell me a little about yourself," he said.

She told him about her husband without giving him a last name, and a little about her life since his death, now almost a year in the past.

"How in the world did you become, well, what you are?"

"I'm not anything," she said. "But if you mean how did I get to be paid for my services? It sort of just happened."

He raised his glass. "To my good fortune."

She touched the rim of her glass to his and listened to the clear ring of the crystal. "I don't usually let anyone carry glass around the pool and hot tub, but in your case I'll make an exception." Actually, her parties had already caused her to relax

Vin's rules about glass around the pool. She had a good, thorough cleaning service and she'd yet to have a problem with breakage.

They kicked off their shoes and with him carrying his case, they walked barefoot through the newly mown grass to the spa. "This is lovely," he said, "exactly what I had in mind when I first talked to Marcy. I didn't think she'd ever be able to pull it off, but here we are. I think the area needs more greenery around it. Give it a more private feel."

She looked around the spa area, and although taken aback by his frankness she allowed as how he might be right. She nodded slowly. She'd think seriously about changing the landscaping another time. Since her various business ventures were bringing in some cash, she might be able to swing some additional landscaping. "Interesting idea."

"Shall we get naked?" he said, setting the case on a bench and quickly removing his shirt, jeans, and underwear. She looked at his well-exercised body, lean and strong, his chest covered with a thin coating of deep brown hair, his cock only semi-erect.

She quickly dropped her skirt, blouse, and underwear on the knee-high rock wall beside the hot tub and watched his eyes as he looked her over.

"Nice. A beautiful body to go with a strong personality."

"Why do you say that?" she asked, turning the dials to make the water bubble and foam. "I never thought of myself as strong."

"Then you're wrong. A weak woman wouldn't be where you are today. She'd have depended on someone else to get her out of whatever crap her husband left her with."

"Why do you say Vin left me with crap?" Vin hated all vulgarity, so she had seldom used such language while she was married and it still felt a little strange coming from her lips. She laughed inwardly. A prudish prostitute? Because of her new business she'd practiced "talking dirty" reading from stories to help her learn her new language. So much was changing about herself. No. So much was changing about the way she appeared to others. Inside she was still the same Pam DePalma, wasn't she?

"I can size people up pretty quickly. I have to in my business." He lowered himself into the heated water. "Your late husband was a weak man and depended on you to hold him together. He needed things like this house to bolster his ego. You were probably always the one who got the lawn mowed, saw that he always had clean shirts, entertained his business associates, kept him going in lots of ways. He probably hated that. Am I wrong?"

She settled beside him and considered what he'd said. Months before, Mark Redmond had told her that Vin had said she depended on him. Chase was probably more accurate. "No, probably not." She'd give his comments more thought later. Right now she had a job to do, one she was being very well paid for.

"Good. I like strong women," he said.

She remembered what Marcy had told her that he liked and knew what he wanted. She'd read a few stories on the Net to help her achieve a persona he'd appreciate. *Get tough*, she told herself. Her voice became more forceful. "Then let's get this show on the road. From now on you'll play by my rules, and rule one says that you're not allowed to come until I say so." She felt his body stiffen.

"But . . ."

"No buts. My rules. No coming." She saw a small smile flash across his lips, then disappear.

They sat side by side, leaning against the side of the tub, up to their shoulders in water. She reached over and took his cock in her hand. It was suddenly rock hard. She knew from experience that keeping an erection wasn't easy in hot water, but she was sure she could help him do that. She wrapped her fingers around his shaft and squeezed lightly. His soft moan told her she was getting to him. They played and teased, then knowing his preferences, she slid her hand between his thighs and grasped his testicles. He gasped as her hand slipped farther back until she touched his anus. Then, using the water as a lubricant, she slipped a finger inside. "Oh God, Pam," he yelled. "Oh God. Get the case."

She left him, Chase's eyes following her, his head propped on the side of the tub, climbed out, and opened the small leather folio. Inside was a slender anal dildo with a wide flange. She took a deep breath. Now she felt like a hooker, and although it felt strange, she knew she could pull this off.

She climbed back into the water and said, "You're a really naughty guy." She slid her hand beneath one of his buttocks and lifted. "Just hold still right there."

She wondered whether the dildo would go in without lubricant, but the spa water proved sufficient and it slid into his ass easily. She pushed it in as far as it would go, then, holding the flange in one hand, she grasped his cock with the other. Marcy had been right. Anal sex and power. She was new to both but it seemed to come naturally to her and she loved it all.

She kept fucking his ass and manipulating his cock as he moaned and thrashed in the water. She timed her strokes so that as she stroked downward on his cock, she pushed the anal dildo in tighter, then reversed the motions. "I might let you come soon," she told him, "so get out and lie on that bench." On a whim, she added, "And don't let that cock in your ass fall out!" She watched him breathe still faster as he stretched out on his back and knew she'd hit just the right note. As if newly born, she climbed out of the water.

She moved beside him and stared down at his cock, sticking straight up from his groin. His eyes were closed with obvious pleasure. "Now remember the rule. No coming until I tell you you may. Right now I'm going to watch you fuck yourself." She was experimenting with words and ideas, watching him to see whether her ideas aroused him and was pleased when they did. "I want you to play with that dildo in your ass while you masturbate."

He opened his eyes, stared at her, then closed them again, his excitement obvious. He reached behind him and held the flange tightly against him, then grabbed her hand and wrapped it around his cock. Then he thrust through her tightly clenched fingers, showing her exactly what he wanted.

His moans and sighs told her he was close to coming, so she used everything she knew about a man's body to hasten his orgasm. "It must be difficult not to come," she said.

"Pam, I can't hold back."

"Just another moment, and I know you can do it. Another minute." She kept him waiting until the strain on his face showed he couldn't keep his climax under control much longer.

"Please?" he begged, his voice trembling, showing the difficulty he was having holding back.

She smiled. "All right, but you'll have to do something to increase your stamina if we're going to be together again."

His bellow told her that he'd let orgasm overtake him, and as she watched, semen boiled up between her fingers. "My God," he said when he was able to catch his breath, removing the dildo from his ass and dropping it on the slate around the bench. "That was quite something."

Although she'd enjoyed watching his excitement, she was relatively calm. Chase didn't appear to care about her pleasure, and she wasn't being paid to come unless he wanted her to. "Certainly was," she said. Unbidden, the memory of what Liza had told her about Vin and how they played together slipped into her mind. It was so sad, she thought, that he couldn't have shared his desires with her. They might have had an enjoyable sex life if he had. She now understood that, for him, Liza was just about sex.

Later she walked Chase to the door, opened it, and as he started down the front walk he said, "Another time?"

"Of course."

"Marcy said you host parties here, too, of all kinds. I'd like to use this place for business gatherings, but I also have several friends I'd like to invite here for fun and games."

"I'm sure I can accommodate you either way."

"Can I invite some of Marcy's girls, too?"

"Sure. The more the merrier." Did she mean that? It sounded like he wanted to set up an orgy. Oh, what the hell. In for a penny . . .

"I'll call."

She knew he would.

Late the following week Rob invited her to dinner at Chez Marcel, a very chic East Side restaurant. She enjoyed his company and they usually ended up in his apartment afterward. Once, however, she'd been surprised when he'd guided her into the elevator of the posh hotel in which they'd eaten. "I like a change of scene now and then."

The hotel had a Jacuzzi tub and, as it filled, Rob had added a generous amount of bubble bath. Bubbles filled the tub, then sloshed onto the floor. They'd giggled like naughty children, then made slippery, slithery love on the bath mat.

Tonight he'd insisted that she wear a dress with a full skirt, so she found a lightweight summer floral print with spaghetti straps and cummerbund-style waist. They sipped fine wine and ate perfectly prepared salmon with a creamy dill sauce. While they talked about nothing of import, they shared the house special dessert, a chocolate gateau with an outrageously rich fudge sauce. Rob licked a bit of fudge from her index finger, sucking it like a small cock.

As she sipped the last of her burgundy, Rob moved from the seat opposite her to the banquette at her side. "Go into the ladies room and take off all your underwear," he whispered into her ear.

She whirled and stared at him. "Do what?"

"Stop stalling. I love the way your breasts jiggle and I want

THE MADAM OF MAPLE COURT   217

to watch that as you return. Then I want to be able to gaze down the front of that lovely dress and see your nipples. I want to know that your pussy is naked, too."

When she looked incredulous, he smiled his amazingly charming, enticing smile. "Please," Rob said.

She grabbed her purse and stood. As she disrobed in the stall she wondered where the little woman was who'd been married to Vin. Gone. Long gone. Now she was a bold, sexually liberated woman, and she liked herself this way. It might not be anyone else's cup of tea, but she was having the time of her life. When she returned to the table she'd done what he asked, and her wispy bra and panties were now stuffed into her purse. She slipped onto the banquette beside him.

"I love to watch your breasts sway, knowing my hands will be touching you later, pinching your beautiful nipples and watching them harden beneath my fingers."

As he talked he stared down the front of her dress. She knew that, indeed, her nipples were tightening. "Delicious," he said. Then she started as she felt his hand on her knee. "Don't look so startled," he purred. "It's just me, touching you the way I know you like to be touched."

"Rob, stop," she protested softly. "Everyone will see." Rather than stop, he slid his hand up the inside of her stocking-covered thigh. So this was why he wanted her to wear a dress with a full skirt.

"No one is paying any attention, sweet," he said into her ear, his breath heating her blood, "and anyway, the tablecloth is long enough that no one can see anything." His fingers found the top of her thigh-high stockings and then the bare flesh above. He was embarrassing her a bit and she wanted to squirm away, but there was another woman sitting at the next table on the banquette facing her dinner companion. She couldn't make a fuss, although Rob was crowding her. She had nowhere to go.

"Just relax," he said into her ear. "I'm having fun."

"I can't think when you do that," she murmured.

"What do you have to think about? Just go with it." He paused and his index finger found her pubic hair and brushed against it. "But don't let anyone know what's going on."

His movements were heating her blood and she wanted nothing more than to stretch out and let him have his way with her. But she couldn't, not here in public. His finger tunneled through her hair and found her wet center. "You know," he said conversationally, "I'd like a liqueur and I think you would, too. Would you signal the waiter?" He chuckled softly. "My hand is a little busy."

She couldn't help but chuckle. "You are so outrageous."

"I know," he said with a grin. "Ain't I the very devil."

She motioned to the waiter, who scurried over. "I'd like an Amaretto," she said. She was almost unable to utter a coherent sentence while his finger was rubbing her clit. She could barely control her trembling voice.

"Make that two," Rob said, still rubbing, keeping her just below explosion.

It took only a few moments until the waiter returned with their drinks and, totally calm, Rob lifted his small snifter with his free hand and sipped. "This is really good," he said. "You really should taste it."

She lifted her tiny glass but set it down immediately when she couldn't control her shaking hands. "Difficult?"

"Very."

"I'm going to make it harder," he said, laughing at his double entendre. "I mean for you, although I'm pretty hard here as well."

Then his finger found her channel and slid inside. His thumb massaged her clit and she knew she was close to coming. "Don't make any of those delightful little noises you make when you come," he warned. "That lady beside you is getting really curious about what's going on."

Pam glanced to her left and, sure enough, conversation at

THE MADAM OF MAPLE COURT   219

that table had ceased and the woman frequently glanced over at her. Pam tented the napkin in her lap lest the nosy lady see anything unusual. She was scandalized but loving every minute of Rob's ministrations. She vowed that she'd never visit this restaurant again.

Finally she gritted her teeth against any outward show of the orgasm she knew was bubbling up inside her. When she came, she knew Rob could feel the rolling waves of pleasure as they echoed through her. The only outward sign, however, was the further quickening of her breathing. Otherwise, difficult as it was, she remained silent.

When she calmed a little she looked over and saw that the front of his slacks bulged with his obvious arousal. With as little movement as she could, she shifted her napkin into his lap and, from beneath, unzipped his fly and maneuvered his cock free. With a grin she squeezed tightly around the base the way she knew he liked it, then moved his erection so it rubbed back and forth against the linen. "Witch," he hissed.

"Right," she said, now able to sip her drink with her free hand.

She manipulated his cock until she knew he was fighting for control. She didn't let him. Instead she began long, slow strokes from base to tip and back, increasing the pressure and frequency until she felt him start to spasm. She moved her free hand until she held the napkin tightly against his cock as he spurted into it.

Staring at him as the pleasure washed over his face, she didn't really believe she'd done something so outrageous. But she had.

Chapter
19

Throughout the remainder of the summer and early fall Pam's life sparkled. She hosted a society wedding and several smaller engagement, birthday, and anniversary parties. The only party she found a little difficult was the baby shower, but she tried to focus on the joy of the mother-to-be rather than the hole in her own life. She discovered a company that made heated tents and had a connector made that could temporarily and warmly attach one to her patio doors. With that, her entertaining continued even as the weather cooled. She had also become an expert in organizing and hosting parties in other locations and became something of a phenomenon in central Westchester. Parties arranged by Pam DePalma quickly attained considerable cachet.

The other side of her life flourished, too, and her bank account began to climb above its low water mark. She thought she might make it without another job, at least through the end of the following year. Pam saw Matt several times and, although they enjoyed each other's company and she often forgot that he was a customer, she was always well paid. She also entertained clients at Club Fantasy several times a month and she'd branched out in her sexual activities, learning to give pleasure with oral and anal sex and old-fashioned hand jobs like she and Rob had done in the restaurant. She now had a collection of toys that she and clients played with.

In mid-October she had a small group to her house, for the first time since Chase's party, for an evening of strip poker. She'd debated using her house for what would certainly turn out to be an orgy, but she'd decided that she'd just do it and worry about the consequences, in the rare event that there were any, later. She wondered whether she should have Linc around, but their sexual relationship made it impossible for her to entertain with him in attendance. She could only be this outrageous with strangers.

A man she and Marcy had met with arranged for everything, paying a small fortune for the evening. He invited six guys and, in addition to Pam, two of Marcy's girls were attending. When Liza arrived she'd taken a moment to whisper, "Quite a change from the first time we met."

With a quiet giggle, Pam had to agree.

The ten of them sat around a large table in the living room, sipping drinks of all kinds. Before the game began, each person had added or subtracted items from their person until each had the same number of articles of clothing.

"Texas hold 'em," the leader, a stick of a man named Jim had said. "Ante will be ten chips. Once you're out of chips, it's up to us to decide what each article of your clothing is worth. It's up to you to make taking off your bra or shorts worth as much as you can."

The game moved along with one of the women and two of the guys eventually possessing most of the chips. A woman named Angela was out of chips and wanted to bet. "Ah," Jim said, "our first casualty." Angela stood up and pranced around the table, wiggling her shoulders, causing her large breasts to jiggle. "I want a hundred chips for my blouse and for a glimpse of what's underneath." The offers grew and eventually, for a considerable stack of chips, she pulled off her jersey top, her prominent nipples obvious beneath her lacy bra.

THE MADAM OF MAPLE COURT   223

Then she pulled one cup quickly aside and flashed the flesh beneath, to the cheers of the guys.

"It's all going too slowly," Jim said. "I'm upping the ante to a thousand chips or a shirt."

Soon several of the women were shirtless and one had removed her skirt and was down to panties and a bra. Pam still wore her panties but had broken the bra barrier, much to the guys' delight. A few of the guys were down to shorts and T-shirts and Jim, who'd had a run of bad luck, was sitting in only shorts. Shorts were covering gigantic hard-ons.

"Okay," a man named Ralph said to Pam, "you're out of cash again. I'll give you a hundred chips for a suck of your beautiful tits."

"Two hundred," she insisted.

A third man chimed in. "I'll give you a thousand if you can make him come in his shorts, using only your hand."

"Damn," Ralph said, "I'll add another thousand to that."

"An offer I can't turn down," Pam said. She was quite mellow from the wine she'd had and it had silenced any little negative words in her head. She knew what she'd become and was enjoying the hell out of it.

"Can I play?" Liza said. "I'm in need of chips, too."

Soon each of the ladies, now naked, was crouched between the bare legs of a man, the two men left over playing with available breasts. "Whoever gets the guy to come first wins his entire pile of chips."

"Hands only? How about tits?"

"Shit," Ralph said to Pam. "I'd love to come between those gorgeous boobs of yours. It would make losing so worthwhile."

"Okay. Hands and tits," Jim said. "Shorts off."

Ralph and his friends removed the rest of their clothing, the poker game forgotten. Pam crouched between Ralph's knees and cupped her breasts, letting his long, slender cock nestle between them. "On your mark, get set, go!"

There was cheering from several of the guys, then the room filled with moans and groans. The strain showed on each man's face as he tried not to climax. Soon, however, a man named Jack came in Liza's hand, quickly followed by most of the remaining guys.

Ralph held out until Pam reached between his legs and cupped his sac, scratching the tender area between his testicles and anus. "Not fair," he said when his breathing finally slowed.

She grinned and winked at him. "Who said anything about fair?"

For more than an hour after, couples wandered upstairs, then came back down, until everyone was sated and ready to depart in the waiting limos. "A hell of a party, Pam," Jim said. "A hell of a party."

As she watched the limos leave Pam said aloud, "The Madam of Maple Court is in business for real."

During the week after Thanksgiving, Marcy called with another client for Pam's escort services. "The guy called and wants to give one of my ladies as a present to a coworker who helped the company big time with some contract or other. Something seems off with this one."

"Legal problems?"

"No, no, that's not it. I wouldn't get involved with anything I was the least bit leery of that way. No, the guy who called me is the younger brother of a very good and trusted client. However, I got the impression that the guy whose present you might be isn't much into women."

"Gay?"

"No, just young and maybe virginal. He said that he had the names of several other escort services and implied that if it weren't going to be through Club Fantasy he'd call someplace else. I'm afraid some poor slob might be the butt of some kind of practical joke, so I need someone like you who can think

THE MADAM OF MAPLE COURT   225

quickly on her feet and make it all work out right for everyone concerned. I thought of you. Interested?"

Pam was complimented by Marcy's words. "Maybe you should just turn him down."

"I will if you won't do it. There's no one else who's right for this. I'll trust your judgement. Frankly, I feel very sorry for the poor guy who's being set up."

An amazing vote of confidence, Pam thought. "As long as you're sure there's no danger, sure," she said. *The Madam of Maple Court strikes again.*

The gathering was set for a suite at an exclusive Midtown hotel, and Pam knocked lightly at the door of room 417. A small, ruddy-faced young man, wearing a lime green sport shirt and slacks answered. "Well, hello," he said appreciatively.

"I'm Pam."

"It's nice to meet you." He extended his hand and guided her into the room. "I'm Phil."

This was a new experience for her, meeting someone in a hotel room. It made her feel more like a call girl. The room had no bed, just a wide sofa, two upholstered chairs, and a few tables with lamps and potted plants. Two couples were trying to slow dance to a CD of new-age jazz and a third woman stood beside Phil, her arm around his waist. "It looks like I'm a little late," Pam said, glancing at her watch.

"Not at all," the man said, looking her over with obvious appreciation. "You're here for Manny." He indicated a small young man, sitting in the corner looking very uncomfortable. "Manny is single-handedly responsible for a great new contract the company just landed, and we wanted to give him a present."

Manny was probably no more than twenty-five, nondescript with unruly, mousy brown hair, soft brown eyes that looked like they'd work better on a basset hound, and soft baby skin that looked as though he didn't have to shave. He also looked like a deer in the headlights. Phil's date glanced at Manny, a wide but slightly nasty grin on her face, as the other two couples looked on, one of the girls appearing very uncomfortable. Pam felt bad for Manny and angry at Phil and his cohorts. She'd make this all work out if it was the last thing she did.

"It's very nice to meet you all." She took off her coat and dropped it with all the others on a chair. She'd worn a red jersey dress that hugged her ample curves and buttoned from plunging neckline to hem. She walked over to Manny and extended her hands. "Shall we dance a little?" With her back to the rest of the group, she winked at Manny and mouthed silently, "It will be okay. I promise."

It took him a moment to answer, then he said, "Okay, but I'm not usually a dancer." She watched him paint on a coat of bravado and stand up, facing his companions. "But for you . . ." His effort to appear unfazed impressed her. *He must be mortified.*

"Dancing isn't much more than moving your feet up and down from time to time, and it's a lovely way to get to hold each other." And break the ice.

"Yeah," one of the other men yelled, "dance with the lady."

"Come on, Manny. Be a sport. This is your party, after all."

Pam extended her arms and whispered, "Please."

He put his right arm around her waist and held her hand with his slightly sweaty left. She took their joined hands and tucked them against her chest, moving very little, allowing him to shuffle his feet and get a feel of her breast through her dress. "Mmm," she purred. "You've got the idea."

She felt him tense and tried a new tack. "Is there a bar in here? I could use a glass of something cool."

"It's in the next room," he said.

She moved toward the connecting door with Manny following. The second room of the suite had two large double beds and the other usual hotel accouterments, including a fully stocked bar. When Manny went to close the door one of the

THE MADAM OF MAPLE COURT

guys winked at him, so he left it open. "May I have a glass of white wine?" she asked, eager to give him something to do to ease his discomfort.

"Of course. I'll have one with you."

He poured, and as he moved to reenter the living room she patted the edge of one of the beds. "I'd rather just sit and talk, if it's all right with you."

Manny looked terribly uncomfortable as they settled on the edge of one of the beds. "Don't worry about all this," she said in a low whisper so only he could hear. "I get it. You won't embarrass yourself." Louder, she said, "Tell me a little about yourself," then sipped the really fine chardonnay.

He seemed tongue-tied. "I'm sorry," he whispered, almost in tears. "I'm not used to this sort of thing."

"I know," she said so the others could easily hear. "First dates are always difficult for anyone. There's really nothing to it. Let me start. I'm almost thirty-five and a widow. My husband was killed in a traffic accident almost a year ago. I live in Westchester County, no kids, and right now I'm a party planner. I organize big weddings, bar mitzvahs, like that."

"You mean this isn't your real job?" He glanced at the door and lowered his voice. "I thought that the guys hired you to show me up, you know, make a fool of me."

"They probably did, but we're going to turn the tables on them," she whispered, then raised her voice to normal volume. "For me, this isn't a job, although I do get paid. Most of the time it's a pleasure. And I'm sure it will be for us tonight." Again whispering, she added, "Say something. Ask me about my parties. It will make them crazy to hear us having an adult conversation."

For the first time that evening she saw the hint of a smile. "You plan parties?"

"Right. Planning weddings is my main occupation." She spent the next fifteen minutes regaling him with stories of the disastrous people she'd had to deal with and the screwups and their fixes. At first his laugh was tentative, then he began to relax and enjoy her stories. The noise from the next room led her to believe that the folks in there had gotten bored and weren't listening too closely anymore. She saw that Manny had finished his wine, so, while his back was turned, she poured some of her drink into his glass.

Slowly the alcohol loosened his tongue. "I'm twenty-five and I'm not very good with girls. I've never been married," he told her. "I'm a computer nerd and, with the help of a production scheme I came up with for the company, Paramount Packaging, our firm just completed a contract with a large manufacturer to take all the production we can turn out for the next two years. Did I tell you that we make plastic packaging?"

"No, you didn't." Softly she asked, "Did you know what was going on tonight?" When he nodded, she continued, "So why did you come if you knew what they were up to?"

His eyes moistened. "I don't have many other friends. Actually none."

"Those guys aren't your friends."

"They're better than nothing."

She raised an inquisitive eyebrow. "Are they?" When he didn't reply, she changed the subject. "Tell me about your company and this great new contract."

He told her a few details. "Without the really unusual production scheduling scheme I worked out, the deal wouldn't have gotten done." He droned on, now comfortable talking about his job, so she listened, seeming to pay strict attention while her mind wandered. Eventually he said, "So when they told me about this little party, I agreed. I kept hoping one of them would break a leg or something so it wouldn't happen."

The others were laughing and telling jokes in the next room, not paying attention to Manny's troubles. Occasionally one of the guys wandered in, stared at them, refreshed drinks, and left. Softly she asked, "Are you a virgin?" His flush told her that her instincts had been correct.

THE MADAM OF MAPLE COURT   229

"I promise we won't do anything you don't want to do, but I'm here for you if you want me." There was a lull in the noise from the next room, so Pam said, loudly, "It's getting a little warm in here and my feet are killing me. Do you mind if I make myself a little more comfortable?" She could imagine six sets of ears straining to hear all the details.

"Not at all," he said, his face terrified.

Don't worry, Manny, she thought, *I won't hurt or embarrass you.* She stood, kicked off her shoes, and rubbed the small of her back. "With no chairs in here, sitting on the edge of the bed like this is a bit uncomfortable. I guess I'm not much of a bed person." She'd said it deliberately but she managed to look embarrassed and giggled softly. "Put my foot in that one, didn't I? You know that's not what I meant."

"Of course not," he said, unsure how to proceed.

She rolled over on her back against the pillows and unbuttoned the top buttons on her dress. She patted the bed beside her. "Why don't you kick off your shoes and make yourself a little more comfortable over here?"

Seeming reluctant but toughing it out, he removed his shoes and stretched out beside her. She found she was enjoying herself, doing a service for this sweet, shy young man. She took his arm and pulled it over her shoulders. "Isn't that a little better?"

He merely nodded and she could feel his hand tremble. She took his free hand and placed it on her breast. "We can get much more comfortable if you like," she said, pulling the tails of his shirt from his waistband.

He stared at the open door to the next room and she nodded. "Why don't we close that door and get a little more privacy?" she suggested, rising and unbuttoning her dress so it hung on her shoulders, revealing a skimpy bright red teddy beneath. She pinched her lips to make them look well kissed, lifted her breasts almost out of the top of the teddy, and pulled at her nipples to swell them. Then she swung her hips as she walked to the connecting door, putting on her most heated, heavy-lidded expression. "Hey guys, refill your drinks if you want to, then we're going to close this door so we can have a little privacy."

Phil stared at her breasts, his eyes widening. "You and Manny?"

"Sure," she said. "And in case you didn't know it, he's got great hands."

"He does?"

She merely smiled and turned her back.

"Hey. We'll want that room, too," one of the other guys said.

"In due time," Pam said. "Drinks, anyone?"

When no one moved she closed the door behind herself and returned to the bed. "Manny, the guys are now pretty sure they know what's going on in here, so we've covered our bases. For the rest of the time, nothing has to happen unless you want it to."

She watched his chest deflate and heard his long sigh. "I really don't know what to do," he confessed.

"After tonight you won't have to lie about your sex life anymore. I've already made sure that you'll be famous around your place. So now we can do whatever you're up for." Laughing, she added, "You know what I mean."

"Thanks. You're really nice. I never expected a"—he stumbled over his words—"woman like you to be so understanding."

"Don't think about that right now." She stood at the foot of the bed, kicked off her shoes, and let her dress slip to the floor so she was now clad in only the teddy and the red stockings that were hooked to its garters. She unfastened the detachable cups so her large breasts were exposed. "Or do nothing." She moved her body slowly, not wanting to scare him but knowing that he wanted what she was offering.

"I like what you're wearing," Manny managed to say around the obvious lump in his throat.

THE MADAM OF MAPLE COURT
231

"In case you hadn't noticed, there's no crotch to this teddy," she said, sliding one finger between her legs.

His eyes widened. "There isn't?"

She walked to the side of the bed. "Want to check it out?" She took his hand and guided it to her wet center.

Suddenly the door to the adjoining room opened and the three men walked in, grinning, camera phone held out. "We thought we'd surprise you," one of them said, then saw Pam's bare breasts and Manny's hand buried between her legs. She took hold of his wrist, lifted his hand and licked his index finger. "You want to watch?" Pam asked. "I don't know whether Manny wants to put on a show or not, but it's his call. And of course I charge more for voyeurs."

"Hey, Manny," Phil said, suddenly serious, "maybe we were wrong about you. We thought you were a virgin and wanted to help you get your first one tonight. You're a good guy and deserve it."

She watched Manny's spine straighten. "Well, obviously we're having a great time," he said.

"At your expense by the way, guys."

"Right," Manny said while Pam unzipped his fly, allowing his large, thick cock to spring free. As she'd discovered while they were dancing, Manny was amazingly well endowed, and the three guys merely stared at his large phallus. She knelt beside the bed and licked the length of him. "Manny and I are busy, so unless you've got more cash so you can watch, beat it."

Looking sheepish, the three men disappeared, closing the door behind them. "I'm sorry about that," Manny said. "They're really nice guys."

"They don't seem like nice guys to me. You're a really nice guy and shouldn't be that desperate for friends, Manny."

"They aren't so bad."

"They aren't? What's the old saying, With friends like that . . ."

Manny dropped his chin. "I guess you're right."

"I suppose you have to work with them, but you don't have

to put up with all their crap. Hopefully after this evening you won't have to."

"Actually, the company that just signed the contract with us offered me a job."

"Really? That must be a great compliment." He blushed and she continued, "Maybe you should take it."

"Maybe I should. I'll think about it." He smiled one of the first genuine smiles he'd had all evening. "You know, you're a wonderful woman, Pam. I like you a lot."

"I like you too, Manny." While they'd talked she'd been stroking his cock. "I'd like to show you things we could do together, but now that we've made the point with your *friends*, the rest is up to you."

He grinned. "I think I'll take the new job and you, too." He stood and quickly removed his clothes. As Pam started to remove her teddy, he said, "Could you leave that on? You look really hot in it."

"Of course." She stretched out beside him and took the lead in their lovemaking. They kissed and she guided his hands to her breasts. She heard his breathing quicken as his hands roamed her flesh. When he started to roll on top of her, she slid off the bed, retrieved a condom from her purse, and pushed him onto his back. Slowly she unrolled the latex over his large cock, squeezing and fondling him as she did so. "You're amazingly well endowed," she purred. Exaggeration was often necessary, but in his case it was true.

"I'm glad you think so," he said, his voice hoarse. He quickly rolled on top of her and plunged inside. Fortunately the condom was well lubricated, so her body put up no resistance despite the fact that she wasn't really aroused. She played the part well, however, and he climaxed quickly. She let out a deliberately loud moan, hopefully audible in the next room.

They lay side by side and talked for quite a while. She learned about his hobbies, his love of classical music and John

THE MADAM OF MAPLE COURT

Wayne movies. "I just saw *Sands of Iwo Jima* for the dozenth time a few nights ago on Turner Classic Movies," he said.

"I watched it, too," Pam said truthfully. "I love that film. The Mexican Hat Dance scene where he's teaching Forrest Tucker about the bayonet is one of my favorites."

Together they started humming, "Da dum, da dum, da dum . . ." Together they had a good laugh. Later they dressed and heard a knock on the door from the other room. "Go away," Pam said.

"Listen, Manny, you don't have exclusive rights to that room." The voice sounded impatient, especially since their little game had gone wrong. "We need it, too."

"When I'm done," Manny called, now sounding confident. Then he said to Pam, "You know, you're right about everything. I don't have to put up with their crap. However, I'm not going to tell them that I'm leaving the company just yet. I want to enjoy the fallout from this evening for a while first. I've never been thought of as a Super Stud. We really socked it to them, didn't we? Would it be all right if we left together? Let's leave them guessing about where we're going."

"Good idea. And thanks for a lovely evening, Manny."

"You, too," he said as he opened the door to the adjoining room and grabbed his coat and hers. "Okay, you guys, we're getting out of here. Sorry we messed up one of the beds, but the other is still *virginal*." He grinned at Pam. "I hope you all enjoy the rest of the evening."

"Uh, yeah," someone said as Manny closed the door behind them.

In the elevator, Manny kissed Pam soundly. "That was quite an awakening in many ways," he said, glowing. "I thank you for everything."

"No problem. Have some faith in yourself and you'll be great."

"Yeah."

Chapter
20

Pam visited the cemetery several weeks after the anniversary of Vin's death. She stood beside the grave and marveled at how much had changed in a year. "You wouldn't recognize me, Vin, and it's a shame how much you missed. We could have had fun together, but thanks for going elsewhere to scratch your itches. Without that, I'd still be the little woman I was."

A few weeks later, on a freezing cold Manhattan evening in mid-December, Pam walked out of a small room on the third floor of Club Fantasy wearing a very short white skirt with a white uniform shirt unbuttoned farther than any real doctor would allow, all covered by a thigh-length white lab coat. She wore white stockings and white pumps with four-inch heels, had a stethoscope slung around her neck, and carried a clipboard. Rather than perfume, she'd dabbed alcohol on her neck and in her cleavage.

She'd been pleased when Marcy asked her to play out this doctor-patient fantasy with a man named Roger, and she'd been coached on the correct ways to use the stethoscope and blood pressure cuff. Marcy had also given her a few stories to read about "playing doctor" to help her with the dialogue.

In the hallway she straightened her back and opened the

door to the club's "doctor's office." This room was seldom changed and, according to Marcy, used more often than Pam would have imagined. It contained an exam table, a doctor's scale, a wall-mounted blood pressure monitor, and a metal desk covered with swabs, gauze, cotton, and other paraphernalia that would be found in any exam suite.

She knew her way around the room: where to find instruments, how to move and tilt the exam table, how to reposition the gooseneck light. "Good evening, Mr. Forbes. I'm Dr. O'Brian and I'll be examining you tonight."

"Oh," was all the portly man sitting on the edge of the table could say. He was dressed in a paper exam smock that didn't quite close in the front. Beneath he wore nothing at all. His naked legs hung over the edge of the table, his bare feet sticking out below. He was mostly bald with a few hairs carefully combed over the top of his head, round-faced with eyes set deeply in his puffy, overweight face. Although she couldn't see much of the rest of him beneath his smock, she decided that he must weigh at least two hundred fifty pounds.

"I see here," she said, studying the papers on the clipboard, "that you've been having some digestive troubles."

Her patient had been given a little information about his "condition." "Yes, I have."

"I'm sorry to hear about your problems. Let's see what we can find out. Lie on your back for me so I can begin the exam."

He repositioned his large body and stretched out on the table. "What are you going to have to do to me?" he asked.

"Just the usual exam," she said, taking the stethoscope from around her neck and placing the bell against his chest. "Take a deep breath for me, Mr. Forbes." He did and she moved the bell. "Again." When he complied, she moved it again and said once more, "Again. Good. Your lungs are clear." She made a note on her clipboard, drawing out the "exam."

She moved to the other side of the table. "Now I need to

THE MADAM OF MAPLE COURT

listen to your heart." She put the bell against his upper chest and leaned down as if to listen closely, giving him a great view down the front of her shirt. She wore no bra, so he got quite an eyeful.

"Your heart seems fine, too," she said, standing up and making notes on his "chart." "I need to palpate your abdomen."

Pam parted his smock and saw that his penis was fully erect. "Hmm," she said as she purposely stared at his cock. "You seem to have no problem with your libido." It jerked. "Don't be embarrassed, sir," she said, squeezing his cock. "It's perfectly normal to have an erection during this sort of procedure. I'm quite used to it."

"I'm s-s-so sorry," he mumbled.

"Don't give it a thought." She pressed on various areas of his abdomen and watched his cock spasm. How many times, she wondered, had he masturbated while he dreamt about this situation? "I need to check your genitals. Please just relax." As if he could. She again squeezed his cock, then cupped his testicles as if weighing them in her palm. "Very good," she said, "but don't get carried away. This isn't a massage parlor, so this isn't at all sexual." This was so ridiculous, but he was enjoying it to the fullest.

"Of course not, Doctor," he said. "I'm sorry. I can't seem to control my reactions."

"You really do need some self-control," she said, playing with him while she talked. "Okay, knees up."

"Why?"

"I need to do a rectal exam, of course," she said in her best, most formal voice. "It's part of the procedure." She slipped her arm beneath his legs and lifted his knees. Then, his eyes never leaving her hands, she slowly smoothed on a pair of latex gloves. "Don't worry. I'll use lots of lubricant. I need to check your prostate."

Pam repositioned the lamp until it shone directly on his

hairy ass-cheeks, then found a tube of K-Y Jelly on the desk and squeezed a large dollop into her palm. Slowly she rubbed her fingers in it, trying not to smile as he stared at her hands, eyes wide. "Do you have to do that?" he asked. She knew the heat on his buttocks was exciting him still further.

"Of course," she said. "Now just relax. I promise I won't hurt you."

She parted his cheeks with one hand and slipped her lubricated finger between, finding his puckered anus. "Just relax," she said again, pushing her finger into him. Then she pressed on his lower abdomen with the other so he could feel every movement of the digit inside him, hand brushing his cock, now dribbling precome onto his belly.

She knew he couldn't hold out much longer so she said, "Remember your manners, Mr. Forbes. No ejaculation."

That did it. As she found and rubbed his prostate he came, semen erupting from his cock and spurting all over his hairy chest. She slowly withdrew her finger and pulled off her gloves. "That completes the exam," she said. "I hope you found it informative."

He couldn't control his trembling body. "God," he said, "that was amazing"—he paused—"Doctor."

"There's a shower across the hall if you want to use it to clean up after your exam."

"Not a chance. The slippery goo will remind me of this for hours yet. Thanks for a great exam. I might need another soon."

"I'll be happy to perform one for you anytime." For my usual fee, she thought, smiling.

Linc arrived early Christmas afternoon wearing a Santa hat at a jaunty angle, lugging a large, heavy box and carrying a shopping bag containing several smaller, gift-wrapped packages. "What in the world?"

"Open the big one and see," he said, pouring a glass of cabernet for each of them.

She stared at him. "I thought we'd agreed on no presents."

"We did. These aren't for you, they're presents for me."

Totally puzzled, she tore off the wrapping and read the words on the large cardboard box inside. "It's a massage table. Thanks, but I'm afraid I don't get it."

"Oh, you will *get it*." His smile had a slightly devious look to it. "Open the rest."

One by one, she opened the gaily wrapped packages. Toys. The boxes were filled with sex toys. She found a set of six soft, squishy dildos in assorted colors, two with wide flanges at the bottom, a vibrating dildo in bubble gum pink with an odd projection from its base that looked very like a rabbit with huge ears, an assortment pack of condoms, several with ticklers at the end and a few that were ribbed, and a bottle of Slippery Stuff–brand lubricant. "You're kidding."

His smile vanished. "I couldn't be more serious. If you're going to be in the business you need to get used to your tools. Like a carpenter knowing his hammer."

"I've played with lots of guys," she said, and added, with a wink, "and I think I know my tools."

He chuckled. "Okay, forget that. I want to play and I know you don't have the toys I want to play with, so I bought you some. Today, in honor of the holiday, I want you to be totally selfish. Wanna play with me?"

She'd never owned a sex toy just for herself, and she was fascinated and aroused by the collection in her lap. Selfish? Her? She'd never had sex just for her. It was always for her client. She didn't know what to say.

"You've always been puzzled as to why a woman would pay for sex. I want to show you yet again."

"You've already taught me a lot about great sex. You don't have to do any more."

"I know that. Don't deny me my present. Wanna play?"

Pam slowly picked up her glass and touched the rim to Linc's. "What could be bad?"

"Great. Go turn up the heat and I'll set this sucker up," he said, hefting the large, heavy box. Linc was still wearing the Santa hat, with a bright red, long-sleeved T-shirt and tight jeans. Pam watched his body as he maneuvered the box into the center of the room. "Get me a bowl of warm water, would you?"

Within about twenty minutes Pam had helped Linc set up the table, put a bottle of oil into the water to warm, and set the toys out in a splendid yet gaudy array on the sofa. "Okay, get your clothes off and I'll get you a towel. To start with, of course."

She coyly turned her back, took off her clothes, and wrapped herself in the bath sheet he brought from the bathroom.

"Have I told you recently that you look hot in a towel?" He patted the leather surface of the table and she stretched out on it, resting her face in an indentation. He filled his palm with oil, rubbing his hands together to warm it, then began with her calves. Pam closed her eyes and surrendered herself to Linc's talented fingers, purring from the hedonistic pleasure of it. When he started to rub her toes she quickly discovered that feet in general and toes in particular were erogenous zones, and the feel of his thumb pressing deeply into her sole made her pussy twitch. Was it that movement or the fact that Linc was doing it?

He worked his way up her thighs, his fingers drifting close to her pussy but not touching it. The teasing was very effective and she made mental notes for the time she might do this to someone else.

Then he began on her shoulders. The core of her body was still draped in a towel which, right now, with the room so warm, she thought was silly, but still, even with Linc, who was intimately familiar with her body, there was an air of expectation. What would he touch next? What would he uncover?

THE MADAM OF MAPLE COURT 241

He used oil to lubricate her arms and hands, then massaged each finger as though it were a cock, pulling and pressing, making her juices flow. Finally, after what seemed like a week, he slapped her lightly on the upper thigh. "Okay. Turn over."

As she did, she kept the towel positioned so it covered her from breasts to upper legs. Again he started on her legs and feet. As she lay there she realized that he was humming softly, enjoying what he was doing. A soft smile played on his face as he made love to her with his hands.

He moved on to her arms and shoulders again, then her face. He played with her ears, using his pinky to simulate fucking them. He stroked her cheekbones, her closed eyelids, her lips. When he slid his fingertips over them for the fifth time she opened her mouth and nipped at him.

Finally he lowered the towel and massaged her ribs, swirling over her breasts, just grazing her erect nipples. His teasing was starting to make her impatient and she moaned.

"Not just yet. I've got a few surprises in store," he said softly.

Suddenly she felt a sharp pain in her right nipple and her eyes snapped open. She saw that he had fastened a clothespin-like nipple clamp onto her flesh.

"I wanted you to feel this before you rejected it, so I didn't show them to you earlier. If the pain isn't pleasurable, just tell me and we can stop anytime," he assured her, "but I think this might make you really hot."

Pain in her other nipple. The pain was not too intense and she felt her vaginal tissues swell and moisten still more. There was a chain between the two clips, and when Linc pulled on it the pain increased slightly. "Good?" he said, asking seriously.

She hated to admit it, but it was. She closed her eyes and said nothing, so he took that as her assent. Then he pulled the towel off altogether and slid his fingers through her pussy hair. She thrust her hips against his hand when he touched her clit but he backed off. "Not just yet, pet," he said.

He left her to consider the effect that the pain in her breasts was having on her body, then returned. "Raise your knees," he said, lifting her legs. Then he pressed something cold and hard between her inner lips and slowly pushed the dildo inside. "You're so wet," he said. "I'm glad this excites you. However, I don't want you to climax yet. There's much more I want to try."

In and out, in and out. "If you do that too much more I'm not going to be able to control myself," she groaned. He stopped, leaving the dildo in place. Then she felt another piece of plastic slippery against her anus. "Shit, Linc," she moaned as the second dildo slipped inside. "That makes me crazy."

"Good. That's my intention."

She heard the rustle of clothing as Linc stripped. "Now, I want mine," he said, moving so his fully erect cock was beside her face.

"You do, do you?" she said, reaching out, grabbing his cock and squeezing. "Will this do?" She pulled at him, then pushed her hand down his shaft from tip to base. Slowly she masturbated him and felt his cock grow still harder. Finally she pulled him to her open mouth and flicked her tongue over his cockhead. While she slowly sucked him into her mouth he played with the chain holding the nipple clamps together. She was so hot and she wanted him to fuck her, but she also wanted to give him the most pleasure she could with her mouth.

It was long minutes of mutual pleasuring before he finally said, "I'm going to come if you keep that up."

"That's what I intended."

"In your mouth?"

He'd always pulled out before climaxing before. "Merry Christmas," she said, scratching his testicles and sliding her finger backward and stroking the tender area between his balls and his anus. That was enough to drive him over the

THE MADAM OF MAPLE COURT 243

edge and he filled her mouth with semen. She swallowed what she could and allowed the remainder to slip out around the base of his erection.

"My God, woman, that was amazing." As she started to sit up, dildos still in place, he pushed her shoulders back down. "Not just yet."

She heard a buzzing and felt the dildo vibrate against her clit. She had cooled a bit while she sucked Linc's cock, but now she soared. "My God," she yelled and orgasm overtook her in a rush. Finally she pushed him away, unclipped the nipple clamps, and, wrapped in her towel, almost crawled to the sofa where they lay intertwined.

"You're fabulous," he said. "I thought I'd teach you a few new tricks, but it seems you're as well educated as you can get."

"That's quite a compliment," she said, basking in his approval.

"You must know that you're good at what you do."

That brought her up short. She was a hooker and should be expected to be a good cocksucker. She let out a long breath. It was okay. She knew what she was and what she enjoyed.

Now she understood why a woman would pay for sex. If a man could give the kind of pleasure Linc had just given her, it was worth a lot. And wasn't it wonderful that she could give so much pleasure to a man she cared about. And she did care about Linc.

Chapter
21

The day after Christmas was momentous for Pam. Gary had been in Sweden much of the fall and early winter trying to fix a project that was, as he put it, totally fucked up. He returned for a weekend each month, but saw her only sporadically. When they did get together they had dinner, talked at length about his life and hers, and often rented a DVD of a recent movie that he hadn't had the chance to see. Often, because of jet lag and the stress of a bicontinental life, he fell asleep on the sofa before they had a chance to make love. However, with her active life outside of this relationship she was just as glad.

Since Gary's daughters were having dinner with Toni's family, Gary and Pam had enjoyed Thanksgiving dinner together at a local restaurant and, over turkey and stuffing, he'd invited her to spend the day after Christmas with him and his daughters. Knowing how protective he was of them, she'd been blown away and had spent the intervening weeks living with stark terror. What if they didn't like her? What if she proved to be a terrible parent-in-waiting? What if they were monsters, jealous that their father had someone other than their mother in his life?

Presents. Christmas presents. What did she know about

buying for little girls? She had no idea what seven-and five-year-old girls might like, and less idea about what they already owned. She wanted to ask Gary, but somehow it was important that whatever she purchased be without their father's help. Clothes? Toys? Computer games? She was bewildered and finally realized that she needed help. Eventually, with sage advice from Marcy and the help of a supplier for Club Fantasy, she thought she'd found a unique present. That afternoon she drove through the neighborhood of houses festooned with colored lights and yards filled with inflatable Santas, elves, and Snoopys. Thanks to a lot of luck, she found a parking spot just half a block from Gary's apartment.

To keep her fears at bay during the drive south, she'd thought over her afternoon with Linc and couldn't help but smile. Her nipples still tingled a little when she thought back to the day before. Not only was it wonderful, but it opened up so many new avenues. It was a wonder that she'd gotten this far without ever playing with toys and erotic massage for herself. Was she misleading Gary about their relationship? He obviously thought there might be more in store for them as a couple, but was that the correct assumption? She had no idea. All she knew was, mistake or not, she really wanted to meet the girls.

At almost exactly two o'clock, she maneuvered into the parking space and lugged a large shopping bag to the front of the two-story building. When Gary opened the door, she asked him to fetch two gigantic boxes from the back seat of her car. He pecked her on the cheek, retrieved the imaginatively gift-wrapped packages, and followed her upstairs. Two lovely, quiet little girls waited in the middle of the living room, dressed in similar sweatshirts and jeans. "These are my daughters," Gary said beaming. "Melissa is seven and Amy is five."

Melissa was the taller of the two, with long, baby-fine, fly-away chestnut hair caught haphazardly in several barrettes. Her eyes were wide and deep brown. Amy was still a very lit-

THE MADAM OF MAPLE COURT   247

tle girl, with long, deep brown braids and the same huge eyes as her sister. Toni must be the straight-haired brunette, she thought, glancing at Gary's blond curls.

Pam had never been more nervous, and she had to set the shopping bag down so that her shaking hands wouldn't be too noticeable. She took a deep breath. "It's nice to meet you, ladies."

The two girls giggled. "We're not ladies yet," Melissa said.

"To me you're very grown-up ladies."

"Daddy never lets us meet any of his friends. Why you?" Melissa asked perceptively.

Pam had thought of answers to such questions for days. Before Gary could answer, she said, "Because he thought we'd get along really well, and I hope we do."

"What's in the boxes?" Amy asked before any more difficult questions could surface.

"Amy!" Gary said. "That's most impolite."

"You never find out anything if you don't ask," the child said.

When Gary frowned, Pam smiled and said, "That's all right. These are for you." She pointed. "Melissa, this is yours, and Amy, this one is for you."

"My name's on the box," the younger girl said. "How did you know our names?"

"Your dad talks about you all the time and I feel as if I know you quite well even though we've never actually met before."

"He does?" Melissa said, eyes wide.

"Of course I do," Gary said. "Say thank you to Ms. DePalma."

"May they call me Pam? Ms. DePalma sounds so grown-up, and for today I want to be a kid again."

The girls looked at their father, and when he nodded, they said in unison, "Thank you, Pam." Then they tore open the boxes and pulled the lids off. Their faces were priceless. Inside each box was a dress designed for a fairy princess, all lace and tulle. With open mouths they lifted the gowns from the boxes and, beneath, each found matching shoes, a tiara covered with rhinestones, and a wand with a sparkling star at the end. "Oh, wow," Melissa said, staring at the dress. "This is for me? It's purple. I like purple best."

"Mine's pink," Amy said, her face glowing with delight and wonder. "That's my favorite color."

"I know. I cheated and asked your dad."

The two girls bounced up and down. "May we try them on? Please, Daddy? Right now?"

"Of course." As the girls dragged the boxes into the bedroom, Gary took Pam in his arms and kissed her thoroughly. "I don't believe what a hit those dresses are. You're amazing. You say you don't know children but you've really hit the jackpot this time."

After the two girls were dressed in their "ball gowns," Pam dug into her purse and found a butterfly clip and several barrettes for Melissa's hair. Together with the tiara, the clips allowed Pam to arrange Melissa's hair into a neat cascade to her shoulders. She wound Amy's braids around her head in a coronet and, with the tiara, she looked quite grown-up. "What's a coronet?" the little girl asked.

"It's another word for a crown."

Amy made a face at her sister. "I've got a crown. You've just got hair."

"I could have a coronet if I wanted to, but I like mine like Alice in Wonderland."

"You both have beautiful hair," Pam said. Finally she used a bit of her lipstick and blush to give the overjoyed girls' princess makeovers a final touch. From the doorway, a slightly astonished Gary watched their every move, beaming.

The three spent the next hour playing Princess and the Pea, with Pam playing the queen mother who needed to find out whether her prospective daughter-in-law was a real princess. Pam was surprised at how quickly the three of them became

THE MADAM OF MAPLE COURT 249

comfortable with each other while Gary sat on the sofa taking it all in and occasionally snapping a picture with his digital camera.

When the game finally lagged Pam said, "I brought something else that I thought we might enjoy together."

"What did you bring?" Amy asked.

"Why don't you change into your regular clothes, wash your faces, and then we'll find out?"

While the girls hurried into the bedroom to change back into their jeans and clean up, Pam settled on the sofa beside Gary. "I'm a little chagrined," he said. "I was very nervous about having you meet my girls. I mean, since you've never had any experience with children I was really worried about how you'd get along. I shouldn't have been concerned at all. You're a magician."

Pam picked up one of the wands from the cushion beside her and tapped Gary on the shoulder. "The magic is those wonderful girls of yours. They're charming and delightful. They obviously have two parents who care very deeply about them and haven't let their personal problems affect them. They're very lucky."

"Thanks."

Before they had time for another sentence the girls reappeared, changed and scrubbed. "Mom and Peter smooch on the sofa sometimes," Melissa said, sounding wise beyond her years. "Are you going to be our new stepmother?"

Pam had spent quite a bit of time preparing an answer for that question. "Right now I hope I'm going to be your newest friend, and that's enough for me."

"What's in the bag?" Amy said, oblivious to the undercurrents in the room.

"Let's find out." Pam scrambled to the floor and sat beside the bag. First she pulled out two old men's shirts.

Two small female faces fell. "What's that for?" Amy asked.

"When I was a little girl, my mother and I used to have a lot of fun around Christmastime. I needed a smock like this to keep me clean, and so do you."

"Are we going to get messy?" Amy asked, suddenly gleeful.

"Maybe a little," Pam answered.

She showed Amy how to put the shirt on backward while Gary helped Melissa. "What's in the bag, Daddy?" Amy asked.

"I don't know. I guess we'll all find out together."

Pam pulled two old nylon stockings from the bag and tied one around each girl's waist to control the yards of extra fabric. "In here," she said, pulling out a large bowl, "is cookie dough." She put the bowl on the floor and pulled out a plastic bag filled with cookie cutters and another with jars of sprinkles of all different colors. "And here are some more of your tools." Another bag followed with tubes of frosting in all colors. "My mother would cut out the cookies in all kinds of shapes and then I got to decorate them. She made homemade frosting, but I'm not good at that so I bought every color at the store."

"Can we bake cookies, Daddy?" Amy begged. "Please? We'll only eat a few. I promise I won't spoil my dinner."

Pam had brought enough cookie dough and pans for at least a dozen cookies each, so she, Gary, and the girls made white snowmen with blue eyes and red buttons down their fronts, green Christmas trees with dabs of frosting for ornaments at the tip of each branch, and gingerbread men. "I'm going to make mine all green, like Shrek," Amy cried.

"He'll look just like Shrek," Gary said, carefully decorating a sugar cookie bell with lines of red and green.

Later, when plates of carefully decorated cookies sat all over the counters and just about every other horizontal surface in the apartment, Melissa said, "We can't possibly eat all these. What are we going to do with them?"

"What did you do with them when you were a kid?" Amy chimed in. "Did you make this many?"

"We had a firehouse around the corner, so we took a big

THE MADAM OF MAPLE COURT 251

boxful over there for the firefighters. They work very hard and it's really nice to say thank you for all that they do to protect us."

Melissa's eyes brightened. "Can we, Daddy?"

"Yes, can we?" Amy chimed in.

Gary could only nod his agreement tinged with pleased amazement, and as she saw it Pam blossomed with her success. Although she'd always wanted children, she secretly worried that she didn't know how to be a mother. This afternoon proved that she certainly knew something. Maybe it was an instinct that she'd had all along and was now allowed to let flourish. She loved this motherly thing. "Let's pack up most of these cookies, then get our coats," she said. "I think I saw a firehouse about two blocks down. And Gary, bring the camera, too."

As she'd suspected, the firefighters stuck with duty during Christmas week were surprised and pleased by the thoughtful gift and took the girls on a tour of the firehouse and the engines. "This is the best day we've had in a long time," Gary said as they took the stairs to the firehouse sleeping quarters. "I would never have thought to bring them here. I always thought this was boy stuff."

"We girls aren't so different," Pam said, professing a wisdom she must have acquired somewhere.

"Daddy," Melissa called. "They have a pole. Can we slide down?"

"Not a chance," a gruff male voice said. "We have to take lots of training to know how to do that safely."

Gary took photos of each of the girls seated behind the wheel of a fire engine, wearing a helmet. "We'll print them when we get home and show them to Mommy," Melissa said and one of the firemen looked at Pam, then raised a startled eyebrow. *Wow*, Pam thought, *the fire guys believed I was the girls' mother.*

Later, back at Gary's apartment, they quickly printed out a

collection of the day's photos on the computer for the girls' mother and one for Pam. She carefully put hers in the shopping bag. Back on Maple Court, Pam would put them somewhere very safe so she could look at them over and over. Then the four shared pizza and had a few of the cookies they'd saved for dessert. "We seem to have planned very well," Pam said to the girls. "There are enough for you to take some home to your mom and Peter. Let's put them into some plastic bags."

While Gary walked the girls back to his wife's house several blocks away, Pam cleaned up the kitchen and dreamed of life as the mother of those two wonderful girls. They could shop together, play games, go to movies, and she could even get involved in their school. She and Toni would have to work out some ground rules, of course, so they didn't step on each other, but it could all be worked out. She could be a mother without any of the labor pains.

She hummed as she wrapped leftover pizza slices in plastic wrap, stuffed pizza boxes into the garbage, and put half-empty soda bottles into the refrigerator. She washed what glasses there were and tossed out sauce-covered paper plates.

"You should have heard them," Gary said when he got back. "Toni had barely opened the door when they began to regale her with stories of their dresses and the cookies. Melissa was still bummed about not being able to slide down the firehouse pole, but the rest of the day was a triumph. Toni says to thank you for the dresses. When I left they were going to try them on for her and Peter."

"I'm so glad the day went so well," Pam said, barely able to contain her glee. "I've been worrying for days."

"You needn't have. You were fabulous. How about a glass of wine?" He poured for both of them. That night she stayed over.

Throughout the rest of the winter and spring, Pam saw Gary more often and spent days with him and his girls at least

THE MADAM OF MAPLE COURT   253

once a month. His business overseas had finally resolved itself and, except for monthly trips to visit various customers, he spent considerably more time in New York. The four of them went to movies, the zoo, visited museums, and used the resources of New York City frequently. The first weekend Six Flags Great Adventure was open, they drove there so Gary could ride the roller coaster. Pam finally confessed that she didn't really want to go on the roller coasters, but Gary rode Kingda Ka and Nitro each twice. "While the rest of the family watches," he said. When Gary used the phrase "rest of the family" there was a lurch in Pam's heart. Then they spent a wonderful day going on as many other rides as they could manage and eating until Melissa confessed that she had a slight tummyache.

On the drive home the two girls slept in the back seat while Pam daydreamed and decided that she'd never been happier.

She also entertained clients with increasing frequency. She'd had a few encounters in her house and many others at the brownstone in the city. She'd also met men in many other places.

She saw Linc several times each month, and managed to find time for Rob whenever his busy schedule allowed. Rob had already surmised what she was doing with Marcy so, since both these men knew about her occupation, it was fun to talk about her experiences, never revealing any details about the men involved.

She watched her bank account grow as well. The town was still debating the future of Maple Court, trying to decide the wetlands issue with little success. A new town board had taken office in January, and everything ground to a halt while the new administration tended to more pressing issues.

Pam didn't mind the delay now, since she didn't want to have to part with her wonderful house.

She was happy, doing what she enjoyed in all facets of her life.

Chapter

22

One evening in late May Marcy asked Pam to come down to the city to meet with a potential client. "Here's the story," Marcy said when they were seated in the brownstone's living room. "I think you'd be great interviewing potential clients. You've got great instincts about people and I'm still hoping to branch out, forming Club Fantasy North. If not, that's fine, but I want you to get a taste for what the discussions are like. Game?"

"Sure. I don't know about the Club Fantasy North part, though. Having the occasional party or entertaining once in a while at my place is one thing. Being the owner of a brothel in Westchester County, only a few miles from the Clintons, is quite another."

"I know that, and you're free to do what you like. This part, however, is the crux of my business, and having another person doing it would help me out, too."

"What about Chloe?" Pam had met Marcy's business partner several times but didn't know her very well.

"She's got a guy and I'm afraid she isn't long for this business. Anyway, she was never particularly good at this part of it. Before I moved down here, Jenna did most of the interviews. It's an art."

"Okay, I'll go along and keep my mouth shut. I'd love to watch you operate."

"I won't reveal any secrets, but there's a personal connection here, too, if James wants to reveal it."

They met in a small luncheonette near the club. James Harris was a small, rather nervous man, all quick gestures and movement. He never seemed to sit still. He was short and reed thin, with thick red hair, very white skin, and green eyes, and appeared to be in his late twenties. "I didn't know you'd bring anyone else," he said.

"This is Pam, and she's part of the club. If she makes you uncomfortable I will certainly ask her to leave, but I think she might have a few good ideas for us."

"Of course, if you say so."

"It's nice to meet you, James," Pam said.

They ordered coffees and chatted about the rainy spring weather until the drinks arrived. Pam watched James put four teaspoons of sugar into the cup. *No wonder he's a nervous wreck.*

"Okay, James," Marcy said, "let's try to discover what would give you the most pleasure."

"This is very embarrassing. I'm not sure I can talk about it with you." He dropped his chin and stirred his coffee over and over. After a few minutes of silence, he slid to the edge of the booth seat and gathered himself to leave. "I'm sorry, but I'm afraid I wasted your time."

"It's not a waste at all," Marcy said. "I think that you might feel better about yourself if you tell me what's going on. I think you'll be surprised at how many others have the same desires you do. People want different things, and there's not much I haven't heard."

"I'll bet," James said, brightening. "But not mine."

"Please," Pam said, violating her resolve to keep still. "It's really okay. Whatever consenting people do is okay."

"Really?" James said.

THE MADAM OF MAPLE COURT

"Of course," Pam said, looking at Marcy, who seemed content for her to do some of the talking. "If you don't want to take this any further than this booth that will be fine, but it might make you feel better if you let some of it out."

"Pam's right," Marcy said. "You can trust us."

James sat for several moments, chewing over what Pam had said. "Okay, here goes. I want to be a girl."

Although Pam was nonplussed she kept her face impassive, and Marcy didn't blink. "Okay. Tell me a little more," Marcy said.

"You're not shocked?"

"You aren't the first man who's told me about his desire to dress as a woman."

He heaved a large sigh. "Can I really talk about this?"

"Of course," Marcy said.

"First, I have to tell you that I'm not gay or anything. I like girls and I'm certainly not a virgin. However, even when I was a kid I liked to play dress-up in my mom's things. I've been reading on the Web about places that will do a makeover, but I don't trust them. The Internet is so impersonal and they wouldn't care about me. They might even take photos and post them on their Web site."

"I'm glad you trust us," Pam said.

"I gather that Manny Greenberg told you about us."

"He told me about a woman named Pam who was so great to him. He's a good friend, and when I finally told him about myself he suggested you." He looked at Pam. "Oh, that must have been you. You were so wonderful."

Manny Greenberg. She'd never learned his last name. "Does he work with you?"

"Yeah. He left Paramount Packaging and joined us several months ago. I work for my dad's electronics firm, Harris Electronics, and we met there. Anyway, when I finally confessed and told him my secret, he suggested you. Can you do it for me?" Pam was delighted that Manny had moved on.

"Tell me exactly what you want," Marcy said. "I want to get it all right for you."

"I want a makeover and a dress, shoes, the works." He pushed the words out in a rush. "Then I want to go somewhere with another girl, maybe you, Pam, and be taken for your friend, not your date. And I want photos that I can keep and I want the only copies."

Pam wanted to ask more about his desires to cross-dress but she held her tongue. She wouldn't pry. He'd tell whatever he wanted them to know. Marcy said, "If we take photos, you can be guaranteed that you'll have the only copies."

"Good. Can you do it? I can afford whatever you charge."

He and Marcy discussed the costs, including the clothing and accessories he'd keep, and they agreed on a price. "Pam," he said, "can you be the one to do it? If Manny trusts you, then I do, too."

Marcy looked at Pam. "Would you do this for him?"

Could she? Why not? She'd do some research and do her best to make him look the way he wanted. After all, she'd done it with two little girls.

Two weeks later, James arrived at the club at a little after seven. Marcy and Pam had rearranged the all-purpose room on the third floor with several full-length mirrors, a dressing table, and a clothes rack with a selection of dresses in what they estimated to be James's size. Several pair of low-heeled sandals with enough buckles to adjust to most sizes sat in boxes in one corner. Undergarment sizes were a little more difficult to judge, but they had enough of an assortment that it should work.

James was shown upstairs and his eyes widened when he entered the "dressing room." "This is wonderful," he said.

Pam had never seen him standing up but now she guessed that their estimations of sizes were pretty good. "James, come in. I think we're pretty well organized. There's no one else on this floor this evening, so you can come and go to the bath-

THE MADAM OF MAPLE COURT 259

room as you wish without anyone seeing you. Why don't you strip down to your shorts so we can get started?"

An hour of body and leg shaving, facial depilatories, and moisturizers satisfied him that he was ready for the next step. His hair was long enough that styling gel and a curling iron created a pretty nice-looking head full of curls. Pam thought he looked a bit like Little Orphan Annie, but he seemed delighted by their progress.

Fitting him for a bra and panties almost made Pam laugh, but he seemed so delighted that she was pleased for him. "You even got breast forms for me," he said, putting the pads into his bra.

When he was organized, she said, "Okay, now let's pick out a dress," and the fashion show began.

Using a digital camera she took photos of him in several dresses, letting him use the pictures to make his final selection. "This one," he said, selecting a spring floral print dress with an off-white background, soft rose flowers, and moss green leaves and vines. They arranged the straps on a pair of off-white sandals and added a strand of green beads with matching screw-back earrings.

Wearing his feminine clothing, Pam thought he didn't look half bad. They'd talked throughout the process and Pam found herself liking the man very much. He was, as he'd said, heterosexual and was planning to be married within the following year. "I wanted to do this before I give up even thinking about it for good."

"You can't necessarily control your thoughts, only your actions."

"I know that, but I can try, for Nancy's sake."

"Now for your make-up." Pam had spent several hours searching the Net, learning tricks for making wide faces look narrower, long noses look longer or shorter, cheekbones look more prominent, eyes look wider, and generally camouflaging facial flaws. She snapped photos as she worked.

She wouldn't let him look at himself as she worked, so she steeled herself for his reaction when she finally turned him to face the mirror. As she looked over his shoulder at his new look she was amazed at what a good job she'd done and what a fairly decent-looking woman he made. "Wow," he breathed. "Wow. Is that really me?" His face was wreathed in smiles and he almost giggled.

"It certainly is. Do you have a name for this persona?"

"Denise. I've always wanted to be Denise."

They took dozens of posed pictures, then Pam said, "Okay, girlfriend, let's get out of here. Oh, and walk slowly. The shoes will take a little getting used to."

Together they went to a small club Marcy had suggested. No one seemed to notice James/Denise, and at one point a man made flirtatious eye contact with him/her. "He's looking at me like he wants to come over. I don't think I'm ready for that."

"Shall we leave, then?"

"I think so."

Back at Club Fantasy, James disappeared into the bathroom to shower and change back into his street clothes while Pam printed several of the pictures, then wrapped his new clothing, shoes, undergarments, and an assortment of make-up in a large box for him. When he returned from the bathroom Pam handed him the camera and a stack of photos. "The camera's yours, so there's no worry about us having any of the pictures. If you notice, too," she said, pointing to a group of snapshots, "I took step-by-step pictures of your make-up so you can duplicate it if you want to."

At first she'd been skeptical about the whole thing, but now, seeing his delight with the photos and the package of goodies, she was more pleased than she might have imagined. "Pam, thank you," he said, then he kissed her on the cheek. "You're wonderful and a lifesaver. Not only did you do this for me, but you made me feel so comfortable about it."

THE MADAM OF MAPLE COURT

261

"I'm glad you're happy."

"Oh, I am. You can't imagine what a thrill it is to become someone so new."

Pam considered the previous year. "Actually, I think I can."

In the middle of June, a man entered the all-purpose room on the third floor of the club, dressed in a sweatsuit and sneakers. He was in his mid fifties, short, with a belly that had started its trip outward. His thinning salt-and-pepper hair was cut short and his face was creased with laugh lines. His most striking features were his deep blue eyes. "Yes, Ms. McAllister, you wanted to see me?" His voice had a hint of an English accent.

"I did, Gordy," Pam said in her guise as the teacher. "You've been tardy to my class three times in the last two weeks." She wore a prim white blouse, straight black skirt, and thick-soled shoes. She had slicked her hair back and twisted the strands into a bun.

"I'm sorry, ma'am. I've been trying to train for the track team. Sometimes I don't get showered in time."

She raised an eyebrow from her seat behind the large oak desk that had been positioned in the middle of the room after the rest of the furniture had been removed. Maps hung on the walls, a flag drooped in the corner, and several smaller desks were scattered around the room. They'd rubbed chalk on two erasers and then banged them together just before he arrived so the room had a schoolroom pall and even smelled like she remembered her school smelling. "That's not really my problem, is it?"

"No, ma'am. I'm sorry for being late to class."

"Good. I'm glad you recognize your difficulty."

"Difficulty, ma'am?"

"The rules state that three tardy reports can get you expelled."

"Expelled?"

His seemingly genuine fear always surprised her. They'd

played this scene several times, and each time he behaved as if it were all new. That was one of the wonderful things about fantasy, she'd discovered. For some men it didn't matter how often they played out the same one, it was as exciting the last time as it had been the first. Some men changed their desires over time, but others, like Gordon, or Gordy, as he preferred to be called in this "classroom," honed it, making it closer to perfect for him each time they played. "Yes, Gordy, expelled."

"But, ma'am . . ."

"No buts, young man. I'll have to call your father."

He looked as if he were going to cry. "You mustn't do that!"

"I mustn't?"

"I'm sorry, ma'am. You can and should do whatever you need to, but he'll kill me if I'm expelled."

"Hmm," she said, picking up a long, slender paddle from the desk. "I haven't reported any of your tardies yet. I guess I could overlook one if you're truly repentant."

Words came spilling forth. "I am. Oh, I really am. I'm sorry about it all and I'll be on time for the rest of the semester. I promise I really will."

"Oh, I'm sure I can impress upon you the importance of being on time." She slapped the paddle against her palm. "I know I can." She stared at him. "Drop them!"

"Do you have to do that?" he wailed.

"Excuse me? You're the one who doesn't want me to call his father."

"I know, ma'am, but it will hurt."

"It certainly will. Do you remember the word?" They'd agreed on a safe word before they played this scenario the first time. If he said the word "red" at any time, everything would stop. That way he could cry, beg her to stop, without worrying that everything would indeed stop.

When Marcy first asked her about playing this scene with a new client, Pam hadn't quite understood some people's desire

THE MADAM OF MAPLE COURT 263

for a little pain. She'd read about it, of course, but this would be the first time she'd actually done it.

"Pain heightens a sexual experience for some people," Marcy had explained. "I don't mind a little swat on the ass from Zack occasionally, but some seem to need more than a little slap."

"It's not my thing," Pam said.

"Mine either," Marcy said, "but a few of my ladies really enjoy being on the receiving end of a power/pain session."

"Why me, then? Why not one of them?"

"Receivers, masochists, bottoms, they don't usually enjoy being on the other side, and the two ladies who do enjoy being tops are otherwise engaged. Do you think this would bother you?"

"I don't know, but I don't think so."

"Would you help me out, then?"

"Sure."

So she'd had her first session with Gordy and had found that although it didn't excite her much, it didn't repulse her, either. Seeing a man get so much pleasure pleased her tremendously, however it happened.

" 'Red' is the word, ma'am," Gordy said now as Pam continued to slap her palm with the paddle.

"Good boy. Now drop 'em!"

Slowly Gordy began to pull down his sweatpants. Through his white shorts, she could easily tell how aroused he already was. "Everything. Quickly!"

He stripped. "Now fold your clothing neatly." Anything that dragged the scene out increased his excitement. With shaking hands he put all his garments in a stack on the corner of the desk. "Good. You're doing well. Now assume the position."

He leaned over the front of the desk, cradling his head on his folded arms, stark white, white behind easily accessible. His cock was long and swollen.

"Now," she said, now slapping the paddle lightly against her thigh, "how many today?"

"Five, ma'am?"

"Oh, come on, Gordy, three tardies?"

"Ten, ma'am."

"Okay. We can start there. Now count. You know how to do that, don't you?"

"Yes, ma'am."

She swatted his naked ass once lightly with the paddle.

"One, ma'am, and thank you for helping me learn."

Again. "Two, ma'am, and thank you for helping me learn."

The next few were relatively soft, gradually increasing in force, but at about eight, she began to spank him really hard. "Eight, ma'am," he said, his voice cracking, "and thank you for helping me learn."

Nine and ten were as hard as she could make them and she found that, by the end, her arms were getting tired and her hand stung from the force of the paddle. Originally she'd used her palm to administer Gordy's punishment, but with his approval she'd switched to the paddle when her hand began to hurt as much as his ass. "Ten, ma'am, and thank you for helping me learn." He stood up almost in tears, his erection looking almost painfully hard.

"Now you'll have to show me how sorry you really are." She sat down behind her desk and crossed her legs. "Touch your dick."

"But, ma'am . . ." He shuddered.

She merely raised an eyebrow and smiled.

"Of course, ma'am." He wrapped his fingers around his erection.

"Now don't make a mess," she said, "while you stroke it."

He took a breath as if to protest, then began to slowly rub his hand over his hardness.

"Oh, Gordy, you can do a better job than that."

THE MADAM OF MAPLE COURT 265

"Yes, ma'am." He began to stroke his cock in earnest, a look of pure bliss on his face.

"Use your other hand to play with your balls."

As he did, Pam tapped and rubbed the paddle on the desk in an imitation of Gordy's motions on his cock. As he stroked, his eyes never left the movements of the paddle. Faster and faster she moved the wooden slat, and his hand moved in time with its rhythm. Finally, when he couldn't hold back any longer, he spurted semen onto the desk, his entire body jerking as he came.

Silently they cleaned up. She checked the hallway, then he crossed to the bathroom and showered. Later, back in the "classroom," he was dressed in a golf shirt and slacks. He picked up his sweatsuit and stuffed it into a small black duffel. "Pam, as always you were wonderful."

"Thanks, Gordon," she said. He was only Gordy to his teacher. "I always enjoy our times together."

"See you next month?"

"Of course."

He closed the door behind him and Pam quickly changed into a pair of jeans and a T-shirt. She knew that Marcy would take care of scheduling and charging his credit card.

Chapter
23

Present

Pam stared at the retreating car, shading her eyes from the setting midsummer sun, barely noticing the streaks of gold and orange in the sky. HOBART3. It had to have been Chase's wife. Although she'd known him for almost a year, she'd only been with him about half a dozen times, most recently the previous weekend to hash out the details of the party and, of course, have sex. Prior to that? Maybe three months before. Not so many times that his wife should be suspicious. *Unless he has other, real girlfriends? Is that why his wife is doing her own detective work? How often, other than with me, does he cheat on his wife?*

Shit. Her lovely life was ruined. What should she do? Maybe she could get married again, leave this life she'd learned to love, start again. Maybe she could even have children. Well, not *have*, but adopt.

Of course there was Gary. His daughters were such wonderful girls. If she married him they'd be hers, sort of, and he might even be enticed to adopt another. Okay, she was getting a little long in the tooth. Would an agency allow her to adopt at thirty-five or older? She huffed out a breath. They'd probably find out about her background and that would be that. Maybe she and Gary could adopt a needy child from another country. It was costly, but between them they would have the money to do whatever they wanted. How would Gary feel about that? *Pam, you're getting way, way ahead of yourself.*

She would have to tell him about this part of her life. What then? Shit, he'd probably toss her out on her ass.

All these thoughts flashed through her mind as the black SUV disappeared around the bend of Maple Row. She reread the note in her hand.

You will be punished again and again for what you're doing.

Things slid into place. One of the landscapers who'd been doing the spring cleanup had mentioned that several of her rose bushes had been pulled up. A long scratch down the side of her car had appeared out of nowhere while it had been parked in her driveway. She remembered thinking that it looked like it had been done with a key. She parked in so many garages that she didn't think much of it at the time, but now all the pieces fit. HOBART3.

With trembling hands she started to crumple the note, then thought, *I should save this for the police in case there are any clues.* Police. Right. The Madam of Maple Court reporting a threatening note. Right. PROSTITUTE ENLISTS POLICE HELP, the headline would read.

Her shoulders slumped as she walked slowly back up the driveway. She was ruined. Of course, she and Marcy had lists of prominent people who wouldn't want their names associated with their business. That would help. *Marcy must know lots of high-priced, talented, high-profile lawyers.*

Her mind whirled. Money. If the shit really hit the fan, she'd need lots of it. Sure. It all came down to money. That's where it had begun and that's the way it would end. Of course

Rob might help. He had more money than God. So did Chase, for that matter, and therefore so did his wife. Could the woman sue? Where would Chase come out if push came to shove? Would he side with his wife or threaten to leave her if she made any of his activities public? Pam's mind was flooded with questions for which she had no answers yet.

She felt anger rise and displace some of the depression. What right did anyone have to judge? Why should she take the heat for Chase's foibles? *Smash him if you must, HOBART3, but keep your hands off me!*

She needed a shower, a hot shower to clean away the fears, the anger, the dread. When Vin was killed she hadn't had the wherewithal to handle things herself. Now she was a different person, stronger, more self-reliant. She remembered a comment one of her teachers in elementary school had made on a report card. "Unable to deal with difficult situations." As she walked up the thickly carpeted stairs she realized that she hadn't thought about that comment in many years. Ms. McNeil. That was the teacher's name. Fifth grade.

Her mind jumped from one fragmentary thought to another. She remembered what had engendered that comment. The brother of one of her classmates had been killed by a hit-and-run driver, and all the ten-year-olds had made sympathy cards and welcomed the little girl back after the funeral. Pam had hung back, unable to figure out what to say. She couldn't just dish out platitudes. "So sorry." "Too bad." It was so much more than that. What could she say to make it better? Nothing. It would get better in its own due course.

"Unable to deal with difficult situations." She hadn't been able to think of anything that would make it all go away for Ruth. That was her name. Ruth Livingstone. Funny, that scene when Ruth returned to class that morning was so clear in her mind. Ms. McNeil standing, watching, judging everyone's reactions. Tears pouring down Pam's face as she hung back. She knew that nothing was going to be the same for

Ruth. Pam had lost her own father when she was four and her beloved grandmother when she was seven. They never came back, and life never returned to the way it had been. *Fuck you, Ms. McNeil.*

"Unable to deal with difficult situations." Now she had to deal with a difficult situation and she was going to do the best she could. As she turned on the hot water in the shower and dropped her clothing in the hamper, she considered. Should she call Marcy? She'd have information about Chase, where he lived, the name of his wife. Not yet. She needed to think it all through. "You'll be punished again and again for what you're doing."

Whatever the outcome of this little drama, she was getting out of the business. That was for sure. She wasn't going to go through this again. It was all too risky. But so much fun. Great sex. Well, admittedly not always. Sometimes it was tedious and sometimes the effort to be charming made her smile muscles hurt. Some men were ham-handed and insisted on entering her long before she was ready. Thank God for lubricated condoms. That was part of the job, however. She wasn't there to give herself pleasure but to please the customer, and she did that well and it pleased her to be able to do that.

Most of her clients, as Marcy called them, became regulars, like Chase. They came for sex and returned for sex and companionship, for someone to talk to without repercussions. And always for hot, sweaty sex and good fun in bed, or out of it.

She climbed out of the shower and toweled her hair almost dry, then sat at her vanity and, on autopilot, used the blow-dryer to style and straighten. What should her first step be? Rob? He had tremendous business savvy and he'd be able to help her organize her thoughts. No. She wanted to think it through on her own first.

Shit, she thought. She had Chase's party the following afternoon and there were still things that needed to be done. This was a business affair. Would his wife be there? Shit. She hadn't thought of that. He'd hosted a few parties before and his wife hadn't attended. At least Pam didn't think she'd ever laid eyes on the woman. He must keep his business and personal life separate.

A scene played behind Pam's eyes. Anna—that was her name—Anna standing in the middle of her living room, screaming that she ran a brothel, that several of the women in the room were hookers. The police storming in at some pre-arranged signal and hauling Chase, his friends, and several of Marcy's employees into a Black Maria. Pam being led out in handcuffs, flashbulbs going off in her face. Pam's hands began to tremble so badly that she had to put the dryer down.

Stop it! she told herself. This was getting her nowhere. She took a deep, cleansing breath. She wanted to call Chase and find out whether Anna would be at the gathering the following day, but as she reached for her cell phone she hesitated. Her question would come out of the blue. She'd never cared before, so how would she explain her interest now? She put the phone down.

She suddenly remembered that she had plans with Gary and his girls to go to the Bronx Zoo on Sunday. Where would she be by Sunday? In jail? Should she cancel? Gary knew nothing of her life as the Madam of Maple Court. He'd introduced her to Marcy all those months ago, but he had no idea they were still friends and business associates. Maybe it was time to come clean. Would that be burning bridges she didn't have to burn? Once he found out about her other life, he wouldn't let her within a mile of his precious children.

She had to stop the merry-go-round in her brain, so she dressed and headed downstairs to pour herself a drink. She seldom indulged and she almost never did so alone, but that would at least calm some of her thoughts. As she poured rum into a tall glass and reached into the refrigerator beneath the bar for ice, her private cell phone rang. She glanced at the screen. Linc. Someone else to confuse things.

"Hi," she said.

"I'm around the corner. If you're alone I thought I'd get a pizza and stop by."

"I'm alone," she said, her voice flat.

"Something's wrong," he said. "I'll be right over."

Five minutes later Linc sat with Pam in her living room, his arm around her shoulders, the crumpled note in his hand. She'd told him the basics of what was going on. "Anna Hobart. Are you sure?"

"The license tag was HOBART3. What more do I need?"

She could feel his long sigh. "I don't know what I can do for you."

"You're doing what I need. Letting me disgorge everything is important for me right now. It's helping me organize my thoughts and sort everything out."

"You have to talk to Marcy. She'll know what to do."

"In good time," Pam said, leaning on Linc's shoulder, her legs curled beneath her. "In good time."

"You can't go to the local police. A woman who used to be one of Marcy's ladies is married to a cop on the New York City force. Maybe he can help."

"Nope. No cops. I can't take the risk, for me or for Marcy."

He thought a moment. "Okay. You're right. No cops. Maybe the best thing would be to scout her out. Find out what you can about Anna Hobart. Isn't that what your friend Gary does?"

"Gary. Right." She hesitated. "I would have to tell him everything."

"Don't you have to anyway?"

Her sigh was long and painful. "I guess I do. He'll hate me." Linc knew all about her relationship with Gary and always seemed to want only the best for her. She talked to him

THE MADAM OF MAPLE COURT 273

at length about Gary's children and how fond she'd become of
them.

"Maybe he will and maybe he won't. You won't know until
you tell him, and I don't think you have any choice about that,
whether you use his sleuthing services or not. If he's a good
guy maybe he'll understand that it was all just sex. No strings.
He and his kids are what's real."

"That's true," she said.

"And if you're ever going to make a life with him, he has to
be told. After all, you want a family and he's got one."

Pam was startled at how perceptive Linc was. "That's not
all Gary has. I do care for his daughters and I think they like
me, but I care for Gary, too. We might make a great family together."

"I didn't hear you say you love him. Don't you need that to
make a future with someone?"

"Of course I love him." *Don't I?*

"Okay. What about Rob? How do you feel about him? You'd
have to give him up, and the business, too, if you married
Gary. He doesn't sound like the kind of man who shares."

Linc hadn't said she'd have to give him up as well. How
would he feel about that? "I'd have to give you up, too," she
said, holding his hand against her shoulder. Had she felt him
stiffen slightly?

"That wouldn't be too difficult. We have great sex, but not
much else. Right?"

She thought about the times he'd helped her through sticky
situations, given her advice about how to handle difficult customers, let her talk when others would have given her gratu-
itous advice. There was more to him than met the eye, and if
she gave him up she'd miss him more than she'd realized.
"There's more to us than sex," she said softly. "You're such a
good friend. I care a lot about you."

"I care about you, too," he whispered.

She smiled. "I know you do." She squeezed his hand.

"We could run away," he said lightly, speaking quickly. "I've always wanted to live in Europe or South America. Between us we could earn enough to keep going. We could even get married."

Pam gasped and her stomach fluttered. "Whoa. Down, boy." Now wasn't the time for any such pledges. "You're not serious and we both know it. At least not about marriage. Anyway, I can't run out and leave Marcy to clean up after my problems and face whatever consequences there are and we both know it, and this mess certainly isn't a reason to make lifelong commitments."

"I suppose you're right," he said sadly. "It would have been such fun."

They talked late into the evening about Pam's difficulties. "I'd like to stay tonight, just to keep you company," Linc said at about midnight.

Pam seldom let anyone stay overnight in her house. This was her private space and, as such, very important for her sanity. She wanted no one to assume they had any more significance in her life than just dates. Not Gary, not Linc, not Rob, not any of the other men who inhabited her active social life. No one. But tonight she needed a haven, somewhere she could be and not think. Linc's arms might just be that place, at least for this one night.

"I think I'd like that. Just for tonight."

"I understand you better than you think, Pam, and I'm not going to make any assumptions. I merely want to be here in case you need someone to talk to at four a.m."

They climbed the stairs and walked slowly into Pam's bedroom. "I've got no pajamas for you," she said, "and I don't wear anything to sleep in."

"That's fine. I sleep raw myself, but don't worry. I won't pounce on your gorgeous naked body. Unless you want me to, of course."

Later, in bed, she cuddled against him until she fell into much-needed sleep.

The following morning, after Linc showered, dressed, and left, while the caterers worked throughout the house, Pam confronted the problem of where to go from here.

Finally she realized that she had to be sure that the car did indeed belong to Chase's wife's and, assuming it did, she had to know what the woman was like. She needed ammunition, and Gary was the one to find out everything there was to know. Her next problem was what to tell him, and how.

She muddled through the party, polite but a little distant with Chase. "You're not quite all here today," Chase said as the crowd thinned late in the afternoon. "Anything I can help you with?"

If he only knew, she thought. "No, just lots of things on my mind." She needed information. "I've been wondering why you've never introduced me to your wife at any of these gatherings."

"She's pretty much of a homebody. The kids take up most of her time and she's not comfortable with my business friends the way you are. I keep the many parts of my life well separated."

"I can understand that, I guess," Pam said. "It's just that most of the other married men I host straight parties for bring their wives occasionally."

Chase looked at her seriously. "What's this obsession with my wife all of a sudden?"

"Nothing, just curious."

"You know I don't like to talk about Anna. She and the kids are in a different segment of my life."

"Sorry," Pam said, disappointed that she couldn't learn more about her enemy the easy way.

His shoulders relaxed. "Later?" Chase said with a raised eyebrow.

"Not today, darling," Pam said, brightening her voice to

avoid any discomfort. "I've got a lot on my mind and wouldn't be good company."

Chase frowned. "That's the first time you've ever turned me down. Whatever's bothering you must be substantial."

"It is," was all she answered. She thought later that he hadn't asked her what was bothering her, nor had he offered to help.

She spent Sunday with Gary and his children. They'd decided to start out really early and drive down to Six Flags Great Adventure. In the car the four had sung songs and played auto scavenger hunt. Amy had been the first to find a license plate from Florida, and Melissa had yelled out when she'd seen a sign with the letter Q in it. "Antiques," she screamed. "I call a Q word."

Gary again invited her to join him on Kingda Ka, but she decided again that she didn't want to attempt a ride. Ever. It made her stomach hurt just thinking about it. "Let's go have an ice cream," she said to the girls, "so Daddy can ride as many times as he likes." They arranged a meeting place, then the three started for the refreshment area. As they walked, Amy slipped her hand into Pam's and Pam's heart swelled. She didn't mention her troubles to Gary.

Chapter
24

At nine the following morning she called Gary at his office. "Good morning, love," he said breezily.

When had he started to call her love? she wondered. "Good morning, Gary. I need some information," she said without preamble.

"You sound very formal. Of course I'll help in whatever way I can. What can I do for you?"

"I need to know whatever you can find out about the owner of a car with the New Jersey license plate HOBART3, and the person who usually drives it."

Suddenly serious, he said, "Okay, will do. What's up?"

"Is it okay if I tell you more when you've got some information?"

"Are you in some kind of trouble?"

Hell yes, she thought. "Let's just let it lie until you know something."

Next she called Marcy. "We need to talk," Pam told her best friend, without preamble.

"Okay," Marcy said without hesitation. "Phone or in person?"

"Can you get away for lunch today? I know it's short notice but it's important."

"Listen, with my nanny in residence, I'm a relatively free woman. Chinese at twelve-thirty?"

"Sure. Same place?"

"Done."

Pam was so worried that she paid little attention to the Sprain Brook Parkway. Fortunately, there was little traffic. Could Marcy forgive her for getting both of them into so much trouble? But what had she done that Marcy didn't do herself, directly or indirectly? Maybe it was making her house so available. If Chase's wife knew about the goings on at Maple Court, would the rest of the world be far behind?

When she arrived at the restaurant Marcy was already sitting at what had become "their booth" dipping noodles into duck sauce. "You look like you haven't been sleeping," Marcy said. "What's up?"

Simply and completely, Pam told her friend about Chase, the rose bushes, the keying of her car, and the SUV that had circled Maple Court. Then she took the note from her purse and handed it over. Marcy scanned the piece of paper silently, then looked up. "Okay, what should we do about this?"

No recriminations, no anger, just a matter-of-fact question. And the word "we." Marcy was a wonder. "I've asked Gary to look into the car's license plate number, but I can't imagine it was anyone but Chase's wife."

"Me neither, but I wouldn't borrow trouble yet," Marcy said calmly. "I've got friends in all kinds of places, and we should be able to contain any incipient trouble. However, you probably will need to consult a good lawyer."

"Yeah," Pam said with a sigh.

"I can see the financial wheels turning, Pam. Don't sweat money. I know you haven't saved enough yet to afford truly high-priced talent. Not to worry. Remember that you're in this partly because of me, and between us we can cover anything that needs doing. I know it's difficult, but try to relax." She reached out and took Pam's hand across the white tablecloth and squeezed. "We can handle it."

"You sound so calm," Pam said, feeling her spirits lift a little.

"Been there, done that."

"You've been in this kind of trouble before?"

"I've skirted the edges of some pretty nasty stuff but it's always worked out. Maybe Jenna, Chloe, and I have been lucky, but with all our brain cells focused on a problem, there's little we can't get through."

Was she actually taking this so lightly? Sharing a burden did lessen it, Pam realized, and Marcy seemed so unflappable. Perhaps she was right and it would all work out. With a wry chuckle, Pam said, "Once this is over, maybe we should all work on the problems in the Middle East."

Marcy huffed out a laugh and patted Pam's hand. "Maybe. We couldn't do a much worse job than what's been done there already."

The following day, after an early-morning call from Gary, Pam arrived in his office, impressed again by its feeling of quiet confidence.

She settled across from his desk and they chatted briefly like relative strangers about the weather and the international situation. Finally he said, "Okay, here's what I found out." He consulted a sheet of printed information. "The car is owned by a man named Chase Hobart and registered to him at an address in Paramus, New Jersey. It should be on a 2007 Lexus LX SUV, color black. Does that sound right?"

"It does. What about the person who drives it? Could you find out anything there?"

"I did some snooping and, using credit card receipts for gas purchases, I gathered that it's usually driven by Anna Hobart, who resides at the same address in Paramus." Pam nodded, eager to hear more. "She's the wife of the owner of the car, and I checked personal stuff. They've been married for about twelve years, three children, Chase Jr., usually called Bud, aged eleven and a half; Tracy, aged nine; and Emily, aged seven, all of whom attend the local school system. The home is on a par with yours, I would guess. Want details?"

"Not about the house. What else could you find out about her?"

"Pam, you know I don't want to pry, but I want to help. What's going on? Are you in some kind of trouble?"

She'd known this moment would come and she'd decided to be as honest as she could and take her chances with Gary's wrath. She told him about recent incidents and then, for the second time in two days, she pulled the note from her purse. Marcy had been so reasonable, maybe Gary . . .

He read it silently. "What have you been doing to get this person in such a fury?" His face was rigid. "Have you been having an affair with someone?" he asked through gritted teeth. "Mr. Hobart, perhaps."

She took a deep, slow breath. "Not exactly." When he remained still, she continued. "Before I tell you anything, I want you to know that I've never lied to you. Omitted a lot, but I've never lied." Then she told him.

She began by reminding him of her need for money when Vin was killed, and his introducing her to Marcy. Being as honest as she could, she continued with the story of her getting into the party business, her entertaining, and her relationship with Chase.

He remained silent for a long time, seeming to gather his thoughts. The skin around his eyes tightened, his expression stony. "You're a whore?" The words hissed out between tight lips.

What could she say? She nodded. "I guess you could call it that."

"Guess you could call it that?" He sat, stunned. Except for the hum of the ventilation system the office was silent for several more minutes. "I can't take it in. I thought I knew you. I had begun to think of you as a mother for my children. I don't understand."

"I don't know how to explain it to you. I do what I do to make money, to make men happy, and I enjoy it. It's just sex."

"I know you well enough to know that nothing's *just sex* about your prostitution." He paused. "My God, Pam. Who are you?"

"I'm the same person you've known all these months. You're right about one thing, though. I do care about the guys I'm with, but it is just sex. There's no permanence." She thought of Linc and Rob but decided against mentioning that part of her life.

"What about me?" Gary said. "You give it to me for free, but am I really just another john?" Bitterness began to seep out through his strict control. "Why do you fuck me?"

"Gary, it's not like that at all." She pictured the lovely life she had dreamed about, two little girls, going to school plays, sharing their report cards. What could she say?

"Okay, what is it? You fuck men for money, so why do you fuck me?"

"I care about you."

"You just said you care about all the men you fuck. Why me? I don't pay."

"Gary, I love you. I don't love any of the other men." Was either part of that statement true? Linc was so much more than a casual man in her life. He was one of the few constants. Did she love him? Rob was fun to be with, and together they'd tasted many of New York's best places. And she liked him. Love? She wasn't sure that she knew what love was. Did she love Gary? She didn't know that, either.

"Nice, neat answer, but we've never mentioned love before." He was now clearly furious. "It's very convenient for you to say those words now. Keep the guy interested. Make him think about a future. You're really good at managing relationships, aren't you?" She watched him glance down at his clenched fists and deliberately spread his fingers. "Okay, enough of this. Let's keep this purely professional." His laugh was bitter. "I mean my profession. Your profession is your business." Another wry laugh. "I can't seem to keep double entendres out of the conversation. What do you want from me regarding the rightly pissed Anna Hobart?"

Tears began to gather behind her eyes. "I don't know."

"Don't give me the teary female bit, Pam. We're in this too deep for that. I'll find out what more I can. I assume you need to find something to keep her from blowing your little business to kingdom come, and I'll help you do that. Personally, I would hate to see your face splashed all over the newspapers. The girls would be sure to find out things and ask questions that I don't want to have to answer." He stood up. "Call me in a day or so and I'll tell you what I can." He extended his hand. "Nice doing business with you, Ms. DePalma. I'll send you a bill when we're done."

She recognized his dismissal and left. Maybe, when he'd had time to digest all she'd told him, he'd come around. *Stop kidding yourself*, she told herself. *Not a chance.*

After twenty-four hours of worry, Pam got a call from Gary. "Nothing in Anna Hobart's background will do you any good, Pam. She's clean as the driven snow. A suburban housewife who sells real estate part time, takes good care of her kids, and is generally well liked in the community.

"I looked into the husband's life and it seems he's got several lady friends besides you. I could give you names, dates, and places, but suffice it to say he's not the upstanding husband he'd probably like his wife to think he is. If she ever wanted to divorce him, she's got grounds up the kazoo even without you."

It didn't surprise Pam that Chase had ladies on the side that she didn't know about. Why should she know about Chase's other women? It was really none of her business. She was

THE MADAM OF MAPLE COURT 283

bought and paid for. She wondered whether he paid any of the rest of them, asked any of them for the kind of kinky sex they shared.

Pam remembered his recent words, tossed off, but in such a way to make most women hope for things he never intended to supply. "How about let's run away together, or get married when I get my divorce?" he'd said just a few days before. She wondered whether he said those to his other women, too. Did any of them actually believe the words? Some probably did, but Chase was very married. Maybe not happily, but married and intending to stay that way. What a con man he was. "You did quite a job, Gary. Will she know someone's been looking into her background?"

"I'm too good for that," Gary said, sounding a bit more reasonable than he had the day before. "I've looked into you a bit, too, and from everything I could find out you're pretty clean yourself. There's nothing anywhere that could or should connect you to anything out of the ordinary. From public records you're a woman who organizes both business functions and parties for rich folks, with a high-maintenance house and lifestyle that you seem to be able to fund from your legitimate business."

Relief almost overwhelmed her. "You couldn't find anything more than that about me?"

"If I dig around a little more I could probably discover your other life, but it's pretty well hidden. Someone else poking around would have to know what he was looking for."

"That's reassuring," she said, slowly letting out a long breath.

"I meant it to be." She could hear his sigh. "I've been doing a lot of thinking. I haven't shared much of this with you, but I've been thinking about my future for several months. Pam, in general I'm a pretty lonely guy with two kids who fill a lot of my life, but don't fulfill my needs in other areas the way you do. I think I can understand why you got into the life in the first place, but your party-planning business seems to be well able to take care of you now that it's thriving. Pam, get out of the rest of it. Tell Marcy that you want out. Will she let you leave?"

"This isn't that kind of relationship," she sputtered, angry at his characterization. "You met her. Marcy isn't a pimp like the ones you see in the movies. It's not like that at all."

"Okay, okay. Let's not go there. Think about what I've said. Get out before it's too late."

It's already too late, she thought. She enjoyed her life too much just the way it was. She pictured Gary, Melissa, and Amy. Her family. Gary seemed to be telling her that she could still have that life if she left Marcy now. Marcy would certainly understand but there were so many other issues, not the least of which was Linc.

Gary's voice interrupted her reverie. "The girls have come to love you and they'd hate it if you were no longer in my life. I would, too."

The girls. She loved them, too. If she gave it all up she could have the life she'd always wanted, a ready-made family. "Let's just let some time pass before we talk about any kind of future."

"That's a sound plan," he said. "Let's both take some time and see what develops. Call me in a day or two, will you?"

"Of course."

She clicked off her cell phone, called Marcy, and relayed what Gary had told her. "I'm glad he couldn't find out anything about me in his cursory search. Maybe that means that Anna doesn't know any of the details about Chase and me."

"That's a comforting thought."

"Maybe I should stop seeing him."

"I think you really should. You could be honest with him and just tell him that you think your wife knows about us and might make trouble. How often do you usually see him?"

THE MADAM OF MAPLE COURT   285

"Actually not too often, but recently he's been a bit more persistent."

"I know you'll take care of things, but if you need any help, I'm always here for you."

"Thanks, Marcy. I'm going to give you the greatest compliment I can give. You're the sanest person I know."

Her cell phone rang later that afternoon and she looked at the screen. Linc. He'd called her every day offering comfort and support, soft words of encouragement and deep caring.

"Hi, Linc." She outlined what Gary had found. "Here I am talking about Chase and Gary. I don't understand you, Linc. Why aren't you jealous?"

"I've often wondered that myself, where you're concerned, and this is the only answer I've come up with. I care a great deal about you and want you to be happy. I think your life as it is makes you happy. That's all I've figured out so far. I just know that I don't resent any of the men in your life. I'm merely glad to be there, too."

"Is it really that simple for you?"

"I've looked inside myself, something I don't do too often, and that's what I find. Simple? Not really. It just is. And, of course, since I'm anything but monogamous myself, I can't say anything anyway. I think I'm just like you, happy. Aren't you jealous of me with other women? After all I'm not so different from you."

From time to time he'd mentioned some entertaining he'd done for Marcy. "I never really think about what you do when we're not together." She listened to what she'd just said and let out a small laugh. "No, I don't mean it that way. I don't think about you and your job, and that's probably the way you think of me, too."

"I care about you. More than I'd like to, but not enough to rock the boat for either of us right now."

She considered, then said, "Me, too."

Chapter

25

Nothing more happened for the next two weeks. At first Pam waited, tense every moment, trying to anticipate when the bomb would drop, but when it didn't, she began to think that maybe it would all blow over. When Chase called and told her he wanted to get together with her the following Tuesday, she couldn't help but ask, "Where's your wife going to be?"

"Anna's taking the kids to our lake house for a week, and anyway she's none of your concern," he snapped.

"Sorry, Chase."

"What's with you and my wife? You've never been so concerned about her before."

"I've had a few incidents, including a black SUV that cruised my block the last time you were here. I think she knows about us."

"Bullshit. She's not bright enough to have figured anything out."

"The license plate was HOBART3."

"That's her car. I'll give it all some thought, but please. At least one more visit. Anna's in the country with the kids, so she can't make trouble right now. And anyway, I can handle her."

"I don't know whether I can. I've got a lot to lose."

"Are you holding me up for more money? Isn't your fee enough for you? And in case you're thinking about talking to her about us, I won't pay you to keep your mouth shut, either."

"Hey. Slow down. Where did that come from?" Pam snapped. *He must be more worried about this than he's letting on.*

She heard his deep, long sigh. "I'm sorry. I was really stressed before, and now this. See why I need you?"

She had to stop seeing him. "I don't know whether I'm free that evening."

"Listen, Pam, forget what I said. I don't know where it came from. I need to be with you." He was almost whining. "Please. You're the only one who understands me and I'm feeling very needy."

Right. The only one, except your other girlfriends. She wondered whether he'd just broken up with one of his other women, but she'd probably never know and it didn't matter anyway. She just knew that she needed to call it all off with him, without making him too angry. She let out a long sigh. Maybe she'd let him have one more visit and then make it clear to him in person that it was over. Resigned to one more meeting, she said, "Okay, Chase. What time?"

"Let's say seven. I'm looking forward to your hot tub and the kind of relaxation that only you can give me."

It was now mid-August and the sun was still above the horizon as Pam and Chase sat in the bubbling water. Several times she'd started to tell him that this was the last time, no matter how much he wanted her or was willing to pay, but each time she'd chickened out. She was good at so many interpersonal things, why not this? She'd have to develop a tougher hide.

The sudden crash was loud enough to penetrate the noise in the spa. "What the hell was that?" she said, climbing out of the water with Chase close behind. She grabbed her sundress

THE MADAM OF MAPLE COURT

289

from the bench and dropped it over her wet skin while Chase pulled on his jeans. Then the two of them headed toward the front of the house.

The scene that greeted them was chaotic. The back end of Chase's car, parked at the top of the driveway, was now joined with the front end of a black Lexus SUV. Pam knew immediately that it was Anna's. A woman tried to open the driver's side door but, since the vehicle was seriously crumpled, had to heave her shoulder against it and, with lots of screaming, straining metal, she pushed her way out. "You bastard!" she screamed. "I knew I'd find you here, or at Cheryl's or at Lynne's. You bastard! Bastard! Bastard!"

Chase's eyes widened. "You're at the lake house."

"You're such an arrogant fool," she yelled. "My lawyer suggested that I use a detective, but I've known about your little friends for months. You're not very discreet."

Chase stood frozen to the spot. "How . . . ?"

"The hows aren't important," she shrieked. "I know that you're a bastard with a bevy of girlfriends." Her gaze shifted to Pam and she glared. "At least this one's not bad looking. But she's short. I always thought you went for tall women. Both Cheryl and Lynne are tall and really stacked."

"You've ruined both the cars," Chase said, as if ruining his marriage wasn't as important as his vehicles. "You're crazy."

"I might be crazy, but I'm not staying here to help sort this out." She pulled her cell phone from her pocket. "I'm calling a local cab and paying the driver whatever he wants to take me home. Don't come back. Let me know which of your lady friends you'll be staying with and I'll send some things there."

"Anna, wait. We need to talk about this."

Anna dialed her phone and gave Pam's address. "I'll pay you whatever you want to get me back to New Jersey. Can you do that?" She listened, then refolded the phone. "Lady," she said to Pam, "he'll be as free as a bird as soon as my lawyer makes the arrangements. But don't think there'll be any money. The kids and I will have it all. If you still want him, he's yours."

"But, Anna, what about the cars?"

"Have your little friend call a fucking tow truck."

The taxi pulled into Maple Court and Anna waved at it. Without another word she got inside and it drove away, leaving Chase with his mouth agape. "You'll need a cab, too," Pam said, unable to decide whether to laugh or cry. Anna knew nothing about her business. She merely thought Pam was one of Chase's girlfriends, and Chase wasn't going to enlighten her.

She was safe! It was over! While Pam called a taxi and arranged for two tow trucks, Chase quickly dressed and retrieved his belongings. Without another word, he walked down to the foot of the driveway, still in shock. Pam couldn't help but wonder whether he was more concerned about his marriage or his cars.

When the taxi arrived she heard the driver quip, "Had an accident?"

Chase growled something, got in, and the taxi took off.

Pam collapsed onto a lounge chair beside the pool with her cell phone. Her first call was to Marcy. She told her about the afternoon.

"You're kidding. An enraged wife caused all this turmoil?"

Pam actually laughed. "Amazing. I came close to doing truly outrageous things and now, overall, nothing's really changed."

"Gary knows about you."

"Yeah. I'll call him next."

Gary was happy for her, glad things had worked out. "Now you can call it all off and get back to leading a normal life."

"Normal life?"

"You know. The country club, your charities, like that."

"You mean give up Club Fantasy."

THE MADAM OF MAPLE COURT

"Of course," Gary said, not seeming to find any problem with that.

"I don't think so."

Gary seemed incredulous. "You mean you would continue with, with, with what you were doing?"

"I like what I do. I know all the downside, but the upside is wonderful and I feel great about it." She took a deep breath, words spilling forth. "I look at it as performing a service, one men want and need, and I'm well paid for it."

"But what about us?"

"Gary, I'm not going to change, at least for the moment. I care for you and for your children. I've had dreams of getting married, being a partial mother to your wonderful girls, but that's not enough for me right now. I'd like to keep seeing you but with no illusions on either of our parts. I like you, we have fun together, and we have good sex. We also have fun with your children and I'd be really heartbroken if I never saw them again, but I'd live with that. I can't be what I'm not, and I'm not ready to settle down and give up what's become an important part of me."

Gary was silent for a long time and Pam let him think about everything. "I don't know, Pam," he said.

"That's okay. I'm not as sure about things as I might appear."

She heard him let out a long sigh. "I'd like to get together for dinner and see whether we can sort this all out."

"I'd like that, too, but don't have any illusions. I am what I am."

"I'm not sure I completely understand, but I'd like to get together."

"That would be great. Why don't you chew it all over and call me in a few days. If you still want to have dinner, that would be great."

"I'll call you."

She called Rob and told him that he needn't continue to worry about her. "Darling, I was never worried. I know you well enough to know that you'll always land on your feet."

She hoped what he said was true.

Her last call was to Linc. She told him the whole story, then said, "Linc, can you come over? I need a friend to celebrate with."

Dear Reader,

I know you've enjoyed reading about the fun on Maple Court and I hope you will miss Pam and all her friends as much as I will. The second book in this series, as yet untitled, will appear sometime in 2009. Check my Web site for further details in the spring of that year.

If you like Marcy as much as I do, you probably want to read her story. Marcy's book is entitled *Night After Night*, but I would suggest that you first read her sister Jenna's tale in my novel *Club Fantasy*. *Hot Summer Nights* introduces a burned-out Club Fantasy employee named Leslie who stirs up the town of Sound's End, Connecticut, when she goes on vacation. You can also go all the way back to the beginning of all the enterprises and meet a delightful woman named Erika in *The Price of Pleasure*.

Phew. There are so many books for you to enjoy, and I've also written quite a few that don't include any of these characters.

Please drop me a note at Joan@JoanELloyd.com and let me know which character I should bring back in later books. In addition, visit my Web site at joanelloyd.com for information about my books and lots of sexual matters, including questions and answers, and zillions of letters from nice folks like you who've added their thoughts over the years.

GREAT BOOKS,
GREAT SAVINGS!

When You Visit Our Website:
www.kensingtonbooks.com
You Can Save Money Off The Retail Price
Of Any Book You Purchase!

- **All Your Favorite Kensington Authors**
- **New Releases & Timeless Classics**
- **Overnight Shipping Available**
- **eBooks Available For Many Titles**
- **All Major Credit Cards Accepted**

Visit Us Today To Start Saving!
www.kensingtonbooks.com

All Orders Are Subject To Availability.
Shipping and Handling Charges Apply.
Offers and Prices Subject To Change Without Notice.